Texas Desire

Texas Desire

A Texas Legacy Romance

Holly Castillo

TULE
PUBLISHING

Chapter One

San Antonio, Coahuila y Tejas
March 5, 1836

S OMEONE WAS IN the house.

The realization was like jumping into icy water. Afraid to breathe, afraid to move, Olivia Torres held herself perfectly still, her hands gripping the bed sheet, desperately straining to hear a noise, praying it had just been a continuation of her nightmare.

A soft thump in the kitchen sent tremors coursing through her blood and her skin became clammy. She sat up quickly—cringing as the bed creaked, counting in her mind, ticking off the time since she had heard the first noise. In the dark, cold room, time seemed to crawl and she feared whoever it was had been in the house for several minutes already.

Her mouth was dry, her hands trembling. Olivia slipped off the bed and knelt on the cold floor, ignoring the ache in her ear as her heart pounded frantically. Her fingers felt under the cornhusk mattress until the smooth butt of a pistol fit into her palm. Gripping it tightly, her tremors slowed and she felt stronger, braver.

The door to her room seemed yards away, though it was only two short steps. Her mind was racing with possibilities and she tried to imagine how she would handle whatever it was she faced. Olivia hoped it was only her grandmother, or perhaps Serena, up and about for some odd reason. The likelihood was very small.

More than likely it was a Mexican soldier or a vagrant seeking shelter, food, or some other comfort she wasn't prepared to offer. The sporadic fighting at the mission had been going on for days now, and it seemed inevitable that Santa Anna was going to make a hard push at the Alamo any day. It seemed every passing moment the Mexican Army built in size.

But the tension was thick and the soldiers were restless. She didn't want to think about the danger her family would be in if the soldiers decided her home would provide entertainment. Cautiously, she opened the door and slipped out into the hall. The insane thought ran through her mind that her feet were cold and she should have grabbed her slippers. Yet her hands were sweating.

Same as in her dream, her heart pounded so hard it seemed impossible to hear anything more than the thundering cacophony. She hesitated for a moment in the hallway, pressing her back to the wall as she tried to gather her wits. This wasn't her nightmare. There were no bullets and cannon balls flying around her. She was in her own home and just needed to discourage someone trying to escape the cold March night.

Her heart lurched as someone bumped into their stack of

cast-iron pans. The curse that floated on the air was one she had never heard before, and her cheeks flamed at the colorful expression from the deep male voice that held a drawl that wasn't familiar to her. Licking her lips, she whispered a quick prayer and crossed herself, then tiptoed silently towards the kitchen.

She couldn't hear any more sounds, which only made her more nervous. Her ear started to throb painfully. She clenched her teeth together. It was bad enough she could barely hear a sound out of her left ear, but it was worse that it continued to ache and throb.

She peered around the corner of the hall, barely peeking her head out into the kitchen. Shadows from the moonlight made it difficult to distinguish anything. Gradually, her eyes adjusted and she began to pick out the familiar objects in the kitchen.

One of the pots had been knocked to the floor. Whatever man had invaded her home that night had certainly been clumsy. But where was he now? Nothing moved in the shadows. Swallowing hard, fingers tightening on the gun, she took a step forward, then another.

Nothing moved, not a sound was made other than her own nervous breathing. She took another step and her foot slipped on something. Surprised, she glanced down and noticed dark spots scattered on the floor. Confusion lasted for only a moment before her mouth went dry.

Blood. She heard an ominous click behind her. Her instinct was to whirl around and confront whoever had invaded her home, her sanctuary. But she had learned the hard way she needed to listen to reason and rational thought instead of blindly following her gut instinct.

"What do you want?" Her voice was nowhere near as strong as she had hoped. It even quivered. She had no idea what kind of madman held a gun at her back.

There wasn't an immediate answer and her fingers twitched around her gun.

"Is this the Torres home?" The voice was deep, rough, and strained.

"What do you want?" she demanded again, avoiding his question. She was proud that her voice was stronger.

There was a sound, as though he took a step towards her, but then stopped. "I was told—a man told me you could help me…"

She turned very slowly, trying to keep her gun hidden within the folds of her nightgown. She didn't see him right away. He was dressed in dark clothes that allowed him to blend in the shadows easily. His dark hat was pulled low over his eyes, and at least a day's growth of beard shadowed his jaw. But it was hard to focus on anything with the large gun he held.

It wasn't pointed directly at her, but she had no doubt the mysterious man would aim at her heart in the space of a breath.

"I've come for sanctuary. If you aren't able to provide it, tell me now so I can get away quickly." His words were curt and to the point and made it impossible for her to dodge the question.

"This is not a boarding house." She didn't know if she

was handling the man the right way or not.

For all she knew she was only provoking him further. For a moment, the gun wavered and Olivia wondered how injured the man was, and how he had become injured. Perhaps he was a thief that someone had caught and he had escaped. Or perhaps he was a Texian. The thought gave her hope. Maybe he had brought others with him and they had come to help the defenders holed up within the Alamo.

His eyes searched her face intently, the creases around his eyes deepened as he squinted in the faint light to really see her face.

Then he nodded with finality. "I will leave you. Just please don't alert anyone that I was ever here."

Curiosity and something else pulled at Olivia, overriding her usual logic. She took a step towards him, then another. "Who would I alert? Whom are you running from?"

The man lifted his chin and stared down at her. Suddenly, she was staring into the coldest blue eyes she had ever seen. She had to restrain herself from taking a giant step backwards. This was a man who had met the devil and laughed.

"Every man with a gun is looking for me," he said softly.

Olivia's lips pulled into a thin, tight line. "Then you must have done something truly terrible."

For a moment something clouded his eyes, an emotion that made her wonder if he actually might still have a soul. "Yes, I did something terrible. I believed in the wrong people."

Olivia watched him for a moment, and for the first time

in her life, was uncertain. "So whom, precisely, are you running from?"

"The entire Mexican Army."

Olivia fingered the high collar of her nightgown. "It would seem we have a common enemy." He was silent, watching her warily.

The creak of a floorboard drew his attention and he spun quickly, so quick she wondered if he really was injured, and his gun was pointed directly at a wide-eyed Angie.

"Stop!" Olivia gasped and raised her gun, clumsily cocking it.

The man glanced between the two sisters then slowly lowered his gun. "They'll be here any minute." He spoke in a rough whisper. "Once I have tended to my wound, I'll leave. You'll not be burdened by me long."

The weight of the gun felt odd in her hand and she brought her other one up to support it. "Tell me why we should trust you."

Small beads of sweat covered his forehead, and she could tell by the way he stood he was in a great deal of pain. But he didn't want to reveal it. "You have no reason to trust me. Nor do I have reason to trust you. But we are rapidly approaching a situation where your only decision will be whether you hand me over to the Mexican Army or shoot me dead right here. At this point, I'd prefer you shoot me, ma'am."

The man was badly injured. That much was certain. Never taking her eyes off their mysterious visitor, Olivia spoke to her sister. "Do your best to clean up the blood.

Throw down a rug if you must. I'll take him down to the basement…"

At her words, the man wavered on his feet, and Olivia rushed forward. He was bigger than she had realized, standing inches over her already tall frame. As her arms wrapped around him, most of his weight pitched forward and she staggered, trying to keep them both from falling.

"I'm fine." He grunted and pushed himself back up to his original height, putting minimal weight on Olivia.

Olivia scoffed, but said nothing. As though things weren't already bad enough, the sounds of men outside suddenly met their ears. The sounds prompted the man draped on Olivia to push from her and begin to head for the back door. "I have to get away. I have to…"

"Come with me. Quickly. Angie, don't light a lamp. We must hurry."

Olivia scrambled towards the dining room, the man following closely behind her. She paused when they came to the dining room and turned just in time to support the injured man as his knees sagged. From the warm dampness she felt on her nightgown, the man was bleeding profusely.

"Can you stand on your own?" she whispered.

The man looked down at her with pain in his eyes. "Yes, I'm fine."

She pulled away from him slowly, trying to make sure he was steady, and realized she was still holding her gun. A glint of light drew her eye and she saw a lantern out in the street. Whoever was out there was getting closer.

Moving quickly, she knelt and pulled back the rug, revealing the small trap door that would take them to the basement. She struggled to pull open the heavy door, and suddenly found a large hand covering hers and pulling for her. She glanced up and the man gave her a tired smile.

"I don't even know your name," she whispered.

"Cade."

She realized the door was open and they were wasting precious time. She tore her eyes off of him and started down the ladder.

"Follow me," she said, even though it was unnecessary.

It felt comforting to issue directions in a situation that was far outside of her control. As soon as she reached the basement she fumbled in the dark for the lantern she knew she'd find.

By the time Cade had made it down the stairs the lantern was lit and Olivia waited nervously for him. When his feet touched the floor his knees buckled, but he forced them to straighten and held tightly to the ladder for several long moments.

Slowly he turned to face her and she pulled in a deep breath. She had been able to tell simply from holding him that he was a large man, but she hadn't really prepared herself for what he would look like.

He was tall, a good three inches taller than her, and he had broad shoulders that tapered down into narrow hips. His clothing was slightly different from what she had seen many of the Texians wear. He wore a rustic shirt and still had his chaps on, making her wonder if he had been part of a small skirmish against the Mexicans.

She moved towards him with determination, though it felt as though her stomach was lodged in her throat. Good God, he was such a big man, and obviously a strong one that had been through hell and back. Once he recovered—if he recovered—would he prove to be a danger for her family?

A sound reached Olivia and she turned her head to the side, straining to hear with her good ear. It was the sound of boots on the porch. A loud knocking at the door caused her heart to lurch in her throat.

Cade cocked the pistol that was still in his hand and stared up at the floor boards above them.

Then he lowered his gaze back to Olivia. "Do you have any other weapons? Any bullets? Knives, even?"

Olivia took a deep breath for courage and wrapped her arm around the man. "First, you need to whisper, in case you haven't noticed there are Mexican soldiers entering my home."

He grunted softly as her body pressed against his side, forcefully guiding him to a cot that lay in the corner. "Second, you are no good in the battle against the Mexican military if you can barely stand."

She turned slowly and eased him down on the cot.

He grimaced in pain, then opened his piercing blue eyes on her. "Why are you doing this?"

"Because I refuse to have a man die in my house. I don't want your spirit haunting me," she snapped back at him, even though she couldn't keep the teasing tenderness to her voice.

The man—Cade—might very well die that night, lying

on the cot in the basement of her home. She began to turn from him but was drawn up short by his hand clasping her wrist. She looked back at him in surprise, her eyes fixated on the spot where his flesh touched hers. She couldn't remember the last time a man had willingly touched her, and the sensation left her more breathless than when his body had been pressed to hers.

"Mr. Cade… I must go help my sister."

"Cade. My name is Cade. Just Cade." His other hand came up and caught a handful of her nightgown. "And how do you plan to explain this?"

The bright red splotches all over her gown were far too obvious to be ignored. A guard would be certain to question the stains. Olivia's mind raced. Would Angie be able to confront the guards on her own? Shaking free of Cade's grasp, she raced for the ladder and went up as fast as her now numb feet would allow. She hadn't heard the front door open yet, and prayed Angie had been successful in cleaning up the blood.

She nearly screamed when her head popped through the opening and nearly collided with Angie. Where was her usual calm?

"Do I let them in? Are you coming out?"

"Did you clean up the blood?"

"Most of it. I covered the largest spot with a rug."

There was a pounding at the door again and, by the sounds, the men outside were growing impatient. "I can't come out. My gown is covered in his blood. Close the hatch and cover it. Don't light a lamp till you're nearly at the door.

Pretend you just woke up and…"

"I know how to lie, Olivia," Angie said, already beginning to lower the door. "Keep your light dim. I don't want them to see through the floorboards. I'll come get you when it is absolutely safe."

The door closed and Olivia said a quick prayer, hoping her decision hadn't just killed her family.

Chapter Two

WITH THE LANTERN barely giving off any light, Olivia confronted their unexpected guest. He sat on the cot, pistol still in hand, listening to the sound of booted feet crossing the floor over them. Every muscle in his body was tense. She wondered if she looked as wary as he.

The only thing to keep her mind off the situation she couldn't control was work. It had always been her way of coping with situations she didn't really want to face. "Where is your worst injury, Mr. Cade?"

He didn't look at her for several seconds as he examined his gun. Despite the cold of the air, a fine sheen of sweat covered his forehead. When he did look at her, he didn't address her question. "I don't think you ever told me your name."

Olivia stood straighter. No one ever asked her name. She was always known as Miss Torres. Or *Senorita Fria*, as the soldiers had named her. It was a nickname she hated with a passion, but it kept unwanted attention away. For a moment she almost told this stranger her name. It was an insane desire that she immediately discarded to the equally insane events of the night. "You already know my name, sir. It's

Miss Torres."

Cade watched her for a few moments then nodded. "Well, Miss Torres, if those soldiers happen to wander down this way, I would prefer to not have my pants around my ankles."

Olivia hoped she wasn't blushing. She had seen and heard much in her twenty-one years of life, and though she didn't consider herself a spinster, she wasn't a naïve, fresh girl, either. "It would be quite a shame for you to have found shelter only to bleed to death."

Cade looked down at this clothes, covered in blood, then back at her. "Not all of it is mine."

Olivia crossed her arms, raising an eyebrow. "A comforting thought. So I have harbored a murderer in my home."

He looked back at his pistol, his fingers touching it with a knowledge only much use could bring. "I'll leave as soon as the soldiers are gone."

Olivia placed one foot on top of the other, trying to warm her toes. The basement floor was like a block of ice, and her teeth were going to start chattering any minute. "I offered you shelter, sir. I am not one to go back on my word."

His eyes rose to hers and he studied her. She desperately wished she wore one of her heavy black dresses instead of the thin night rail.

"I never thought you would," he commented, shifting on the cot, a grimace of pain on his face. "I've been told that you are extremely honest, to the point of fault."

Their hushed voices were creating an intimate environment she wasn't used to. Olivia switched feet, trying to warm the other. "Precisely whom have you been speaking with who is so quick to speak of my family?"

A thump on the floorboards above drew their attention and both stared as though they could see through the thick wood.

"Come over here," he whispered.

"I'm perfectly fine right here, thank you."

The gaze he pinned on her held no room for reproach. "If they find us and come down the stairs, you will be their first target standing there."

"I have my gun. I'll be just fine." She wished she was as convinced as her words sounded.

The gun was a weight in her hand that she wanted gone. Every time she moved she was afraid she would accidentally discharge it. It wouldn't be the first time.

"Well, I won't have my last dying thought be that I let the woman who offered me shelter die without my protection. So, come over here." His words were clipped and irritated.

She had no reason to trust this man and every reason not to. He had broken into their home in the middle of the night, had brought the Mexican Army into their house, bled from multiple wounds, and, upon his own admission, had injured others.

And yet she felt she could trust him. She felt certain he would do her no harm. But she also felt it unwise to push him too far. There was anger within him that she didn't want to see.

Slowly, hesitantly, she walked towards him, her arms still folded across her chest. When she stopped near him, he reached out suddenly and grabbed her wrist, turning her around and placing her next to him on the cot. It happened so quickly she had barely had a chance to draw a breath before she found herself sitting next to him.

He still sat calmly, staring up at the floorboards as though nothing had happened. But now he was directly between her and the path of any intruders.

Shaken, Olivia pulled her knees towards her chest, trying to warm herself, and observed the man who had suddenly disrupted her home. His hair was long, pulled behind his neck with a strap of leather. From underneath his worn hat, the color appeared light, almost gold in color. His face was pale, though she was certain that was due to how much blood he had lost. His scraggly beard was dark, though, making the paleness of his skin even starker. He was thin, though not gaunt. But she was fairly certain it had been a while since he'd had a good meal.

He cut a glance sideways at her and she jerked her eyes up to the floorboards, feeling like a child that had been caught peeking. She jumped when he reached towards her and gasped when he grabbed one of her feet.

"A sensible person would not be barefoot," he murmured as his fingers lazily rubbed over her toes.

Olivia was having a hard time catching her breath. The touch was so intimate, and so unexpected, she didn't know how to react. His eyes were still focused above them, and she became vaguely aware that there hadn't been any sounds for quite some time. "I—I didn't think to grab my slippers when I was trying to catch a thief."

The faintest of smiles crossed his lips as he grabbed her other foot and began to warm it. "Is that what you thought?"

"Considering all that has happened in the past few days, anything was possible." Her previous thought that he could be bringing help grabbed her attention. "Are you here to help? Have you brought more men to fight?"

A cloud covered his face. "I want to help. I will if I can make it through this. But no, I don't have anyone with me." He turned to look at her, his eyes intense. "Is your husband there?"

She shook her head, trying to hide her disappointment. "No. But my sister's husband is. He went to join them just last week."

Cade sighed heavily. "It's an unfair fight. I've seen how many soldiers Santa Anna has. If we don't get more..."

They were silent, Olivia enjoying someone taking care of her for once. Her feet were beginning to warm up, and she was wondering how much longer she should allow the inappropriate contact.

The door above lifted suddenly, and Cade and Olivia tensed, both lifting their guns.

"Olivia!" Angie's voice floated down to them, and Olivia scrambled off the cot, oddly disappointed in breaking touch with Cade.

Angie peered down at her, relief all over her face. "They're gone. They didn't suspect a thing."

Olivia let out a breath she wasn't aware she'd been holding. "Good. Then I need you to go ahead and boil some water. I'll get bandages, and—"

"That won't be necessary, Miss Torres," Cade spoke from close behind her. "I'll be on my way now and won't endanger your family any further."

Olivia turned to face him, planting her hands on her hips. "I'm not about to let you leave now when you'll probably die a few steps from our home."

He tipped his hat back, revealing an array of bruises on his chin and forehead that she doubted he was aware of. "I'm not really in the mood to argue, so if you'd just step aside…"

He was already wavering on his feet and, if he went down, she wouldn't be able to get him up again. She took a deep breath and stepped towards him, forcefully grabbing his arm. "You will do as I say, Mr. Cade, and no further arguing."

She forced him back on the cot and he stared at her as though she had grown a second head. She was thankful that he was weak enough to push around. Angie had already vanished to do her bidding and she was left to handle the difficult man on her own.

"Now, tell me what your worst injuries are."

"Miss Torres, I…"

She reached for his jacket and tugged, successfully getting it off one shoulder before he grabbed her and she found herself on his lap, her nose touching his.

"I don't need your help, Miss Torres."

Olivia tried to breathe evenly, but was finding it incredibly difficult. His eyes watched her closely, and she felt a flush growing up her neck.

"Very well," she whispered, "then I won't help you. But, for the record, I believe you're quite the fool." She turned sharply and pushed against his chest to break free of his grasp.

His low moan drew her attention and she turned back, feeling the slick warmth of his blood under her fingers. She looked at his chest and saw the dark stain of blood on his shirt and her eyes shot to his face.

It had gone terribly pale and was covered in sweat. "Mr. Cade, are you—"

Before she could finish, his eyes rolled backwards and he passed out cold.

IT DIDN'T TAKE long to realize the man was lucky to still be alive. His wounds were numerous; a deep gash in his left side, bruises all over his chest, and numerous cuts on his arms and hands. The wound on his chest was shallow, but long, and she had no doubt it had pained him greatly when she had pushed against it.

He had been in a terrible fight; that much was obvious. And she hadn't yet had the courage to pull his pants off to examine his lower wounds.

She gnawed on her lower lip, standing next to the cot, staring down at the man who had invaded her sanctuary and now needed her help. She had never turned away from someone in need, and she wasn't about to start. But the man's size and stubborn will gave her pause. If he became obstinate enough, she wouldn't be able to control him.

With a determined squaring of her shoulders, she began to work on the laces of his breaches, thankful he was unconscious and not being difficult. By the time she had worked his breeches down to his calves, she was out of breath from the exertion. He was all man, and she now knew his body better than she had ever known another man's.

She forced herself to ignore his nudity as she tried to examine the long, jagged cut that marred his leg. The golden hair that covered his body was crusted with dried blood, and more fresh blood seeped slowly from the cut. She sat down on the edge of the cot, her fingers gently searching around the wound. It was deep and she closed her eyes briefly at the site of his torn muscle. It was a miracle he had been able to walk to their home from wherever he came, and it would be even more of a miracle if she would be able to heal him.

She had never been squeamish before and she wasn't about to start. Grabbing the bowl of warm water Angie had brought down to her, she began cleaning him, working as quickly as possible. Soon he was clean and the only blood on him was the fresh blood seeping from his cuts. Without the dirt and dried blood on his skin, the bruises stood out prominently, and she wondered how he had ever escaped whoever was beating him.

She watched his face as she ran a damp cloth over his forehead. He was a large man. And he was obviously stubborn and determined, having planned to walk out into the night once again with the entire Mexican Army and God knew who else looking for him. She fought the shiver that slivered down her back. What had this man done?

With a clenched jaw, she held the bottle of whiskey over the deep cut in his leg. It would hurt—badly. She had treated herself with the whiskey when she had been hurt, and the pain had been so terrible she had momentarily lost consciousness. She watched his face closely as she began to tip the bottle. He was already oblivious to all that was around him, perhaps…

His deep, guttural moan of pain made her jump, sloshing the burning fluid on his thigh and hip. He lurched upright, grabbing her wrist before his eyes were even open.

Olivia was breathing like she had just run three times around the house. The fear pounding through her veins made her temporarily immobile, but finally sanity returned and she began to yank on her wrist.

"Be still." He growled. "For the love of God… please, just be still."

Once again she froze, her mouth dry, watching him. He still hadn't opened his eyes and his forehead was covered with dots of perspiration. He, too, was breathing hard. Slowly, slowly, his breathing eased.

"Couldn't you have given me some sort of warning?" he finally said his voice low, his eyes opening and gradually focusing on her face.

"You were already…"

"I know, I know." He shook his head. The motion must have hurt, though, because he froze, his jaw clenched tightly. He let his breath out slowly through his teeth. "It just wasn't a fun way to wake up," he said, forcing a half smile to his lips as his eyes once again focused on her.

Olivia stared at him, feeling drawn by his striking blue eyes. "I know it hurts," she said softly, remembering all too vividly the agonizing burning before blackness.

Her heart was pounding so hard in her chest that she thought it might be visible through her night rail. Her hand rose to his face and she lay her fingers softly against his cheek, touching the rough whiskers, smoothing her thumb over the soft skin right under his eye.

She had never touched a man in such a way, and she didn't know why she was so compelled. Perhaps it was the pain in his eyes; perhaps it was because she knew the pain he was feeling. Perhaps it was because she wanted to touch him.

His eyes watched her intently, confusion now mixing with the pain. "Why are you helping me?"

She couldn't stop touching him. It gave her a heady feeling, as though she had an unbelievable power. He was hers to touch, hers to explore. He belonged to her, at least until he was strong enough to walk away.

"Because you need me," she whispered, knowing her words were true. She felt his grip slackening on her wrist and knew he would pass out again soon.

"I must finish cleaning your wounds. You know it will hurt. Do you want…"

His eyes locked with hers, the pain clearing momentarily as he released her wrist completely. "I know what must be done."

She wanted to take it away from him. She didn't want to cause him this torture. But if she didn't, he would surely die from infection. And suddenly, the thought of this stranger dying was completely unbearable. Keeping her hand on his face, her eyes never leaving his, she tipped the bottle.

His muscles jumped and his face became terribly pale, but he kept his eyes locked with hers. His hand came up and caught the wrist of the palm on his face and held her there, making sure she didn't pull away from him.

She had no intention of doing so. His leg done, she poured the liquid over his chest, and a muscle in his jaw twitched.

"Shh. It's almost over. Almost." Quickly she finished treating the wound on his chest and breathed a soft sigh of relief.

The man she held was trembling and she wanted to cry for the pain he was in. She couldn't believe he was still conscious.

"It's over," she said, her fingers still lightly caressing his face.

He was now covered in a fine sheen of sweat. He swallowed, his eyes closing for a few moments, the exhaustion from the experience obviously pulling at him.

Her fingers moved up to his hair, brushing it off his forehead. "You will get better, now. I promise. You won't even feel it when I put in the stiches."

His eyes opened, sharp and focused on her. "Tell me your name."

It was spoken as an order, and Olivia had long ago decided she was the one who issued orders. But it seemed so far all of her rules had been broken with this stranger.

"Olivia. My name is Olivia."

Chapter Three

T HE CANNON FIRE was a familiar sound. It had been tearing through the silence surrounding San Antonio sporadically for days. Nor was the gunfire unusual.

What startled Olivia out of her bed was the roar of thousands of men, shouting, screaming, crying. Breathless, her body quivering, she raced to the window, her fingernails digging into the wooden sill as she stared out into the slowly spreading light of dawn.

Like a restless sea, the Mexican Army attacked, charging on the small mission that had withheld the attacks so far. The sick churning in her gut told her it wouldn't hold off the Army any longer.

For several moments, she couldn't pull her eyes off of the scene unfolding before her. Line after line of soldiers in red and white uniforms charged the mission, their bayonets raised, their rifles firing madly. Returning gunfire streamed from behind the walls, but as one line of soldiers fell, another took its place. There were just too many. Far, far too many for the Texians within to hold off.

Taking a deep breath to control the fear and overwhelming sadness pulling at her, Olivia shoved away from the window, racing out her door to find the family. They needed her now. There was nothing she could do for the men within the Alamo.

The hall was empty, but she could hear movement in the kitchen. Heart pounding, she ran down the hall, forgetting that she still only wore her night rail. She glanced down at herself and shook her head. It didn't matter. Nothing mattered. If the soldiers came pillaging after the battle was over, what she wore would make no difference to how they treated her.

She skidded to a stop when she saw her grandmother calmly making tortillas on the cast iron stove. The only hint that she was aware of the events unfolding around her was the tight press of her lips. But her rhythms were smooth as always; flip, tap, and flip again.

"*Abuela*! What are you doing? We must get to safety. Where are the others?"

Her grandmother's grey eyes lifted to meet hers, and the fierce stubbornness in them reminded Olivia of her own hard head. "The fighting has been going on for days. What is any different today? I will cook my tortillas as always, and I will feed our customers just as I have every day."

Olivia ran a hand through her hair in frustration. "What customers, *Abuela*? There hasn't been anyone here in days."

"They will come back. They cannot stay gone forever."

Olivia didn't have the heart to tell her that nearly everyone had fled San Antonio. She was fairly certain her grandmother already knew, but she was just fighting the truth. "The soldiers are storming the Alamo. We must hide. There is no telling how they will act once the fighting is over."

The older woman's actions slowed, and she carefully pulled the last of the tortillas off the pan on the fire. "*Bueno.* Then we must get you and the girls somewhere safe. Perhaps…"

Olivia fought from rolling her eyes. Her grandmother was oblivious to all that Olivia did around their *cocina*, and she should be glad. But there were times when she wished her grandmother would realize she could take care of things.

"Where are Angie and Serri?"

Her grandmother was moving quicker, banking the fire and gathering up necessary items, apparently finally able to hear the terrible screams coming from the mission. "I saw Serena earlier… she was working on one of her *loca* projects outside. I haven't seen Angie all morning." Her motions froze and she looked up at Olivia with concern. "You don't think—"

Olivia didn't wait for her grandmother to finish the thought. Racing towards the back door, she was praying to every saint she could remember that Angie hadn't done something incredibly foolish. Her mind screamed at her to run faster; knowing her sister, she was halfway to the Alamo with only her bravery and stupidity as a weapon.

The scene in the backyard made her stop so suddenly she fell back on her rump. Serena, her hair in tangled disarray as usual, sat in the mesquite tree, her feet swinging back and forth, watching her sister with detached amusement.

"Serri, I swear by all that's holy, if you don't come down this instant—"

Angie's face was beet red; her hair falling all around her face, her fists waving threateningly at the thirteen-year-old perched above her. She swung back and forth slowly, suspended above the ground by her ankle tied securely to the tree Serena sat in.

Olivia didn't know what to address first; the fact that Serena's "project" had probably more than likely saved her sister's life, or that they needed to get to safety as soon as possible. "Serri, cut your sister down. You can explain yourself later. Angie, I don't want to know what you were planning on doing, but get the thoughts out of your mind."

Angie turned her bright red face to Olivia, revealing the tears her older sister hadn't seen earlier. "He's in there, Vi. I have to go to him."

Olivia's heart ached for her sister, but there was nothing for them to do now. "Do you think he would want you to get killed, too? No. Lorenzo is a smart, courageous man. If anyone can get out of there alive, he can. There's no reason to endanger your life too."

With a snap, Serena had cut through the rope and Angie fell the short foot to the ground with a thump. "You little hellion! Just wait until I get my hands on you. Come down from there. Right now!"

Olivia grabbed Angie and spun her around, wiping at the tears that covered her younger sister's beautiful face. "Angie, I know you are scared. We all are. But I need your help. You must be strong. Lorenzo would have wanted it."

Angie drew a deep, quivering breath. "Did you see it, Vi? Did you see all of them? It was the most horrible—"

"We knew it was coming," Olivia snapped, then pressed her lips together, trying to regain her composure. If anyone was going to hold this family together and keep them safe, it would have to be her. "It is terrible what is happening. We must take care of each other. Get inside the house. Take Serena. I'll be there shortly."

Angie's eyes narrowed. "And what are you going to do? Don't leave me out of it this time. Don't exclude me."

"I'm going to board the windows. Maybe if they think no one is here, they won't search as much. Everyone else that left did just that. Maybe it will look like we left, too."

Angie drew in a deep breath. "I'll help."

Olivia wanted to tell her no. She wanted to tell her to hide in the safety of the house with everyone else so that she wouldn't have to worry about her. But Angie needed to take her mind off the terrifying cries drifting on the wind.

She nodded. "*Vamanos*. Get everyone to safety and then come help me."

Angie nodded then caught Serena as she tried to race by. "I'm not through with you." She growled, hauling the girl towards the house by her ear.

"Some thank-you." Serena snapped. "I kept you from doing something stupid... again!" Her words ended on a small yelp as Angie shoved her through the back door.

Olivia turned to follow them then paused, listening. The cries were dwindling. The gunfire was becoming more sporadic. She choked back a sob. *Por Dios*, it was already over. The Alamo had fallen.

THE SOUND OF gunfire echoed all around Olivia and her palms began to sweat. She shouldn't be here. She had been out of her mind to grab her father's old rifle and head out to join the fighting.

How many times had she told Angie to stay safe and keep away from the battle? Olivia hadn't listened to her own advice, and now she was surrounded by men shouting and screaming, guns firing in every direction, and death all around. The gun smoke burned her eyes and throat, and she flinched as another cannon exploded nearby.

She wanted to run away. She wanted to flee the terror and carnage, wanted to get far away from the horror of war and believe there would be peace and happiness once more. But she had made her choice, and she would have to face the consequences. She had come here to fight, and she would do everything she could to help these brave Texians.

A soldier stood up over the rise, aiming at her. Her arms rose slowly, as though moving through thick mud, lifting her gun, and cocking it in one motion. It seemed so easy to pull the trigger, the kick in her shoulder an aching testimony that she had just taken someone's life by moving her finger. The soldier pitched forward, his face a grotesque picture of blood and bones where a youthful expression of fear had been just moments before.

Her fingers trembled as she tried to reload. She didn't

want to think about it. She didn't want to think the boy had been just as terrified as she. She didn't want to think about the boy's mother, finding out that her son had died in battle. But she did think of those things, and they whirled through her mind, churning and spinning with her own fear, making her ill.

Time seemed to stand still as the battle raged on around her. Suddenly she was running, trying to escape the cannon ball that was headed towards the small dugout she had been hiding in.

The explosion shook everything and, for a moment, she was flying, the sounds of the battle dying away below her. Her moment of flight ended quickly, though, and she crashed to the ground in a bone-jarring heap, cringing as debris rained down upon her.

The sound of the battle had stopped, though. There was nothing but utter and complete silence. Her head ached, a pounding throb that made her focus on keeping her eyes open against the pain.

She pushed herself to her hands and knees, then fell back on her stomach, looking around in confusion. The Texians were running forward, pushing past her, their mouths open in silent yells. She shook her head, hoping to clear the fog, but it only increased the pain. Several men around her fired their weapons, the smoke mingling with the already cloudy night air. The sound of the gun fire seemed far away, barely distinguishable.

Frustrated, she rolled over, and terror seized her. A Mexican soldier raced towards her, his bayonet raised, his face twisted in anger and fear. He was going to kill her. The thought should have chilled her. But suddenly she felt incredibly calm, her fingers finding the gun at her side easily, wrapping around the trigger smoothly as though the gun was made to be held by her hands.

An insane desire to fight and live captured her. She wanted to destroy the anger and hatred she saw in his eyes. She wanted to defeat him, and then defeat every other Mexican soldier that was trying to steal her freedom from her. A sound finally reached her ears, a dull thud, and she realized it was her own heartbeat. Her arms lifted as though she had no control, her aim centering on the soldier's heart. And then she heard the click of the gun.

Sound seemed to explode around her—the cry of the man as the bullet ripped through his flesh, the screams of others on the streets as they, too, met an unpleasant end. As the man pitched towards her, she could see his face, all covered in soot, and she wanted to scream in her own agony.

He was just a child, no more than fourteen. He hadn't even had the chance to be a man. He fell on her, his body limp, his eyes glazing as his life slowly faded. She fell under his weight, horror gripping her.

The boy's haunted eyes lifted to hers as his blood covered her. She wanted to look away, but she couldn't.

"Why?" he whispered. "Why?"

And his body went still, his eyes empty. "No!" she cried, finally finding her voice. "I didn't know." She sobbed. "I didn't…"

A hand slapped down over her mouth, cutting off her

cry. Olivia's eyes flew open and she realized she had been consumed by the nightmare again, a nightmare that plagued her every time she slept.

Her eyes struggled to adjust to the dim light in the room and she realized someone actually held their hand over her mouth. "Don't panic. It's just me."

Olivia forced her sister's hand away. "I never panic," she snapped. "But something must be wrong with you to sneak around the house like this." She ran her hand lightly over her left ear, cringing at the ache, and made sure her hair concealed the wound she never wanted her family to see.

Angie sighed heavily and folded her arms over her chest. "I couldn't sleep. Besides, you were having a nightmare."

Olivia felt a wave of remorse slip through her and sat up, making room for Angie to join her on the small bed. "It can't go on much longer. The fires are bound to go out soon." But, even as she said that, Olivia looked towards her bedroom window where the orange glow still burned in the distance. It had been going nonstop for three days. She, too, wondered if it would ever stop.

Angie was shaking her head. "The smell is so awful; I gag every time I step outside."

Olivia knew how Angie felt. She had never imagined what the smell of hundreds of burning bodies would be like. Now she wished she didn't know.

"I know he's okay." The quiver in Angie's voice drew Olivia's attention back to her sister.

"Angie..." She began hesitantly.

"Don't say it, Vi. Don't. I know no one lived. But what

if...I mean it's very likely he got out before the fighting began."

"Lorenzo would never desert and you know it."

Angie twisted the thin gold band on her finger. "I'm not saying that. He would never abandon them. But what if Bowie..."

"Angie, you will play this what-if game in your head until it drives you crazy. There's nothing we can do except pray."

Angie looked at her, dangerously close to tears. "We didn't see his body."

Olivia pressed her lips together firmly, not wanting to tell Angie how foolish her hopes were. Santa Ana had made certain none of the Alamo defenders lived to tell their story, and disgraced them even in death by not allowing them a proper burial. The bodies had all been piled together in two great fires that still burned.

Though they had joined the few other townsfolk in moving the bodies from the Alamo, they had not discovered Lorenzo among the gruesome corpses, giving Angie a glimmer of hope.

Angie continued, her voice firmer. "He cheated death before. I know he can do it again. He's so strong, and he—" She drew in a deep breath, halting her speech before she collapsed into tears. "What about the man downstairs? What do you think his story is?"

Olivia rubbed at her eyes as she slid out of bed, wishing for a moment she could take her mind off of the man who had entered their lives. He preoccupied her thoughts day and night, though.

He had been asleep for two days. She almost envied him. He had missed the fall of the Alamo, had missed the deep sadness that clung to the air, had missed the horrible way Santa Anna had burned the bodies of the brave Texians.

Though he hadn't moved or made a sound, his fever had risen, and she feared her promise of recovery would be one she couldn't keep. Finally, though, in the middle of the night, while she dozed off in a chair next to the cot, his fever had broken. Her promise would be kept. She had gone to her room to get a few moments of rest and realized she had only slept for an hour before Angie had interrupted her hellish nightmare.

"I don't know his story and I'm not going to ask for it. He said he came to help at the Alamo. For some reason, God decided it wasn't his time to die." It made her skin chill to realize that whatever mistake Cade had made that landed him in her home had actually saved his life.

Angie was snuggling down into Olivia's bed, her face marked by dried tears, her eyes heavy-lidded with exhaustion. "How much longer will he be here? Grandma and Grandpa are going to start wondering why you disappear to the cellar so often."

Olivia pulled on her skirt and buttoned up her shirtwaist. "He's badly injured, Angie. His leg…it's a miracle he even made it to our home. I don't know how he walked with it torn up so." Angie nodded, but she was already falling asleep.

Aching for her sister's loss, Olivia leaned over and brushed a kiss over her forehead then slipped out of the room, heading back to the man that dominated her thoughts.

STARING AT HIS sleeping face, Olivia nervously fingered the high collar of her shirt. Sitting on the edge of the cot, she had to shake her head at herself. While daylight grew outside, he still slumbered. She had no idea what she would do with him once he awoke.

Carefully, she peeled back the linen she had wrapped around his leg, exposing the wound that had caused him so much pain, and probably would for the rest of his life. Lightly she ran her fingers around the edge of the cut, noticing that her stitching held the wound together tightly, and thankfully the heat of fever and infection were gone. There would be a scar, though it was too soon to know just how severe it would be.

Her fingers smoothed the coarse blonde hair that covered his leg as she watched his face. She didn't know if she wanted him to wake up or stay asleep. She had long ago become used to his nudity, though she had done her best to cover him with sheets. His wounds had been too many, though, and his chest and legs still lay bare to her. She had never seen a man nude before, and found she couldn't stop looking at him. She felt as though she knew his body better than she knew her own.

The sound of boots overhead forced her eyes to the rafters. Their customers had been returning slowly. Most were

Mexican soldiers and, though it pained her greatly, they would provide money the *cocina* desperately needed. It was past noon, and Angie was making sure the last few diners were pleased with their meals before they closed for the day.

Frowning, Olivia looked back at Cade. She had spent far too much time with him, and it was taxing Angie and her grandmother. Though she still helped with the breakfast and lunch preparations, she vanished downstairs after most of the soldiers had left to tend to the stranger that had disrupted her life.

Sighing, she rolled her neck on her shoulders, hoping to find the strength to return upstairs and help with the chores. Her mystery man didn't need her now, and she needed to see to her responsibilities.

Her sigh turned into a startled gasp as her body was yanked forward, her arms pulled behind her. Unable to stop her fall, she collapsed on top of Cade, her nose touching his. Her startled eyes met his cold blue ones.

"Where is my gun?" His voice was raspy, but his intent was clear.

A shiver of fear went through her and she tugged at her wrists. "Why? Planning on killing someone?"

His eyes narrowed and his grip tightened. "Where?"

For a moment, it crossed her mind that she could dig her knee into his wound and would instantly be free. But she immediately dismissed it. For some reason, the thought of causing him pain wasn't something she wanted, no matter what the price.

"If you let me go and stop acting like a child, I'll bring it to you."

His eyes searched her face and his grip loosened. "Don't I know you?"

Olivia swallowed hard. Had she healed his body just for him to lose his mind?

"Don't you remember the other night—" She froze when his other hand reached up quickly and caught her hair.

With a few small tugs, her bun came loose, and her hair fell down over them.

Recognition crossed his face. "Olivia." He spoke so softly she almost didn't hear him.

But she did, and the heat of a blush crept up her neck. "Yes, well, I'm glad you've regained your memory. Though for your sake, I hope you've forgotten what was done to you."

He was watching her, an odd expression on his face, and she realized she was still sprawled across him. She once again tried to tug unsuccessfully on her wrists. His hand slid through her hair, down her arms, and to her waist, and though his grip on her wrists was finally loose enough to pull away, she felt completely trapped.

He held her waist, his hand spanning so his thumb touched her ribs and his small finger brushed her hip. "You were here... all that time...Why?"

Olivia swallowed hard and hoped her tremors would stop soon as she tried to draw in a deep breath. She wondered if her face looked like a beet.

"I-I suppose... It appears..." She pressed her lips together for a moment then tried again. "Have you forgotten about your gun, then?"

He shook his head slightly, and his breath blew over her lips. He surely could feel her heart pounding against his chest. "Do I need it? Should I be afraid of you? Now that you've healed me, are you planning on fighting me to the death?"

There was humor in his voice but it didn't show on his face. The man could be carved from stone. She latched on to the only logical thought she could find. "You are hardly healed. It will be weeks before you can try to walk—and it will be terribly painful even then."

The statement seemed to shift his focus and, for the briefest moment, Olivia was disappointed. Using his hand on her hip, he shifted her to the side so he could see down the length of his body and view the damage. Before she could say anything, he sat up and began to swing his legs off the cot.

"Stop!" She grabbed a hold of his shoulders, fully expecting to have to forcefully push him back onto the cot. She had overestimated his strength. The small movement of just sitting up had obviously exhausted him, and he fell back against her, and she found herself pinned against the wall, his massive back against her chest.

The warmth of his skin pressed against her made her suddenly breathless. With shaky hands, she tried to push her hair out her face, trying to tell herself she was annoyed he had taken it down.

"Well, I hope you're happy now."

His back moved against her as he tried to once again

stand and embarrassment flamed her cheeks as she felt her nipples harden against him. "I'll be much happier when I've got my gun." He grunted, moving forward slightly, then with a moan fell back on the cot. He ran a hand down his face then turned a hard glare on her. "How long have I been asleep?"

Olivia was trying to pull her skirts out from under him and realized the sheet was also underneath him. He was completely nude. She closed her eyes and counted slowly to three, then tugged on her skirts, hard. She found herself in the same position as a few moments ago, sprawled across his chest.

Blowing her hair out of her face, she glared down at him. "If you would just do as I tell you we wouldn't be having this trouble."

"What trouble?"

Olivia opened her mouth and couldn't think of anything to say. Careful to avoid hurting him, she climbed off of the cot and turned her back on him, taking a few moments to pin her hair back into the bun, hoping her heartbeat would slow down. Drawing a deep breath, she straightened her back and whirled back to face him, ready to give him a stern lecture on manners, propriety, and his lack of both.

Her mouth clicked shut. He was asleep. For a moment she had the insane desire to laugh. He probably wouldn't even remember the past few minutes, except that he still didn't have his gun. Nervously patting her hair, she eyed his face. This man was trouble. And the sooner she believed that, the better it would be for all of them.

CADE WAITED UNTIL he heard the door close above him before opening his eyes. Fortunately, she believed he was asleep and had left. Slowly, carefully, he pushed himself to a sitting position and was amazed at how exhausted he was. He shook his head as he looked at his body. He was a disaster that much was certain.

His lips twitched slightly as he saw the sheet she had draped over his midsection before leaving. Olivia was her name. He remembered fragments from the night he had come to their home—remembered her holding the gun on him. More than that, though, he remembered her speaking to him, her eyes locked with his as she poured the whiskey on his wounds.

He ran a hand through his hair and turned to prop himself against the wall, surveying his surroundings. He vaguely remembered descending the stairs into their cellar, but most of the events of that night were foggy. The cellar was obviously used for storage, with bags of potatoes, onions, and yams piled on a shelf. Another shelf held jars of preserves and pickles and other delectable items that made him realize it had been a long time since he ate.

His eyes settled on a small table in the far corner, and he leaned forward, but the lantern light was too low for him to see much. It looked like... guns. Pushing himself forward slowly, he reached for the lantern, and lifted it higher. A rifle, shotgun, and three pistols were on the table, cleaned and oiled; bullets and primer stacked next to them. One of the pistols he recognized as his own, and he struggled to his feet.

The pain that tore through his leg blinded him for a moment and he nearly dropped the lantern. Gasping, he dropped back to the cot, setting down the lantern with a thump. The pain nauseated him, and for several moments he thought he was going to be sick. Slowly it faded, easing into a throb that made his jaw clench.

Sweat covered his forehead and he wiped away at it as he lifted his head to look down at his leg. The bandage was bloodied, and a thin trickle was seeping down his thigh. Breathing deeply, he untied the linen and pulled it back, revealing the long, large gash and the delicate stitching that held it all together. He thought for a moment he would be sick again. He had seen men torn up before, seen their exposed muscles and tendons. It hadn't bothered him then. It was entirely different when he saw his own flesh torn so badly.

He wondered how he had been able to make it the few hundred yards to the Torres's residence that night, and realized his frantic adrenaline induced race to their home had probably caused the wound to tear even further.

With a muffled groan, he lay back on the cot, wanting to yell... wanting to break something. The frustration consuming him made him feel like he couldn't breathe. Gradually his breathing slowed and the room didn't seem to be smothering him. He stared up at the rafters and heard women talking; a young girl giggled.

His hands clenched into fists at his side. He would not let this stop him. He would heal. Too much was at stake for him not to.

Chapter Four

"SOME FOOD WOULD probably do you good."

The voice was one he wasn't used to, and his eyes shot to the stairs where a young woman descended, carrying a bowl in her hands. She smiled at him, though she looked wary. A memory flashed through his mind and he realized she was the woman he had almost shot when he first came to the Torres's home. No wonder she looked afraid of him.

"I know Vi has been taking good care of you, but we had some food left over from lunch, and I thought you might be hungry."

Cade pushed himself to a sitting position slowly, making sure the sheet covered most of him. He hated to admit it, but he didn't want her, or Olivia for that matter, to know that he had tried to stand and caused his wound to bleed. "Yes, ma'am. I am rather hungry."

She hesitated for a moment, landing at the bottom of the stairs, a half smile touching her lips. "I like the way you talk. Are you from near here?"

Cade avoided her gaze as he ran a hand through his hair, hoping he didn't look too much like the worn leather he felt like. "East. East Texas."

"Vi says you like to be called Cade. I hope I'm not being too forward to do so." She stepped closer and the smell of whatever was in the bowl wafted to him. His stomach growled audibly and she smiled. "You should enjoy this."

He wanted to curse when he saw his hands shaking as he reached for the bowl. Damn, but he was weak. He couldn't remember the last time he had been so exhausted. He looked at the bowl with skepticism. He would probably spill the contents all in his lap.

The young woman appeared to be thinking the same thing as she pulled the bowl back, her lips pursed thoughtfully. "Well, I don't think this will work. I can…"

"I can feed him. What are you doing down here anyway?" Olivia was coming down the steps quickly, her manner brisk. "I don't know that he should be eating so soon anyway. Perhaps just a tortilla."

Cade's stomach growled in protest. "I think I can handle a bit more than that. Whatever is in that bowl smells mighty good."

The young woman stepped back and handed Olivia the bowl, then cast Cade a rueful glance. "I'm Angie, by the way." She placed her hand to the side of her mouth and whispered, "The nice one."

Cade's eyes followed Olivia as she approached him with the bowl, noting that her hair was back in its severe knot, and her expression was devoid of emotion. The woman was hard, and he still couldn't believe she had sacrificed so much to care for him.

Olivia carefully sat next to him on the cot and hefted a

spoonful of what looked like stew towards his mouth. For a moment, he felt like telling her he was perfectly capable of feeding himself. When he lifted his hand, though, the tremors were still there. Concealing a weary sigh, he opened his mouth like a babe and took the food she offered.

The flavors that washed through his mouth were intoxicating, and the textures made his stomach growl for more. "What is this?" he asked, swallowing quickly and opening his mouth for the next spoonful.

"It's called *menudo*," Angie said, beaming. "*Abuela* makes the best you will ever eat."

For a several seconds, Cade was lost in the blissful experience of consuming the herb enhanced sauce and meat. "*Menudo?*"

"It's a little like what I suppose you call stew." Angie spoke up again, preventing Olivia from elaborating. "But when she adds the goat eyes, it makes it so perfect."

The next swallow was a little more difficult. "Goat eyes?"

Olivia pivoted on the cot and glared at Angie. "Is there a reason you are still down here?"

Angie clasped her hands behind her and rocked back and forth on her toes. "What are you doing here in San Antonio, Mr. Cade? I know you wanted to help at the Alamo. You're so fortunate you didn't make it."

Cade's eyes locked on Olivia. "What is she talking about?"

Olivia's lips were in a tight, thin line. "The Alamo has fallen, Mr. Cade. There were no survivors."

The mouthful of menudo in his mouth was nearly impossible to swallow. "None of them?" he said, his throat tight. "None of them made it out?" A vague memory tickled his mind and his eyes shot over to Angie. "Your husband…"

Angie's chin quivered, but she forced a smile to her lips. "My husband is a very strong man. He's gotten out of some terrible scrapes before. I know he did it again."

Again, Cade looked at Olivia and saw the expression on her face. She didn't believe as Angie did, but obviously didn't want to voice her thoughts out loud. Cade didn't blame her. The hope in Angie's eyes was enough to make anyone hesitate before speaking against it.

Angie's eyes dropped to the menudo, and her face paled. "I'm sorry," she muttered. "I think I'm going to be sick." She turned as though to head for the stairs, but quickly turned back and grabbed the chamber pot, retching loudly.

Cade's appetite completely vanished.

Olivia set the bowl to the side and shook her head at her sister. "You worry yourself sick. Look at yourself! This is the third time this week you have been sick like this."

"It's not her fault," Cade said softly.

Olivia glanced over at him, a puzzled look on her face. "Did you say something?"

Cade frowned, wondering why she hadn't heard him. "I said it's not her fault. All women go through this."

Olivia pressed her lips into the thin line he was coming to expect and shook her head. "Not all women handle stress and worry so badly. She just needs to—"

"It's because of the babe."

Angie's head snapped up and she hastily wiped at her

lips, looking at Cade as though he had betrayed her. The look in her eyes told him he had just said something she really wished he hadn't.

"What?" Olivia looked between Cade and Angie then focused on Cade. "What are you saying?"

Cade watched Olivia, not willing to say anything more. He had obviously hit upon a subject Angie wasn't ready to discuss, and he didn't want to put the woman in any further turmoil. Losing her husband was bad enough. Having to face the world without a father for her child was far worse.

Olivia focused on Angie, obviously realizing Cade wasn't going to supply her any answers. "What is he talking about, Angie?"

"I—I had wondered… I wasn't certain…"

"We'll talk about this at another time. Go lie down and rest. Be sure to drink some water. I'll be up there soon."

Tears welled into Angie's eyes and she stood, heading towards the stairs. "I'm going to my room. Sorry I can't stay. Mr. Cade, it was nice meeting you… without the gun this time, of course…"

Olivia sat in silence for several moments, staring at the chamber pot. Finally, slowly, she turned back to Cade.

"Would you like anything more to eat?" Her manner was calm, formal… cold.

"I thought you would have known…" He didn't know how to apologize or even if he should.

Olivia grabbed up the bowl and stood. "I didn't. You don't know me or my family, Mr. Cade, so please don't make assumptions. Your stay with us might be brief, but you will be with us, nonetheless. I ask that you stay out of our affairs during that time. I have taken care of this family for many years and will continue to do so without your assistance."

Cade felt as though she had slapped him. "For someone who has taken care of a family for so long, I would think you would know a little more about what goes on with them."

The flare in her eyes made Cade very thankful she wasn't holding her pistol any longer. "I will be down to check on you later. In the meantime, I recommend you try not to stand again. I'm sure the last time was excruciating."

"ANGIE, YOU WILL answer my question. You will not ignore me about this! Are you really pregnant?"

"Yes, Vi, I'm pregnant. I've known for the past week. Is that what you want? I didn't know how to tell you. But now you know. And don't get that look on your face. Lorenzo is coming home. You don't have to worry about a thing." Angie's last words ended on a sob.

Feeling responsible for her sister's distress, Olivia wrapped he arms around Angie, rocking her back and forth from where they sat on Angie's bed.

"The baby should be born in October. At least, that is what I expect. Maybe as late as November. But I started getting sick right after the soldiers began to arrive. That means I'm already at least a month or more along," Angie said between sniffles.

Olivia sat listening to her, but unable to fully absorb what was being said. A baby. It was unfathomable. With Lorenzo gone, and very little hope of his returning, Angie would have to raise the child on her own, with the help of family, of course. But it would have no father.

Olivia pressed her fingers to her forehead and rubbed slowly, trying to ease the ache. "What are you planning on doing?"

Angie leaned back in her arms and shot a look at Olivia. "What else would I plan on doing? This baby is coming, whether we want it or not. And, frankly, I want it." She moved out of the embrace with Olivia and dabbed at her eyes with her apron. "What are you planning?"

"I just…" Olivia hesitated.

She didn't want to tell her sister that Olivia was fairly certain her husband was dead. Though Angie clung to the thought she didn't see Lorenzo's body among the dead at the Alamo, Olivia realized they didn't see everyone that died, and some of the bodies were so mangled and unrecognizable, they wouldn't have known if it was Lorenzo or not.

"We need to make plans for your pregnancy. You can't do as much work in the *cocina* as you have been. I don't want you on your feet all day anymore."

Angie paused and smiled at Olivia. "I'll be fine. The work is good for me. It keeps me from…" Angie's voice trailed off, and both knew what she was thinking of. "It keeps me from noticing the sickness as much."

Olivia rubbed more furiously at her forehead and drew a deep, though shaky, breath. "Still, not as much work. Serena can help out more. And what about your home? I can't let you go back out there like this. It was hard enough with just the two of us. Pregnant, you won't be able to really get anything accomplished."

Angie fluffed her pillows needlessly and focused on picking some lint off of the bedspread. "I've been thinking about that." Her gaze finally lifted and connected with Olivia's. "I think you should go stay out there for a while."

"And leave you and Serena to care for things? Hah! This babe is already addling your mind."

"And take Mr. Cade with you."

Olivia froze. "No. Absolutely not."

Angie turned in the bed and leveled a look a Olivia that clearly stated there was no room for negotiation. "Vi, you know the soldiers are looking for him. It is just a matter of time before they start looking around here. You saw they were searching the marketplace this morning. They still believe he is nearby."

"We've deceived them in the past. We'll do so again."

"I don't think it will be so easy this time. They are actually hunting for him, Vi. And if they find him here, everyone will be at risk. I don't know what he did to make them want to find him so badly, but we will absolutely protect him. You need to get him away from here. For the sake of the family."

Olivia scoffed. "Don't try that ploy on me. You know I will do whatever I think is safest for the family, and right now that would be for me to stay right here."

"You are not being logical. If you just take him out there—"

"I will not sacrifice the Torres good name by staying alone out there with a man I don't even know, much less am wed to…"

"Exactly who do you think is even going to care? No one is around, Vi! Open your eyes. Everyone has left. Our cousins, our *tias*… everyone is gone. No one is watching us except the Mexican Army, and they think we are hiding someone they want to execute!"

Olivia stood and headed for the door. "No. Absolutely not. I won't even consider it."

"The man is injured. He can't do anything. He can't even stand on his own. What possibly could happen?"

Olivia stopped halfway to the door and whirled on her sister. "You have no idea the terrible things men are capable of. And you don't know because I've hidden them from you. But it's time you opened your eyes, Angie. We don't know this man! How do we even know if we can trust him?"

"Then why have you let him stay in our home, under the same roof as your sisters and grandparents if you don't think he can be trusted?"

Olivia's mouth opened then clicked shut. She folded her arms over her chest, her foot tapping madly on the floor.

"He needed me," she said finally, then corrected, "He needed us. We are the only thing keeping him from that army. I—I will not see him come to harm by them."

"Good. Then you're already looking at things more logically. Now realize that you need to get him away from here." Angie stood and began to straighten the bedspread.

"You are one to talk about logic! All your life you've

done everything backwards and against the rules!"

"Your rules, Vi. Your rules."

Olivia stood frozen for several seconds, breathing heavily, so angry and frustrated she couldn't move.

Slowly, she turned, her hands shaking as she reached for the door handle. "I have always done what is best for this family. And I will continue to do so."

"Then you will take him out to my home."

"And do what, Angie? Leave him out there? Wish him a speedy recovery?" She shook her head, looking over her shoulder. "I don't think so."

Angie frowned, placing her hands on her hips. "What are you scared of?"

Olivia nearly choked on her tongue. Without another word she yanked open the door, slamming it loudly behind her.

"VERY BRAVE. WHY didn't… the others? It would have…"

Olivia stepped closer to the door leading out into the dining room, straining to hear the conversation that kept eluding her. Casually glancing out at the diners, she saw a soldier… an officer, speaking to Angie, and her heart skipped a beat.

"San Antonio is our home, *senor*. It always will be." Angie said, smiling sweetly at him.

There was a fine tremble in Angie's hands, though, as she poured coffee.

"Ah." The Officer leaned back in his chair, smoothing his hand over his mustache, his eyes watching her. "Now that order has been restored, I'm sure your neighbors will return soon. It must have been uncomfortable with those heathens running this town."

Olivia cringed when Angie's spine straightened and Olivia hurried to the table, hoping to prevent a disastrous situation. "Sister, we are running low on empanadas. Do you think you could make some more? I will make sure these *senors* have their breakfast."

Angie hesitated only a moment, then nodded, smiling at Olivia as she handed her the coffee pot. "I was worried we wouldn't have enough. Do you think a dozen more?"

Olivia shook her head. "Two at least." She turned a smile on the soldiers at the table. "You know how much our customers love empanadas." It wasn't hard to smile as she made the comment.

Angie burnt her empanadas more often than she made them right, but the soldiers had no way of knowing that.

"What can I do for you today, *senor*?" she said, addressing the officer first. "We just made a new pot of *menudo*, or we could cook you a batch of *juevos*. What would you like?"

"Some answers, *Senorita* Torres."

Olivia hoped her face didn't not show how nervous she was. The man made her uneasy for more reasons than one. The blatant way he stared at Angie had made Olivia's skin crawl, and now he stared at her in the same way. "I will do my best to assist you," she said politely.

"I came to your home the other night. We were looking

for someone. Your lovely sister assisted us in our search."

"Yes, she told me about it. I am sorry you didn't find what you were looking for."

His dark brown eyes were speculative, and his finger continued smoothing his mustache. "Why didn't you greet us, *senorita*? I was under the impression you ran this household."

Olivia forced a smile to her stiff lips. "We all share in the responsibilities, *senor*. My sisters would be impossible to live with if they thought I believed myself to be in charge. My sister is a light sleeper. You had come and gone before I could even get my wrapper on."

His fingers slowed their movements as his eyes moved slowly down the length of her body, and she the heat of a blush touched her cheeks. "Had I known such a beautiful woman was here, I would have waited."

Olivia prayed her smile was still in place, but she was contemplating spilling the entire contents of coffee in his lap. "You are too flattering, *senor*. Now, what can I get you for—"

"I have heard that many of these homes have cellars. Do you have a cellar, senorita?"

Olivia couldn't move her lips to speak. Her grip tightened on the coffee pot as her palms suddenly became damp with sweat. "Y-yes." She swallowed. "Of course, *senor*."

"Ah." He watched her for several moments, then leaned forward in his chair. "What do you keep in the cellar?"

"*Senor*, I do not understand your curiosity over the use of our—"

"We still have not found what we were looking for the other night, *senorita*."

"Precisely what is it that you are looking for? Perhaps I can direct you where you might have misplaced it." Olivia instantly regretted her words. The officer was not one to be toyed with, and she was pushing the limits.

He appeared amused, the corners of his mustache twitching. "I'm looking for a man. He is a very dangerous man who killed three of my soldiers. I would not want your family to be in danger."

"We have seen much in the past year, *senor*, and have taken care of ourselves just fine. I truly appreciate your concern, and I wish you the best of luck in finding this man. Though I doubt he would still be in San Antonio if he knows you are seeking him."

The officer finally smiled, and Olivia thought he would be an attractive man if only he didn't wear the uniform of an officer in the Mexican Army. That and the fact that there seemed to be no warmth, no soul within him. She had thought the same of Cade when she first saw him. Was it still the same? Or had her feelings towards him changed in the short time she'd been with him?

***

"HE HAS NOT left yet, *senorita*. He could not."

Olivia cocked her head to the side, feigning interest. All she wanted to do was to get away from the man. He frightened her in a way she couldn't explain.

"Why not, *senor*? A man on foot or horse could easily leave town."

His smile turned frighteningly cold. "Because I cut him… I slashed him with my blade. If he is still alive, he cannot walk. I made certain of that."

Olivia felt ill. "Then how could he possibly have escaped you, *senor*?" She tried to appear concerned. "He did not hurt you, did he? Is that how he was able to get away?"

The officer looked uncomfortable and avoided looking at her. "Like I said, he is a dangerous man." His gaze lifted back up to hers. "I think the devil gives him strength. What else but a demon would attack my men with nothing but a pistol? He is possessed."

Olivia nodded in agreement. "Then may God be with you. I'm sure you will need something to eat to help you continue your search—"

"I want to see your cellar."

Now Olivia knew she was going to be sick. "*Perdone*? I beg your pardon?"

The officer was already standing. "For your own safety, I want to be certain he has not taken refuge in your cellar."

Olivia drew a quivering breath and turned towards the kitchen. "Certainly, *senor*, just follow me." A thousand things raced through her mind as her eyes made contact with Angie's. *Dear God, help me through this*!

Chapter Five

C ADE WIPED AT the sweat covering his brow with the back of his hand and eyed the guns again. He had to get to them. His life and that of the woman who offered him shelter were at stake.

He had awoken to the sound of boots on the floor above him and the delicious aromas of breakfast. Down in the cellar, he could only tell time by the scent of the meal cooking. His nerves were on edge. It had been nearly three days since he had awoken to find the strong-willed woman tending to his wounds. He had been close to losing his mind for the past two.

The *cocina* had become incredibly silent halfway through the breakfast meal, though, and the hair on the back of his neck had stood on end. Something wasn't right. Sitting upright, he strained to hear something—anything that would tell him what was happening. The conversation he heard caused him to break out in a cold sweat and count the minutes he had left to live.

He looked down at his leg and tried to run the possibilities through his mind. If he tried to stand again, he would likely pass out. If he didn't do anything, he would be shot where he lay.

Gritting his teeth, he swung his legs over the side, his jaw muscles so tight he thought his teeth would break. Panting, he once again wiped at the sweat on his face and focused on the small table only a couple of short feet away. He could make it. He had to.

He heard footsteps above him, heard Olivia's voice followed by the deep rumble of a man's voice—a man that had destroyed his life. It was now or never. Throwing himself forward, he landed face down on the ground, turning slightly so he landed more on his right side.

The impact was still brutal and his hands bunched into fists and he squeezed his eyes shut, counting slowly until the pain became a bearable throb. The footsteps overhead stopped and he heard a latch being lifted.

Using his forearms to drag himself, he moved faster than expected, cringing as his leg drug across the dirt floor. If he lived through this, he didn't know if he would survive the lecture he would get from Olivia.

He pulled himself up by the legs of the table and groaned as he felt a pull on the skin around his wound. His pistol fit into his hand perfectly, the weight a solid reassurance. He quickly checked the chamber as he heard the hinges of a door above begin to creak open, and Olivia's voice reached him clearly. "Like I said, we just don't use it…"

And he knew he was good as dead. His pistol wasn't loaded.

OLIVIA STEPPED BACK so the officer could look down. "We stopped using it many years ago, and began to have trouble with critters making homes down there. After the last time my mother was scared by a raccoon that built his home down there, my father did this." Olivia gestured towards the hole in the floor and was relieved her hands weren't shaking too much.

The bricked over hole was obviously useless, and she prayed the officer would come to that conclusion. Frowning, the man kneeled down, his fingers touching the surface as though feeling it would make it more real to him. He looked up at Olivia. "Then where do you keep all of your goods? Surely you must…"

"Oh, of course! We have a small shed out back. I hadn't even thought…Well, I haven't been out there in a couple of days. Do you suppose he could…This man, I mean…"

"Oh, Olivia, surely not. Why would he take refuge in there?" Angie walked up beside her and placed a hand on her shoulder, her face a worried mask. "Do you really think…?"

Olivia turned to face the officer who was slowly standing, still frowning down at the hole. "Would you mind terri-bly…Would it be too much to ask of you to check… I must confess you have me rather worried…"

The officer turned and looked at her, and the measuring skepticism in his eyes wasn't reassuring. But quickly his eyes turned merry. "Don't worry, *senoritas*. I will be sure you are kept safe. This man is as good as dead. Think nothing more of it. And I'm sorry I've troubled you so much this morn-ing."

Angie stepped up to him quickly. "You haven't been any trouble. I am only thankful you are watching out for us. Now with so many restless soldiers, I worry what more could happen here…"

The soldier smiled, enjoying the attention of a beautiful woman as they walked back out towards the dining area. Once they were out of sight Olivia sagged against the china cabinet, her heart beating so hard she felt like it had lodged in her throat. Tears burned at the back of her eyes.

They had never come this close to discovery before. No one had ever questioned about their cellar and for so long they had been safe. Her father had known, years ago, that the cellar would be the wisest place for them to keep things out of sight. But, being the wise man that he was, he had also known there would come a time when someone would search their home.

And so he had created the false door that looked like bricks.

⚜

CADE REALIZED THAT God worked in very, very bizarre ways. When faced with certain death, his maker hadn't given him the loaded pistol he desperately needed. Instead, He had given him a half full bottle of whiskey that tumbled off the table and directly into his lap.

Listening to the door open overhead, Cade took the longest swallow of the burning liquid he had ever taken in his life. Perhaps, then, if Officer Shitface, as he had named him, decided to torture him, he wouldn't feel it as much.

But the door never opened. With half of the liquid already burning a path to his stomach he leaned forward, staring up the stairs at the door where Olivia's voice traveled clearly. What the hell was going on?

His hand clenched around the useless pistol and he took another long draw on the whiskey. It was just a matter of time, and surprisingly enough, his leg wasn't hurting as much as it had been. Maybe alcohol wasn't such a bad thing.

The room wavered for a moment and he blinked slowly. Thank God he wasn't going to need to defend himself. He would probably shoot the roof instead of the man that had made his life miserable.

It had grown quiet once again upstairs, and the alcohol had hit his empty stomach hard. He wasn't sure if it had really gone quiet or if he was already entering an alcohol induced stupor. He deliberately set the bottle to the side and tried to push himself forward, hoping to get back to the cot before Olivia came down. If she came down.

A new thought entered his mind that brought clarity and made his palms sweat. What if they were abusing her? What if they were angry because she wouldn't tell them where he was? What if she needed him up there?

He glared at his leg then scanned the room, wondering if there was anything he could do. His eyes landed on the discarded sheet, and he pulled himself towards it, sweat dripping into his eyes. He was out of breath and his arms were trembling by the time he reached the sheet, but he couldn't lose focus. Grabbing the sheet, he began to wrap it around his leg, wrapping tighter and tighter, trying to give his torn muscle some support... something so he could try to help Olivia.

He tied the sheet in a knot, his eyes squeezed shut against the pain. Olivia needed him. She had stayed beside him all this time and tended to him, putting herself and her family at risk. He wouldn't let them hurt her. Too many people had already been hurt because of his actions.

He leaned back, resting against the wall for a few moments, wishing the room would stop spinning. It wasn't helping his already wavy balance. Inching his shoulders up the wall, he brought himself to a half leaning, half stooping position and looked at the stairs. For a moment he felt helpless. How was he going to get up those stairs?

He shook his head. First things first. He needed a weapon... a loaded one. Pushing away from the wall, he lunged forward, dragging his leg behind him. He hadn't thought it would be so difficult, given that he was hardly putting any weight on his leg. But the pain was making it difficult to see straight. Either that or the whiskey.

He nearly fell on the table and used it as a brace, wincing at the sound of the wood creaking beneath his hands. If the table broke and he went down, he wouldn't get up again. He was breathing heavily, and his hair had pulled free from the leather tong at the back of his neck and covered his face. Raking his hand through it, he brushed it off his forehead and focused on an assortment of weapons and artillery on the table. Finally spotting what he was looking for, he frantically tried to load his gun.

The door above creaked again, and his stomach fell to his feet. They had defeated her. She had cracked and said where he was. More than likely they had already killed her. He had managed to load the gun and turned to face the stairs. He would at the very least kill one of them before they took him down.

Steps sounded on the stairs and he cocked the hammer back, his hand wavering slightly. He leaned his hip against the table, adding balance, and brought his other hand up to support the pistol. Damn, he hated being weak.

He blinked as sweat dripped in his eyes and could feel his nerves jarring with every squeak of the boards. When a pair of small booted feet and a calico skirt came into view, he nearly dropped the gun.

Olivia hesitated, seeing the empty cot. "Mr. Cade?" She hurried down the next few steps, nearly tripping over her own feet in her haste. She froze on the bottom steps, staring at the pistol he held, then at his pale complexion. "What are you doing? Have you lost your mind?"

"Where is he?"

"Who? You're going to fall." She stepped down the last few stairs but stopped when his gun wavered. "I'd prefer you set that gun down before you shoot me."

"Where is he?" he shook his head when she opened her mouth. "The officer! The man looking for me…"

Olivia shook her head. "He left. About ten minutes ago. The *cocina* is empty now. We won't get another rush for at least an hour. You are safe."

Cade lowered the gun and couldn't contain the harsh

laugh that escaped. "That's the biggest lie I bet you've ever told." He pinned her with his eyes, leaving no room for her to argue. "Safe is a world I'll never know."

More of his weight shifted to the table and it creaked loudly. Olivia hurried forward, lifting one of his arms and draping it over her shoulders. "Lean on me. I'll get you back to the cot."

He didn't want to. He didn't want to depend on this woman that had given him so much already. The longer he stayed, the greater the risk to her. He could push away from her and force himself up those stairs. He could do it.

He let some of his weight lean on her and her soft body pressed into his. He looked down at her, wishing he could see her more clearly. The lamplight gave him enough of an idea what she looked like, but he wanted to see how her skin and hair looked in the sunlight.

She hesitated, glancing up at him, concern on her face. Was she really concerned for him? It was impossible to believe. But he wanted to think someone cared. Even if it was someone who didn't know all the terrible things that had happened to people because of his actions.

"Mr. Cade?"

"I need to leave."

Her eyes widened at his comment. "Eventually, yes, I agree. I'm not planning on harboring you down here forever. Though you do make an interesting patient."

Cade was curious, he couldn't help it. "Have you had many patients here before?"

She shook her head, smiling slightly. The smile did wonders for her face, drawing him closer. "So far, only one. I hope it remains that way."

Her arm wrapped around his waist and the feel of her cool fingers against his skin reminded him he didn't wear clothes. "Are you always this comfortable around naked men?"

A blush touched her cheeks and she encouraged him to step forward. "Thank you, Mr. Cade, for pointing out the obvious. I was doing my best to ignore it. How is your leg?"

"I think it is strong enough for me to leave." He leaned more heavily on her as he tried to drag his leg behind him.

"Yes, I can see that," she said dryly, stiffening her shoulders to try to support his weight. "Where exactly are you in such a rush to?"

She tried to pivot with him so that he could sit on the cot, but it didn't work. He pitched forward and she stumbled backwards, pinned beneath him. For a moment he couldn't move. He didn't want to move. She smelled of warm cinnamon and bread and woman, and he couldn't think of a better aroma. With his face buried against her neck, he took a deep breath, then another, feeling light-headed.

He felt her heart beating faster, and her fingernails dug into his arms. "Mr-Mr. Cade..."

His head lifted slowly and he gazed down at her, his eye-lids drooping drowsily. "It's just Cade. Just Cade." His hands reached up and she watched him as though transfixed while he caught a loose strand of her hair and wound it around his finger. "Why don't you leave it down?"

"What?" Her eyes were fixated on his fingers caressing her hair. Then she blinked and stuttered out a response, "I-I don't like it loose. It gets in my way."

"I like it down. You are beautiful."

His words seemed to change her mood towards him entirely, though he had no idea how. "Just how much of that whiskey did you drink? Don't look surprised, I saw the bottle." She pushed at his shoulders. "Will you please get off me? I will not be part of your drunken escapade."

Cade pulled back, surprised by her actions. "Drunken escapade? What the hell are you talking about?"

"Only a fool or a drunk would have tried the stunt you just did. If that officer had come down here do you really think you could defend yourself? You can't even stand on your own." She shoved at his shoulders again, panting with the exertion.

"For your information, I was coming to help you." Even as he said it, Cade realized how foolish it sounded. Yeah, the whiskey probably had been most of the motivating factor behind his... escapade. "And I'm sober now."

Olivia pressed her lips together. "Get off of me."

He didn't know what made him do it. Maybe it was because she needed a little reminder that he was a man. Maybe it was because *he* needed a little reminder that he was a man. But before he could think twice, he dropped his head, his lips sealing with hers.

She gasped in surprise and he took advantage to press further, his tongue lightly tracing the delicate skin just inside her lips. Her body became stiff, her fingers slowly curling into fists. He moved his lips over her slowly, gently, hoping to coax a reaction from her, but if anything, she became stiffer.

Finally, he lifted his head, looking down at her with frustration. She glared up at him.

"I suppose I won't do that—" His words ended on a grunt as her fist struck his jaw—hard.

He pitched to the side quickly, drawing up his arms to defend himself, but obviously she was done.

She stood quickly, adjusting her skirt and shirt, calmly smoothing her hair back in place. "I'm sorry for doing that. But I told you to get off of me and you just would not listen."

Cade touched his jaw tenderly and knew he had another bruise to add to the multitudes. "Lady, one day someone will teach you to thaw out. But I pray for mercy on the man that has to do it." He glanced up in time to see a flash of pain in her eyes before she turned quickly towards the stairs.

"I'll come back later to-to check your leg. I'll bring you..." She paused, clearing her throat. "I'll bring you something to eat." And, with that, she hurried up the stairs, leaving him to figure out just what he had done wrong.

Chapter Six

*B*EAUTIFUL. HE HAD called her beautiful. She hesitated while folding the towels as her mind traveled back to the moment when his lips had first touched hers. She had tasted the whiskey, but she had also tasted him—warm, rich, heady. She could have gotten drunk from the kiss alone.

But then he would begin the groping, the ripping of her stockings and, if she didn't do exactly as he ordered, there would be pain. She knew the experience well, and had prayed that she never again had to go through such an ordeal.

And it was only the alcohol that had made him call her beautiful. She knew how unappealing she was. Ever since she was a teenager she had dressed in clothes that hid her body from a man's eyes. What man would ever crave a woman that was thin and muscular from years of hard work? They wanted a woman that was soft and supple, with all of the right curves. She had curves, but she was embarrassed by them.

She had developed early in life and the boys at school had enjoyed tormenting her over her body. At first she had been able to ignore them. But when the girls began to hurl insults at her as well, she learned to dress in a way that no one would ever know what her body looked like.

Shaking her head, she returned her attention to folding the towels. She hadn't thought about her body or what men would think of it in years. She had been too busy building her wall. She would never again be hurt like she was before. She would never let anyone that close to her heart again.

HE HAD STARTED to doze off when he heard the door above him lift. Wearily rubbing at his eyes, he adjusted the sheet, making sure he was covered. He frowned at the red stains. He hadn't intended on ruining her linens in his haste to wrap his leg.

Tiny feet skipped quickly down the stairs and a young girl he had never seen before smiled at him before jumping off the last two steps, the bowl in her hands sloshing liquid onto the cloth wrapped around it. It didn't seem to bother her.

"*Hola.*" She grinned, sitting on the edge of the cot next to him. "I brought you some broth and tortillas." She squinted. "Maybe if you aren't so hungry you'll stop glaring like that."

Cade hadn't been aware of the scowl on his face, but immediately forced his expression to loosen up. "Where's Olivia?" he asked, accepting the tortilla she handed him.

The young girl began to wiggle her foot. "Does she let you call her Olivia? That would be a first. My name is

Serena, by the way. Everyone just calls me Serri."

The girl talked fast and loud and his head began to ache. With difficulty, he swallowed the tortilla. Never had he tasted something so wonderful, but his mouth was still parched, and the swigs of whiskey hadn't helped. She seemed to know what he was going through, because she grabbed the jar of water nearby and pressed it to his lips. He had no choice but to swallow or have the liquid splash over his face.

Finally, she pulled it away and he drew a deep breath. "Are you... Is Olivia your mother?" He hadn't thought Olivia was old enough, but...

"Hah! She acts like it doesn't she? She's my sister. Hard to believe, I know." She began to braid her hair, her foot still wiggling rapidly.

The girl was dressed in such an odd fashion he wondered if she wasn't entirely right in the head. Her worn skirt had what appeared to be torn pieces of painted tarp pinned on in several places, and she wore a thick red sash that wrapped all the way up her torso over her shirt. She was smiling at him when he looked at her freckle-covered face.

"I just painted the tarp yesterday. I couldn't wait any longer to wear it. What do you think?"

He thought he was in a madhouse. "Where is Olivia?" he asked again.

She sighed and let her hair fall loose from her fingers. "Upstairs. She's been too busy to come down here, so I thought I would come visit."

His brow wrinkled and he hoped Serena wasn't going to make another comment about his expressions. "Does she know you're down here?"

Serena scoffed and stood, walking around the room and rummaging through everything she could get her hands on. "They don't know where I am half the time." She grinned. "Which is a good thing—for me at least." She paused when she came to the gun table and turned back to him.

He quickly swallowed the broth he had put in his mouth, wishing she would keep looking around and not make him the subject of interest again. It wasn't to be. She flounced back over to him and sat down on the cot so hard his leg bounced. He gritted his teeth and tried not to look at her, certain the scowl on his face this time would get a reaction.

When he cracked one eye open to look at her, she was leaning forward, her chin propped in her hand, watching him closely. "So what happened to you?"

He took another long sip of the broth, trying to ignore the eyes that were watching him so intently. He swallowed the soothing liquid and wanted to sigh in contentment. Though he really wanted a huge meal to soothe his hunger, the broth was satisfying and he was feeling warm and relaxed.

She was still watching him.

He frowned. "How old are you?"

"Thirteen. So what happened?"

She was relentless. He glanced longingly at the stairs. Where was Olivia?

He could take her silence and glares easier than the inquisitive girl sitting next to him. "I was in a fight."

"Angie said it was with the Mexican soldiers. Did you

kill any?"

Cade took a large bite out of his tortilla and chewed it slowly. She never looked away.

"Yes," he mumbled around the food.

Her eyes lit up. "Good. They all deserve to die."

He narrowed his eyes at her, cautiously setting his nearly empty bowl on the floor next to him. "Why would you say that?"

She shrugged. "They aren't good people. Did you see what they did to our men in the Alamo? No... I guess you didn't. You're fortunate. And they call us heathens."

Cade shook his head. "Someone has filled your head with a bunch of crap."

Her eyes widened with surprise. "How can you say that? Aren't you a Texian?"

"There have been terrible things done... on both sides. It's a war. Men follow their leaders. Most of those out there right now are just boys and all they know is that Mexico is their home and they must take care of it. If you hate them just for following their leaders, then you need to hate most of the Texians, too."

She frowned deeply at him. "But they're wrong."

"Have you ever thought they might be saying the same thing about us... about you? They think you're supporting greedy Americans."

She folded her arms across her chest and lifted her chin. "I support freedom. They want to take all of that away from us!"

"And the Americans want to break their rules. Sometimes you have to see things from both sides."

She chewed on the inside of her cheek, watching him, frowning at him. "Whose side are you on?"

The corner of his mouth lifted and he lay his head back on the pillow. "Mine."

She stood up and leaned over him, looking down at him. "That's not a very good answer."

"I think it is."

She seemed to be thinking about it, mulling it over in her head. "I don't think I like you."

Cade sighed heavily and closed his eyes. "Not many people do." He cracked one eye open at her. "On either side," he added and she smiled.

She nodded towards his leg. "Is it bad?"

Cade closed his eyes again. "You don't need to worry about it."

"What makes you think I'm worried? Can I look at it?"

Cade's eyes snapped open. "No, you don't want to…" She was already lifting the sheet up and he grabbed the edges just in time to prevent curious thirteen-year-old eyes from seeing his full anatomy. Her face had turned pale.

"That's really ugly," she said, swallowing hard.

"Thank you. I needed to know that." He was struggling to cover his leg up again, but she wouldn't let him.

"It must hurt a lot." She kneeled down next to the cot, trying to get a closer look at his torn flesh. She pursed her lips and drummed her fingers on the sheet. "I could make something for you."

"Make something…?"

She turned back to look at him, a wicked smile on her face. "If I decide I like you, that is. I need to think about it."

"Serena!" Olivia's voice was loud in the small space, and Serena jumped as though she had been struck by a whip.

She gave Cade a nervous grin. "*Adios*, cowboy." He had never seen a girl scramble so fast, dodging around the stairs as Olivia hurried down them and quickly slipping out of her sister's attempted grasp.

For a moment it looked like Olivia was going to charge up the stairs after her, then she stopped, shaking her head. He watched her draw a deep breath before turning to face him, but her eyes wouldn't quite meet his.

"I'm sorry. She shouldn't have come down here. I hope she didn't bother you too much."

"You were more worried about her than you were about me. Do you really think I'm a threat?" Cade wanted to laugh but he was too irritated.

He hadn't done anything to this woman, and yet she had obviously been afraid for her sister.

Her eyes shot to his face in surprise. "Of course I do! You come into my home uninvited with a loaded gun, you threaten to shoot Angie, and you have admitted to killing others. How could I not believe you a threat?"

Put in that perspective, Cade wondered why she hadn't already shot him. Curiosity gnawed at him. "Then why do you let me stay? Why are you taking care of me instead of forcing me out on my way?"

Her eyes left his face as she bent to pick up his bowl. "I made a promise," she said softly, almost too soft for him to hear.

"What promise?"

She smoothed a hand over her hair, making sure the bun was still slicked away from her face. "I-I promised you that you would get better. I need to keep my promise."

Irritation bubbled inside him. "Well consider your promise kept. I'm better. Now I'm leaving." He struggled to push himself to a sitting position, wincing as pain shot up his leg.

"I'm glad to know I've saved a rational man. God knows we need more of them." Her voice dripped sarcasm as she turned her back on him and went to the corner.

Teeth gritted, he kept struggling to pull himself up while she continued talking.

"You don't have the strength to make it up those stairs, much less out of this house. And when you pass out on the back steps the wrath of the entire Mexican Army will come down on my family." She shook her head as she pulled a sheet out from under a pile of blankets and shook it out. She pinned him with a dark look that made him momentarily pause. "I won't let you do that."

He was finally sitting up straight and slowly, painfully, swung his legs over the side of the cot. "I heard that officer upstairs this morning. Or yesterday morning. Hell, I don't even know what day it is. I'm getting out of here before I put you in any more danger."

Olivia approached him, her expression unusually neutral. He should probably apologize for his comment earlier. He hadn't meant to offend her, but her reaction had been unnecessary. He rubbed at his jaw where her fist had struck him. She was definitely wound too tight.

She drew a deep breath as she stood in front of him, holding the sheet loosely at her waist. "Mr. Cade—"

"Cade. Just Cade."

"As much as I would love to argue with you, I must agree that it is not safe for you to stay here any longer."

He hoped the surprise didn't show on his face. "Good. I'm sorry about this sheet. Some day, maybe, if I ever come back, I'll buy you some new ones. I could use another one to cover up, if you don't mind." He nodded towards the sheet she held.

She pulled it closer to her, as though afraid he would take if from her. "I don't want or need anything from you, Mr. Cade. I offered my home to you for your protection and I would do it again if need be. But the officer came back again this afternoon asking more questions. I cannot put my family at risk. So we're leaving."

"*We're* leaving? As in you and me?" He didn't know how to react to her statement. She nodded firmly, then reached for his sheet and pulled it away before he could snatch it back. "Damn it, woman, what is it with you wanting me naked all the time?"

Her cheeks flamed red as she kneeled next to the cot and examined his leg. "I have seen you in the nude plenty of times while you were asleep. Though I did not enjoy it, I did what needed to be done for your health."

Cade forced himself to stop grinding his teeth. He had never met a more hardheaded, downright stubborn woman in all his life. "There is no reason for you to come with me. I'll find a horse or mule and be gone before daylight. Or dark. What time is it anyway?"

Her cool fingers were running down the outside of his leg and he suddenly found it very difficult to focus. Her touch was gentle, soothing, and almost as though some of the pain was being pulled through her fingertips.

"It's beginning to heal," she said softly, "though it's going to take some time. I really wish you hadn't tried to walk on it."

"I thought you were in trouble."

Her fingers hesitated and she looked up at him. He hadn't noticed how many colors were in her eyes before. He counted at least ten before she spoke. "And what would you have done, if I had been? You can't even get up the stairs."

"I was going to try."

"Why? Why were you going to do that for me?" She watched him with a furrowed brow.

He was confused by her question. "Why wouldn't I? You've given me shelter... you've taken care of me when most would have given up."

"You don't owe me anything."

Cade was silent for a few moments, trying to make a decision. It was difficult with her touching him, her eyes watching him. "Lady, I wouldn't be alive if it weren't for you. I'd say I owe you quite a bit. So I'm willing to listen to whatever it is you're planning. I'm not saying I'm going to go along with it, but I'm willing to listen."

A half smile touched her lips. "I don't think you have

much of a choice."

God, she should smile more often. It made him want to touch her, to unpin her hair, to risk getting punched in the jaw again.

He leaned back on his elbows and stared up at the rafters. "I'm listening."

Olivia's attention returned to his leg and, after several moments of silence, he was beginning to wonder if she was going to tell him. "My sister, Angie... her husband is building her a home a couple of miles from here. It needs a lot of work, and it's not a fitting place for a pregnant woman right now, even if he was here."

"Was he the one at the Alamo?"

Olivia hesitated then nodded. "Yes. She believes he's still alive, but I know..." Her words halted and she visibly swallowed.

"Don't give up hope. You can't ever give up hope."

He said the words with such conviction that it made her head jerk up to look at him, but he only made brief eye contact before he was back to staring at the rafters.

"I'm going to take you out there. It will be a good place for you to recover, and the soldiers won't be looking out there. At least I don't think they will."

"And then are you coming back?" Cade lifted his head and looked at her.

"No," she shook her head. "No, I'm going to stay out there with you." Her eyes wouldn't meet his.

"I can take care of myself."

"I made you a promise. I never break my word. Until

you can walk again, I'm not going to leave." Her voice quivered slightly.

Cade watched her for several moments then winced as she began to tie up his leg once more. "A single woman doesn't stay with a man alone. It isn't done."

"Yes, well, I guess it's a good thing I'm an old maid and nobody cares about my reputation anymore."

His eyebrows shot up. "Old maid? Is that what you call yourself?"

She finished tying up his leg and turned to face him, her cheeks crimson. "I don't want to do this. But I will not have my family in jeopardy. And I will not break a promise."

"I've already released you of your promise. You have no obligation to me." He meant what he said. But a part of him knew that it would be virtually impossible for him to do anything on his own. At least for the time being.

She draped the new sheet over him and straightened, smoothing her hands over her skirt. Either she hadn't heard him, or she had chosen to ignore his statement. He leaned more towards the latter. "We'll leave tomorrow," she said with finality. "Try to rest as much as you can."

"Your sisters? How will they get by without you?"

"As much as I would love to think they need me…" She hesitated then continued, "They will probably get along better without me here." She turned to grab the bowl she had set aside when his hand shot out and grabbed her wrist. She looked down at him with surprise.

"What I said…" He hesitated, trying to look for the right words.

"Your assessment of me has been correct, Mr. Cade," she said, with a forced smile on her face, but it didn't reach her eyes. "The townsfolk have given me the nickname *Senorita Fria*. Cold woman." She shrugged. "I don't mind."

Cade's eyes watched her closely, unable to release her wrist yet. "I think you do."

Her smile faltered and she pulled free of his grip. "It would be best for both of us if you think of me that way for the rest of our time together."

"Why? Why would you want me to think that about you?"

She was breathing rapidly, and the rise and fall of her breasts drew his attention. "Because you make me nervous, Mr. Cade."

His eyes jerked to her face. "I would never hurt you. Never."

"I'm not afraid of you, Mr. Cade. I'm afraid of myself when I'm around you. You make me want...You make me..." She swallowed and turned, hurrying up the stairs. "Get some rest, Mr. Cade."

Chapter Seven

THE HEAVY DRIP of water off the roof mingled with the soft fall of rain, creating a muffled silence over the town. A lantern light flickered far up the road, otherwise all was dark.

"It's too cold. Why don't you wait—at least another day?"

Olivia clutched her shawl tightly around her shoulders, frowning into the damp darkness. Her breath plumed in the air and a slight shiver ran over her skin as she turned back inside the house, closing the door forcefully behind her. "No. We'll leave tonight. The rain should keep the soldiers under shelter and we'll have a better chance of not being seen."

Angie was chewing on her lower lip. "Do you think he'll make it? His leg—if it doesn't heal, he'll lose it for sure."

"He's going to be just fine," Olivia said in a rush, then drew a deep breath, squeezing her eyes shut momentarily. When she opened them, her face was the picture of determination. "He'll be just fine."

"This cold won't be good for him."

"You talk as though I'm not even here. Do I get a word in this conversation?" Cade's irritated voice didn't bother the women as they continued staring out at the rain.

"We can wrap an extra blanket around him. The rain isn't that heavy, so he shouldn't get drenched—at least not right away."

"Or I could just set myself on fire. That should keep me warm *and* dry."

Olivia glanced over her shoulder to where Cade sat in an old wicker chair, his leg propped up on another chair next to him. The journey up the stairs had taken him nearly an hour and it had destroyed her to see him in so much pain. She had forced him to drink some corn whiskey to numb the pain, but now he was acting sullen, and she didn't have time for him to be difficult.

"If you can't add an intelligent comment to this conversation, keep quiet."

The look on his face would have been comical if the situation hadn't been so serious. "Intelligent comment?" He chuckled harshly, his eyes wide. "You two crazy birds are talking about hacking off my leg while I sit right here and you talk about intelligence?"

He shook his head, still chuckling, but the sound was forced. "I must have picked the craziest home in all of Texas to hide."

"How much corn liquor did you give him?" Angie whispered to Olivia.

Cade threw up his hands in disbelief, groaning and shaking his head. It didn't help that pain throbbed through his leg and made it near impossible to have a rational thought. But the two sisters were going to drive him insane.

Sighing heavily, he dragged his hands down his face, trying to wipe away the frustration and exhaustion pulling at him. When he lowered his hands, it took everything he had not to yell in surprise.

"*Hola*, cowboy." The young one, Serri, sat on the floor in front of him, cross-legged, watching him with luminescent eyes.

He hadn't even heard her enter the room. His skills must be deteriorating in this home, he thought as he eyed the feathers protruding from her hair. He was in a house of lunatics.

Serena was watching him closely, a half-smile tugging at her lips. It was obvious she was excited about something. "I have something for you."

She was whispering so softly he could barely hear her, and he glanced at the two women standing at the back door. They were still lost in their own conversation, going over supplies and concerns for the *cocina* in Olivia's absence.

Serri pulled a fire-charred clay pot from behind her back, cupping the small container in her palms. When he didn't immediately reach for it, her smile took a dip and she thrust it towards him. "It's for your leg," she whispered, agitation building in her features when he still didn't reach for it.

Using her same hushed voice, he asked, "Does this mean you've decided you like me?"

Her lips lifted again, but this time her smile was mischievous. "I suppose you'll find out."

Cade didn't know whether to laugh or slam his fist through something. Everything around him made little sense, and he kept thinking that at any moment he would awaken from his hellish dream. He reached for the clay pot and was rewarded with a pleased smile from the girl he believed the oddest creature he had ever met.

Warily he pried open the clay lid but quickly pulled back in disgust, his eyes watering from the powerful aroma. "What in God's name did you put in here?"

His reaction drew Olivia's attention and, when her eyes fell on Serena, she whirled, her fists planted on her hips. "What are you doing?" Her voice nearly seemed a shout in the silence and Serena jumped a good foot.

She stood hastily, throwing an angry glance at Cade. "I just came to say goodbye. I knew you were going to leave without telling me."

For the briefest moment, Olivia looked guilty, a light flush creeping up her neck.

But then her eyes fell on the pot in Cade's hands and they narrowed with suspicion. "Where did you get that?"

Serena smiled. "I made it."

Olivia walked over and leaned forward, carefully lifting the clay lid. Cade had been about to warn her not to, but his mind emptied of all thought. She had placed her hand on his shoulder and was leaning over him, apparently unaware that her breast pressed against his arm. His mouth was suddenly dry.

"Oh!" Her startled exclamation and the recoil of her body drew his focus back on the subject. "Serena, I want to know where this came from."

She still stood against him, the intimate contact of her

body against his making him yearn for more. It felt so right to have her against him, her hand on his shoulder—almost like... home.

"I told you I made it," Serena said, talking around the thumbnail she was chewing on.

"Did Talking Wolf help you? He did, didn't he? I told you not to go see that old man anymore—"

Serena's eyes flared with anger. "He knows more about medicine and healing than anyone around here. You're just scared of him."

Olivia straightened and her breast brushed Cade's ear. He felt light-headed.

"You should be afraid of him, too! He's an Indian! I don't care that he's no longer with his tribe." Olivia shook her head, already prepared for her sister's argument. "He has snakes hanging on posts outside his hut!"

Serena stopped chewing on her nail and pursed her lips in a fashion similar to Olivia. "That's to ask for rain." She made a broad gesture towards the back porch where lightening briefly lit up the sky. "And it worked, didn't it?"

Olivia's hand tightened on Cade's shoulder and he felt the tension in her body. "Olivia just wants you to be safe," Cade said softly. "She knows you're smart enough not to put yourself in danger." The heat of Olivia's eyes watching him could almost be felt. But he kept his eyes on Serena.

Serri watched him with narrowed eyes then slowly nodded. "I know." She covered her mouth with her hand, stifling a yawn. "I'm going to bed."

Before Cade could object, she stepped forward and embraced him, carefully avoiding his leg. "*Adios*. When you come back, I'll make you some empanadas. I don't burn them like Angie."

The swift kiss on his cheek left him stunned, but she was quickly moving out of the room. She paused in the doorway and glanced back at Olivia. "Be careful, Vi. I'll... I'll miss you."

The room seemed to lose some of its light at her departure, and Cade slowly, slowly lifted his eyes to Olivia. She was just looking away from the doorway and her eyes clashed with his. Her eyes widened as she became aware of the intimate way she pressed against him. A blush crept over her skin as she began to push away from him, but he caught her hand on his shoulder, unwilling to break contact with her so soon.

Her breath caught, and her pulse visibly pounded at the base of her neck. He let go of her hand as though he held a hot coal and she backed away from him, confusion all over her face.

Then she turned and faced Angie who watched both with raised eyebrows. "Let's finish getting everything in the wagon." Olivia spoke firmly, though her fingers tugged on the high collar of her dress. "We've wasted enough time as it is."

꙰

OLIVIA COULDN'T CONTAIN the shivers that caused her teeth to chatter as she stepped back into the house. She tried to avoid looking at Cade, but his eyes were on her, same as his muscled arm pressed against her body.

She hadn't been aware of the way she had leaned against him, the way she had instinctively reached for his warmth. She had become comfortable with his physical presence, too comfortable. But she had also leaned on him for an emotional need; the need for human contact and extra strength. She had never sought out strength from anyone other than herself. Why now? Why Cade?

"We should be ready," she said softly to Angie, shaking tiny droplets of moisture from her shawl. "Did you find an extra blanket for him?"

Angie nodded towards a dark heap of fabric on the table. "It should be thick enough to keep some of the rain and sleet off."

Olivia nodded and drew a deep breath. "Now we just need to get him to the wagon." She turned to face Cade and his eyes watched her darkly just as she knew they would. She had felt the heat of his gaze all night.

As she started towards him he began to try to push himself to his feet. Olivia moved up on one side and Angie on the other, and he reluctantly accepted their help. Both women braced themselves for his weight and moved slowly out the door.

Olivia was intensely aware of the tension in Cade's body and knew the pain he was suffering. He dragged his leg behind him, for once following Olivia's instructions to use it as little as possible. She had her arm wrapped around his back and her other hand braced against his chest for support and felt his muscles straining. She looked up at his face, and despite the chill in the air, several drops of sweat beaded his brow. "Do you need to rest? Do you need…"

"No." His voice came out harsh, strained. "No, let's just get to the wagon."

Cade's weight shifted and Olivia looked over in concern at Angie, only to be surprised by her grandfather's face, full of determination.

"Just lean on me, *hijo*. We'll get you to that wagon," he said.

"G-Grandpa!" Olivia stuttered, then swallowed hard and her feet faltered in the mud. "Grandpa, what are you—how did you…"

Grandpa didn't look at her as he helped move Cade through the mud towards the wagon. "You girls think we don't know what goes on in that house? Ha! I'm not too old yet that I don't notice."

The panicked look on Olivia's face drew Cade's curiosity.

"You've known?" Her voice was shocked. "All this time? Why didn't you say something?"

Her grandfather cast her a disgruntled look. "I didn't say we approve. You're old enough to make your own mistakes without the advice of two old people." He shook his head. "Besides, you wouldn't listen to us anyway. If we forbid you from helping those damned rebels"—he glanced up at Cade and frowned—"we would have just driven you away where we couldn't keep any eye on you."

"I take it you support Mexico," Cade said, the strain of

his discomfort becoming even more obvious.

"I support keeping this family alive," the old man said firmly. "I lost my son and daughter-in-law because they supported you rebels. I'll not lose the rest of my family, too."

"Grandpa, I never meant disrespect—I never…"

Her grandfather looked at her with tenderness. "I know, *hijita*. I know. I can't tell you what to believe and how to live. I won't drive you away." He looked away from her and moisture filled his eyes. "It's what I did to your father and now I'll never have him back."

Olivia was speechless. She hadn't known her grandfather felt responsible for her parent's death, nor had she even suspected he knew she and her sisters carried on their parent's drive to help the Texians. But she realized she should have. Her grandfather was an incredibly bright and astute man, and had served in the Mexican Army when they fought for independence from Spain. His loyalty to Mexico was admirable, even though she couldn't support it.

They had finally reached the wagon and Cade pulled his arms off their shoulders, leaning heavily against the wheel. Getting Cade up into the wagon proved to be the most difficult task of them all. By then they were being pelted by small sleet and a few soft snow flakes fell around them. With her Grandfather's help, they were able to hoist Cade into the wagon, though Cade groaned loudly, and Olivia knew it had hurt him tremendously.

Before he sat down she was able to wrap the extra blanket around him, and she noticed that his eyes were out of focus, and she doubted he was even aware of what was going on due to the high level of pain he was in. He sighed with relief when he finally sat down on the bench.

Trying to control her shivers, Olivia turned to her grandfather and gave him a fierce hug and kissed him on the cheek. "Thank you, *Abuelo*. Please don't worry about me and don't let *Abuela* worry about me. I'll be perfectly safe at Angie's home. And I'll come into town every few days to make sure everything is going well."

Her grandfather cupped her face in his hands. "Don't worry so much, *hijita*. We will come through this just fine. Now you must hurry. We can't risk getting caught, and you are freezing already. *Via con dios*."

Olivia's eyes blurred with tears but she nodded and sloshed through the mud to the other side of the wagon. Angie stepped forward off of the porch where she had been sheltered from the sleet and snow. She embraced Olivia, but they exchanged no words. They weren't necessary. Just the way they looked at each other said everything. Olivia nodded firmly, then quickly climbed into the wagon.

She quickly grabbed the jacket she had hastily tossed up on the buckboard when they had been packing it with provisions and slid into it, the sleeves hanging past her hands. It had been her father's jacket and it meant a lot to her. She felt safer already just having it wrapped around her. With a final nod to Angie and her grandfather, she took the reins in her cold hands and snapped them, and the mule, startled out of a light slumber, lurched forward.

The ride out to Angie's home proved to be more difficult than Olivia had expected. The ground was pure slush, and the wheels had a hard time gripping into the mud to propel them forward. The mule was doing its best, but it was a daunting task. Finally, Olivia realized they needed to change something, and the only thing she could think of was to lighten the load.

Cade seemed to be half aware of his surroundings, and she was worried the journey was already too much on him. Tying the reins into a knot, she jumped down into the mud and, holding onto the mule's harness, slid forward until she was at his head. She pushed forward, pulling on the mule's reins from its head, struggling to get it to move with her.

Several times she fell to her knees in the mud and cringed at the jar to her body, but pulled herself back up and continued pressing forward. On the plus side, she became numb to the cold around her and no longer noticed the sleet and the snow that fell.

After over a thousand sliding steps in the mush—she had learned to distract herself by counting her steps—she was beginning to wonder if she had passed the small break in the trees that led to Angie's house. Squinting through the snow and sleet she tried her best to make out the tree line. The lack of light was both a curse and a blessing. A curse because she couldn't see anything even if she could keep a wick dry long enough for a lantern. But at the same time it was a blessing, for no one else could see them. Their vision was just as limited as Olivia's.

Following her gut instincts, she pulled the mule closer to the tree line. With frustration, she stared up and down, praying to see a break in the trees, but the visibility was horribly limited. Taking a risk, she chose to backtrack, and trudged through the mud back towards town.

Fortunately, it had been the right guess. After walking for several slippery steps she could just make out a break in the trees, and they plowed forward. She was relieved they were close, but anxious about all that she faced ahead.

Before turning between the trees, she stopped the mule and went back to the wagon. Cade was huddled in his blankets, and it appeared he was asleep. Concerned, she stood on the step to the wagon and reached her hand up, gently cupping the side of his face. It was warm against her cold skin, and that spoke of a possible fever.

At her touch, his eyes snapped open and she was staring into his blue eyes that, lately, seemed to occupy her mind more and more. "I'm sorry it has taken so long. You'll be in a warm bed soon."

He closed his eyes again, but when they opened, they held a pain that was far beyond the physical turmoil. "You shouldn't be doing this. This isn't your problem. I'm not your problem. I released you of your promise."

Olivia shook her head. "No. I won't leave you."

Without waiting for a response, she turned and pulled the shotgun from its sheath on the side of the wagon, then carefully stepped down from her slippery perch. Sliding through the mud, she made it back to the head of the mule and began to pull him forward, her eyes probing the darkness as much as possible.

It had been more than two weeks since they had been at Angie's small, building in progress, home. With all that was happening in San Antonio, it would be the perfect place for vagrants or other unseemly characters to take refuge. Olivia was determined she would clear them out if she had to.

The frame of the house came into view slowly and, much to her relief, there wasn't a fire lit or any kerosene lamps providing light to the house. But she remained wary. Just because she couldn't see anyone didn't mean they weren't there. She pulled the mule up to the far side of the home, then turned back to look at Cade. His eyes were closed again, though she could see him shivering. She needed to get him inside with a hot fire going in order to warm him soon.

She looked back at the house and drew a deep breath. Squaring her shoulders, she cocked the gun and headed for the house.

Chapter Eight

CADE SILENTLY CURSED. He felt utterly and completely useless as he watched Olivia moving about, sliding and frequently falling in the mud as she moved their supplies into the home. His heart had been racing when she had gone into the house alone, with only the shotgun for protection. Damnit, he should have been able to protect her!

When she had been gone for several long minutes, he had come very close to climbing out of the wagon and stumbling, crawling even, if it meant getting to her and... and doing what? He was useless. It had only been a couple of minutes later that he saw lights beginning to illuminate the house and he smelled the smoke of a freshly made fire in the hearth.

Relieved wasn't the right word to use. If anything had happened to her... He had failed to protect his loved ones already. He wouldn't fail Olivia, too. Not after all she had done for him. That, and the fact that he was drawn to her in ways he had never expected to be drawn to a woman. She fascinated him, and her simple acts of care brought him so much pleasure. Just her touch, or an accidental smile from her usually stern face, made him want to know more, to see more of who this woman was.

Suddenly, she was by his side, her hand cupping his cheek again. It was the sweetest touch he had ever felt.

"It's time to get you inside," she said softly, her eyes searching his face. "It won't be easy, and the mud only makes it worse. Try to put as much of your weight on me as you need. I'm stronger than you think."

A smile tugged at his lips. "I already think you're one hell of a strong woman."

Even though the cold had made her cheeks red, they seemed to become even more so at his comment. She pulled off the blanket they had wrapped around him when he had gotten into the wagon and he was instantly struck by the cold and wind and sleet.

He looked down at Olivia in disbelief. She had been fighting through this mess with only a worn leather jacket to protect her. She had to be freezing. Gritting his teeth with determination, he swung his legs around and began to slide off the seat and placed his weight on his right leg on the step. Olivia was already waiting for him, braced for his weight when he stepped down.

It hurt like hell. He wanted to shout out the pain that ripped through his body. He wanted to beat something. But the soft body that gave him support didn't deserve to listen to him rage about his pain. She quivered a little under his weight, then found her center, and together they began to move towards the house.

Cade tried his hardest, but he couldn't stop from cursing every time they slipped in the mud, pulling his leg. Olivia only said encouraging things, motivating him to keep moving. He focused on her voice, the soft, husky tone with the hint of a Mexican accent. And soon, sooner than he would have expected, they were stumbling up the short set of three stairs and into the part of the house that had been completed.

Warmth instantly greeted him and he nearly sighed in relief. The room was larger than he expected, and well-built by someone with great care for those who would live in the home. Angie's husband. Obviously a good man, a good man who had probably perished at the Alamo, no matter how much Angie refused to believe it.

In a corner near the hearth, there was a large bed, and he felt renewed energy to get to it. But Olivia slowed him down, stopping him in front of the hearth. "You must get out of those wet clothes." Her voice was low and her eyes wouldn't meet his as an embarrassed flush covered her face.

"You've seen me naked plenty of times, now," he said with humor. "Why is it any different this time?"

Olivia's chin lifted and she looked at him with determined eyes. "Whatever made you think I have a problem with it now?" While still supporting his weight, she began to unbutton the large jacket he wore. It took some odd posturing and balancing, but she went about the task as quickly and efficiently as possible.

When he finally stood before the fire nude, he basked in the warmth that washed over him. His clothes weren't helping him fight the cold, but he hadn't expected for it to feel so wonderful to be free of them.

Olivia wrapped his arm around her shoulders and slid her other arm around his waist. He tensed at her touch and realized she still wore her wet clothes. "You need to get out of those wet clothes as well," he said in a tone that was not to be argued with.

"Cade—let's just focus on getting you to the bed, first."

"Are you trying to seduce me, Olivia? Has that been your plan all along?" He couldn't help himself... it was too easy of a situation to tease her about. But her reaction was less than humorous. She stiffened and he could almost feel her features harden.

"My *plan* is to tend to your health, sir, and that is all. If you are expecting something else, my shotgun will teach you otherwise."

Her reaction puzzled him. He had expected her to be a bit prudish, but this was something altogether different. She seemed—afraid. He should have expected it. He was a stranger that had shown up at her home without any real explanation, and she had no idea what type of man he was.

"Olivia, I..." His words died off as she came to the bed and carefully pivoted, and he soon found himself lying on the incredibly comfortable mattress. The relief to the pain in his leg was overwhelming, and for a moment the room spun around him. His hearing faded and dark spots blurred his vision. He felt cold and clammy suddenly, even though the room was warm and dry.

"Cade. Cade, look at me. Cade!"

It was the feeling of her delicate and gentle hands on his face that pulled him back from the precipice of passing out.

Slowly, her face came into his vision and she had both of her hands on his cheeks. When his eyes finally connected with hers, she smiled and one of her hands ran through his still slightly damp hair. A shiver slid down his spine, but it had nothing to do with feeling cold.

Her smile was mesmerizing. It made her eyes lift in the corners, and the stern lines of her face relaxed into a soft youth. He had assumed she was in her late twenties, but now, after seeing her like this, he realized she was far younger than she seemed. She had unfortunately been forced to grow up far too fast. He wanted to know why her youth had been stolen from her.

She was still smiling; her hand continued running through his hair as her other hand cupped his face, her thumb smoothing over his whiskers. "I thought you were going to leave me all alone there for a moment," she said softly. "You're not allowed to pass out unless I give you permission."

She was teasing him, he realized with shock. She was the most perplexing woman he had ever met. "I'll never leave you alone," he whispered, his hand coming up to hold hers against his face.

Her smile slipped and he saw surprise on her face, then confusion, then embarrassment. Slowly she pulled her hand away from his and stood back. "I'm going to get some meat and cheese for you. Angie made sure to pack us plenty of food."

It was while she was in this vulnerable state that he noticed she was shivering violently, and her lips were blue.

There were dark circles under her eyes, speaking to her exhaustion. "You need to take care of yourself, first," he said sternly. "If you get ill out here, we'll both be doomed."

Olivia shook her head. "Don't worry. I'm stronger than you think."

Cade tried to focus on her, but the warmth and comfort of the bed were warming him to the point of lethargy. "It's too cold, and you're shivering." Even to his own ears he was mumbling.

Her answer sounded far away and he couldn't completely understand it. His eyelids felt heavy and he was trying desperately to stay awake. Suddenly, she appeared beside him and, much to his surprise, she had switched into dry clothes, though she still shivered. She held a plate full of meat and cheese and he felt more than heard his stomach grumble.

She was fighting the urge to help him prop himself in the bed, and was holding back so he could regain his strength. But he felt as helpless as a baby and hated depending on her for everything. But, at the moment, his mind was focused on the food, and that gave him the energy to prop himself up and grab a couple of chunks, eagerly tearing into the dried venison.

He ate as much as his stomach would allow, oblivious for the moment that Olivia didn't eat anything. Instead she checked his bandages and made minor adjustments over some of his cuts. But then the bed started calling to him again, and the lethargy that had been pulling at him was a warm, large hole opening up in front of him, and he was ready to take a dive directly into it.

Olivia, as always, knew what his body needed and repositioned the pillows around him, then watched him settle into the bed. He tried to stay awake, tried to stay alert to what she was doing to the cabin. But the warmth of the room and the comfort of the bed and the fullness of his stomach proved too much and he passed off into blissful slumber.

THE SHIVERS WOULDN'T stop. No matter how much she moved around, no matter how much she tried to warm herself by the fire, the shivers just wouldn't let up. She feared she'd be losing her teeth soon if they didn't stop chattering.

It wasn't as if she would be able to sleep even if she could get warm. The large man sleeping in the bed at the end of the room was the primary reason why. Every time she looked over at his slumbering form, her heart stuttered.

Which was completely irrational. Yes, he was an attractive man. But she knew all too well the nature of men, and for her to want to be near him, to crave his attention, was absolutely ridiculous. And yet she wanted those very things.

Getting him out of his wet clothes had made her feel things—things she had never felt before, and it frightened her. While his form was lean, it was all muscle. She had already seen him naked before and there was no reason for her to get light-headed as she had peeled off his shirt.

This time he was awake. That had been the difference that had rattled her. She shouldn't have let it. Like he had said, she had seen him naked many times. She began to arrange items to make breakfast for him when morning came, which wasn't far off.

But this time had been different. This time his startling blue eyes had watched her movements, had watched her hands sliding down the buttons of his shirt, and then had clashed with hers as she eased it off his shoulders. There was a heat smoldering in his eyes, and she caught her breath. She nearly forgot about his shirt as her movements slowed and she stared into the warmth of his eyes, feeling butterflies low in her stomach.

She had just barely enough willpower to pull her eyes away from his and finish the task of removing his shirt. But she hadn't been able to stop herself from running her hands lightly over his muscular chest, feeling the damp curls of golden hair that covered his torso. She followed the path of those curls as they descended down his body until they narrowed at his waist and formed a fine, tapered line into his pants.

He sucked in his breath as she slid her fingers lightly under the band of his britches, and she told herself it was only because her fingers were cold. Slowly she untied the laces of the pants, fighting her shivers, wondering if they were from the cold or from her nerves. She could feel his eyes boring into her head, and nearly jumped as he lay a hand on her arm, holding her as she moved to slide the britches down his hips.

She chalked up his touch as a need for balance as he tried to stay off his injured leg. But his actions were causing her heart to race, and made it even more difficult to focus on pulling his clothes off of him. As she slid the clothing off of him, she tried to avert her eyes, even though curiosity gnawed at her.

Yet, as she slipped the clothes off his hips, his hands caught hers and her eyes jerked to his.

"Olivia," he said huskily, then swallowed and closed his eyes briefly. "Olivia, let me do this myself."

"You can't! You can barely stand on your own."

"Just support me. Let me do the rest."

She shook her head. "I will take care of you." He was trying to save her from any embarrassment, and it only made her respect him more. Swallowing hard, she proceeded with taking his britches off, and was especially careful with his leg that she had tried to wrap and protect so carefully. It was hard not to look at him, but she forced her eyes to focus on his legs until she finally had him completely undressed.

She straightened slowly and met his eyes. There was a darkness to them, and she realized it was desire that stared back at her. She felt herself turn deep red even though she was still shivering. No man had ever desired her. No man had ever found her even remotely attractive. And yet this man stood before her, his eyes speaking clearly that he desired her.

But his next words were like cold water. "I'm sorry, Olivia. I don't mean to make you uncomfortable. It has been a long time since a woman has undressed me…"

It seemed he wanted to say more, but he had said enough. He had been without a woman for too long. She should have known that was the reason for his reaction to her. No man found her attractive or desirable. She had been a fool to think that he did.

"It's fine," she said, damning her voice for quavering.

She would not cry in front of this man. She wouldn't cry in front of any man. They had hurt her enough for her to know not to ever be vulnerable in front of them.

And so she had gone back to business, focusing on getting him into the bed, checking his bandages, and feeding him. He hadn't said anything further about the incident, and neither had she. Perhaps he was just as embarrassed as she was.

Olivia paused and looked at all the items she had set out for breakfast. She nearly laughed at herself, but the chills stopped her. She had put out enough to make breakfast for the *cocina*, not for the two of them. Carefully, she repacked some of the items into the pantry that Lorenzo, Angie's husband, had so caringly built for his wife.

Olivia closed her eyes for several moments and wrapped her shaking arms around herself. How was Angie going to make it without Lorenzo? Of course, Olivia and her grandparents would help take care of the baby once it arrived. But Angie's heart would never heal.

At the thought of the baby, Olivia looked down at her flat stomach and felt tears well up in her eyes. She had wanted a child so much. She had always wanted to be a mother. But it seemed it was not to be. She simply didn't have enough to make a man want to marry her. By all standards, she was an old maid.

"Olivia."

Cade's deep voice startled her and she turned sharply and saw that his eyes were open and he had propped his head up with a pillow so he could see her. How long had he been watching her?

Olivia smoothed her bun back with a shaking hand and gave him a feeble attempt at a smile. "I wasn't expecting you to wake up so early. Are you hungry?"

He shook his head slowly. "Come here, Olivia. Please."

She didn't hesitate at his request and moved quickly towards him. "Are you in pain? Has one of the dressings slipped off a wound?" She came to the edge of the bed, her eyes searching his face for answers, and she began to draw the covers back so she could examine his wounds.

She couldn't contain the tiny squeal she let lose when his hand wrapped around her wrist and she was suddenly on the bed beside him, her body spread along his. He tossed the covers back over her and held her in place when she tried to move away, using both of his arms to keep her pulled close to him.

"Wh-what do you think you're doing?" she demanded, anger and fear in her voice. "Unhand me this moment!"

"You're shivering to death. You need to warm up or you won't be in any condition to take care of yourself—or me, for that matter."

Olivia briefly stopped struggling and her eyes flew to his face. "You have no right to handle me this way. I've already been trying to get warm and will do so successfully as I go about my chores. Let. Go. Of. Me." Her last few words ended in a growl, and she was desperately fighting back the fear that was clawing at her.

Was he going to rape her? He had said it had been a long time since he'd been with a woman. Maybe he was desperate enough to use her as his plaything until she either escaped him or he grew tired of her. She felt the mad desperation clawing at her heart, making her want to scream, making her want to cry in fury. She had been known as *Senorita Fria* in town because all of the men thought she was frigid. If only they knew why.

Chapter Nine

CADE SAW THE fear and panic building in her eyes. Weren't they past this stage? She had actually teased him earlier, revealing a playful, soft woman that he hadn't imagined existed. Why now was she so afraid of him?

He lessened his grip on her, but still kept her close to him. "I will never hurt you, Olivia. You should know that by now. Why are you so afraid?"

He could tell she was fighting to control her emotions. "Cade, please..."

Her plea was so desperate he released her, and he saw shock and confusion cross her face. He had expected her to bolt, and she did move away from him until she was at the edge of the bed, but she didn't get out. Subconsciously she rubbed her wrists from where he had held her, and he wondered if his grip had been too strong. Her eyes were wide as she watched his face, but she said nothing.

"What is it, Olivia? Talk to me."

She shook her head, then closed her eyes for several moments, and when she reopened them she seemed to have gathered her wits about her.

"Why did you do that?" she demanded, though her voice

quivered.

"You're practically shivering to death. It is incredibly warm under these blankets and close to the fire. I can't lie here and watch you freeze."

"You... you wanted to—"

"I wanted to take care of you, Olivia. You've done so much for me... it's the least I can do for you right now."

Her eyes were wary, but he could see she was tempted to move closer to him. Her eyes roved over the blankets covering his body and he could see a blush touching her cheeks. "It-it's highly improper... I shouldn't—"

"There isn't anything proper about this, Olivia. You've been with a naked man. And now you are living with him without a chaperone. Proper behavior was thrown away the moment you said you would take care of me. Why are you so afraid to lie near me? And don't give me another foolish excuse about being proper. We're way past that." His tone was slightly gruff, but he was also gentle. She reminded him of a trapped deer—afraid of which way to go that would lead her to safety.

"You won't understand—I can't tell you..." Tears welled up in her eyes, though he could tell she was fighting very hard not to let him see them. "This is terribly embarrassing," she whispered, unable to meet his eyes.

Cade reached out and ran his knuckles lightly down her cheek and her eyes shot to his.

"I was afraid—I thought—" She closed her eyes and drew a deep breath. Finally, she opened her eyes and looked at him directly. "You said it had been a long time since you had been with a woman. And since I'm the only one available, I thought you meant to…" She swallowed hard as she searched for the words. Finally, she just blurted it out. "I thought you were going to rape me."

Cade tried hard not to recoil from her out of surprise and anger. "Rape you? You think I am the type of man that would rape a woman? Is that what you think of me?"

"No! I mean… I don't think so, but you frightened me. Your reaction to me undressing you earlier—"

"Was purely because an extremely attractive woman who has been driving me crazy with her gentle caresses and soft touches that are more than just caring for my injuries was undressing me with desire in her eyes. I couldn't stop my reaction to your touch, and I'm sorry if that frightened you."

Her eyes widened and he reached out to caress her cheek again. "I would never hurt you, my sweet angel. Never."

Her cheeks were bright red as she slid under the covers and moved closer to him. When she was close enough, he wrapped his arms around her and began to rub his hands up and down her back. She stiffened in his arms, but she didn't pull away.

"Talk to me, Olivia. Why are you so afraid? What happened to you?"

"What do you m-mean?" Her shivers fought with her emotions for control of her voice.

"You are more than just scared of being close to me. You've touched me and soothed me for hours and it didn't seem to bother you. But now that I reach for you… there is genuine fear in your eyes. What happened to cause you to fear me so much? What have I done?"

Olivia shook her head and he could have sworn she subconsciously moved closer to him. "You've done nothing at all, Cade. If anything, you've been a true gentleman. You had many opportunities to take advantage of me, but you didn't, and for that I am forever grateful."

"But someone else did take advantage of you. Someone hurt you." Anger built inside his chest. How could anyone hurt this incredible woman?

"Cade, I can't tell you. I've-I haven't told anyone. It's too painful to talk about. No one knows. And I should keep it that way."

Her eyes were large with a plea to him and brimming with tears she clearly didn't want to shed. But he couldn't let it go. He had to know what it was that had traumatized her so much she was still trembling viciously in his arms.

He reached up and ran his knuckles down her cheek, a gesture he was quickly learning seemed to calm her. "Talk to me, angel. Tell me what happened," he spoke softly, and then regretted pushing her as a tear slid down her cheek.

"I was fifteen," she said, her voice shaking as another tear slipped free. "I had to run to the market to gather items for the *cocina* and felt fortunate that we had a wagon and a mule to help me haul all of the things. I went behind the homes as a shortcut to reach the kitchen. I should have... if only I had been more careful! I was such a little fool!"

"Shh." Cade tried to soothe her gently, but she was shaking even harder, her teeth clicking together. "Olivia. Olivia!" He finally caught her attention, and her eyes that had been seeing something that tormented her slowly refocused on him. "It wasn't your fault. It wasn't."

"How can you say that? You don't even know what happened."

"I have a rough idea." He tried to keep his face passive, even though he was furious.

He could only imagine what had happened to her, and what he was picturing made him want to hurt the bastard or bastards that had hurt her.

"They were waiting for me. They had seen me in the market and followed me on the other side of the homes, and then moved ahead of me so they could stop me before I made it to the kitchen." Olivia was breathing heavily and, from the look on her face, she was reliving the horror she had faced years ago.

"One of them climbed up into the wagon and forced me to stop. He put his hand over my mouth so I couldn't scream. A couple of them were officers, and a couple were regular infantry. They pulled me from the wagon and slammed me up against the side. It knocked my breath out of me, and they used that as an advantage to begin... to begin..."

"You don't have to tell me anymore, angel. You don't have to tell me anymore." He didn't know if he could listen to any more.

She had experienced something horrific, and didn't need to relive the experience. He didn't want to make her go through this.

It seemed Olivia wasn't even able to hear him as the tears

slid silently down her face. She was completely reliving her nightmare, and he had pushed her too far to pull her back and get her to stop. He felt like an ass.

"They began trying to kiss me. I tried to pull away, but they were too strong. And then they hauled me to the back of the wagon and... and..." She drew a deep breath. "They forced me to bend over the wagon and hiked up my skirts. Their hands were all over me—touching me in places... I just tried to imagine I was somewhere else. I just wanted it to be over as fast as possible. I knew what they were going to do."

Olivia's eyes suddenly focused on Cade's and she clenched the muscles in her jaw. "But then I decided to fight. I wasn't going to let them use me and discard me in the trash. So I kicked the man directly behind me in the... well, you know where. He made an odd sound and moved away, giving me the chance to pull my blade out of my boot. And I didn't even think twice as I sliced the officer in a way that would make certain he would never have children.

"He screamed louder than I ever would have. The other men jumped away from me and I raced back to the front of the wagon and jumped in. I raced to the back of the *cocina*, and ran inside and hid in my room for God knows how long. Grandma found me curled up in the corner of my room, rocking back and forth. She thought I was being lazy and was furious with me. And I was just so relieved it was over."

Cade shook his head. "You are the bravest woman I've ever known. To have survived that, not only to survive, but to avoid rape…"

Olivia closed her eyes briefly. "I may not have been raped, but they took away a part of me… I don't feel like… I don't think that I'm a true woman any longer. They took that from me and I'll never be able to get it back."

Without her realizing it, Cade had unfastened her bun at the nape of her neck and fanned her hair out, the soft black silken length clinging to his hand. "They've taken nothing from you. You defeated them."

She lowered her eyes and tears streamed down her cheeks and he wondered if he had said the wrong thing.

When she lifted her eyes, they were full of pain, and regret, and—self-loathing. "I can't come to a man pure and innocent anymore. I know what a man wants to do with a woman now… I know the vulgar things a man thinks and does—"

"Not every man. Not every man is like that, Olivia."

"REGARDLESS," SHE SPOKE softly, her throat strained. "If I ever had a chance to find love, it would be destroyed as soon as he learned of my past. The whole town knows about me cutting that man. That is one of the reasons they call me *Senorita Fria*. They think I'm a cold-hearted old maid that will cut a man's *juevos* off if he tries to get near me. No man even looks at me twice, even if he doesn't know my past. I was not blessed with beauty, which has probably saved me through all the years."

"Olivia, you are incredibly beautiful. These men are fools to miss out on the chance to be in your presence." His brow was furrowed in confusion.

"I do believe that your fever has damaged your vision," she said, giving him a slight smile through her tears.

"What makes you think you aren't beautiful? Who has hurt you so much to make you look at yourself in such a way? Was it the men that tried to rape you?"

Olivia shook her head and wiped at the tears on her face. "I'm feeling warmer now, so I'll just—"

"At some point you're going to have to tell me. I won't let it go until I know who has hurt you."

Olivia's hands began to tremble, but not from the cold.

She clasped her hands together tightly. "There was a man one time... a young man who was so handsome. He knew how to talk so sweet to a girl. And I fell for him. Hard. I was only sixteen. He was relatively new to town, so he wasn't as fazed by my actions, but I never could tell him the whole story of what had happened."

She paused suddenly and looked up at him. "You don't want to hear this. There's no reason. All you need to do is rest."

"Tell me, angel. Tell me what happened."

"One day he asked me on a picnic and my grandfather agreed to let me go. I thought we were having a marvelous time until his friends showed up. They were all very mean boys that got in trouble around town most of the time. I was shocked that he was friends with them." She closed her eyes then slowly opened them again. "They began to throw mud and dirt at me, calling me a whore. They were relentless. But it was as if something broke off inside me. My ability to care, to have feelings… I felt like ice on the inside."

Cade caught a stray hair from her face and smoothed it back into place. "Angel, I'm so sorry…"

"That was only the beginning. The young man I thought I had fallen in love with began to punch my face repeatedly, until I nearly passed out. I was so confused. None of it made any sense to me. It was later that I found out he was the nephew of the man I had sliced when I was fifteen."

Cade grabbed her hand and held it tight, giving her the strength to finish her story. "They then stripped me bare and tied my hands in front of me. They all looked at my body with disgust. The boy I had been with led me forward at a fast walk while the others followed behind, throwing rocks at me. They paraded me down the main street of town, crying out that I was the town whore and I deserved to be punished for my sins. I thank God that there was a kind, older woman who ran out of her house with her shotgun and drove them all away. Then she hustled me into her home for protection and wrapped my nude body in a blanket."

She glanced up at Cade and smiled slightly. "To this day, I still make sure to have a *tripas* and egg taco ready for her."

"And what happened to the boys that did this to you?" his voice sounded gruff.

Olivia shook her head. "Nothing. No one would come forward against them, because they all had influential parents who could make our lives rough."

"Look at me, angel," he said softly and her eyes focused

on his face. She knew she probably looked atrocious.

"You are the most beautiful woman I've ever met. I thought that the first night I saw you. I truly thought you were an angel that had saved me. What those boys did to you back then… you can't let that define your life. You're the one that chose to become Senorita *Fria*. You chose it as a protective cloak. But it is a cloak you hate and it is weighing you down every day."

Olivia's eyes searched his for several long moments "I'm sorry I misjudged you."

"After what you experienced, I'm surprised you even took me into your home to care for me. Why did you? I'm a complete stranger and I was running from the army. Why have you done all that you have for me?" His fingers played in her hair and she knew her face was showing several different emotions before focusing on him.

"You were hurt. And you were fleeing the Mexican Army, my enemy. I had to help you. And once I saw your injuries… well, I just couldn't risk letting you die after escaping certain death already."

"Why did you trust me in the first place?"

"I don't really have a good answer for that," she said softly, her eyes searching his face, watching his expressions closely. "There is something about you—something that I can't explain with words—that makes me want to believe you." Her fingers reached up and lightly touched his cheek. "I want to trust you," she whispered.

Cade gave her a soft smile. "Then let's start tonight," he said softly. "Stay with me so that I know you are warm."

Olivia felt an odd fluttering in her chest. "Alright. But if you try anything…"

"Trust me, I've seen the knife you carry. I value my *juevos* a little more than that other guy did."

Olivia's soft chuckle was the last sound before they both drifted off to sleep.

"I HAVEN'T DONE anything to you yet, so there's no reason to go jumping out of bed now, is there?" His voice was low and slightly slurred with sleep. His hand was in her hair, slowly combing through the long length with his fingers.

He had felt Olivia jump when she had realized she was asleep in his arms, but he wouldn't have it any other way. He looked down at her and grinned. "You haven't answered me."

"Just so you know, I am not in the habit of waking up in bed with strange men."

"I should certainly hope not. Because I'm far from strange." Her lips twitched, which made his grin even bigger. "Let's just lie here and enjoy the warmth of the bed before you start running around in the cold again."

Olivia looked as if she wanted to disapprove, but then she just groaned and settled back in against him. "How is it that you talk me out of the most logical things I should do?"

"I don't know," he said, looking down into her eyes, wondering how many different shades of color he could find in them if he tried to count them again. "Perhaps it is my charming personality?"

"Mmm," she replied before lowering her head, tucking it directly under his chin. She fit against him perfectly, and the feeling of her curves pressed along his side were causing his body to have an immediate reaction. He wanted nothing more than to kiss her and caress her and demonstrate to her exactly how beautiful he thought she was.

But, after everything that had happened to her, the wisest thing to do was to hold her gently, never letting on how much he desired her. So he continued running his fingers through her hair, forcing his body to stay relaxed. With her prior experiences with men, he was shocked that she was comfortable enough to lie against him as it was.

"Do you… well, do you often find yourself in this situation?" she asked hesitantly and he nearly laughed at how cautious she was about broaching the subject.

"Waking up in bed with strange men? No, no, that hasn't really ever happened to me." She swatted at him playfully, then let her hand fall on his chest, exploring the whorls of blonde hair that covered him.

"No," he said, his voice thick with growing desire. "No, I don't often find myself in this situation. I don't know that I've ever been in a situation where I have such an incredible woman that is interesting lying next to me." He was beginning to feel light-headed. Probably because all of the blood in his body was headed towards one place.

Olivia chuckled softly. "I hate to tell you this, but you have awoken with a quite ordinary woman who is not very interesting at all."

Cade's fingers tightened in her hair. "You are more woman than any I've ever known before," he whispered in reply, then leaned down and kissed her forehead, then her cheek.

He felt her tense slightly, then slowly relax, her fingers continuing their caress of his chest. Much to his surprise, she moved closer to him, sliding her leg down the length of his, and he had to control his moan of approval.

She moved her fingers up to his face and explored the lines, tracing his eye brows, then his cheeks, then finally his lips. Their eyes clashed and he searched her face. The temptation was too much to resist and he lowered his lips to hers. He was gentle and tender with her and his heart began to beat rapidly as she began to respond, her lips moving against his.

Her body fit his so perfectly and his hands pressed against her ribs, sliding them around her body as he continued slanting his mouth over hers. Her small sound of pleasure made his body react uncontrollably, and if she moved any closer she would find out exactly what it was that he wanted from her. His hands moved around to her chest, and slid slowly up to gently press against the lower portion of her breasts.

She gasped and her back arched towards him, her lips breaking away from his. For a few moments he was afraid she was going to pull away, that he had pushed her too far. Instead, she pressed back to him and sought his lips again. His surprise did not stop him from accepting her seeking query, and he slanted his mouth against her harder, and his hands slid up slightly, softly and slowly caressing her breasts through her gown.

She was still hesitant with him, but when he lightly plucked at her nipples, a shiver slid down her body and he wanted nothing more than to pull her clothes off of her and feel her skin against his. He began to tug on the ties of her dress, and quickly slid the fabric off her shoulders. His lips tore away from hers and began traveling down the length of her neck, inhaling her sweet scent.

Olivia whimpered and moved restlessly, and his other hand slid down and began to pull up her skirts. She moaned when his hand came upon the skin of her thigh. She whispered his name and moved even closer to him, but her body suddenly stopped moving as she became very aware of exactly how his body was reacting to her touch and her movements.

She was breathing heavily and her hands froze on his shoulders. His eyes searched her face, and her eyes reflected the same desire that was pulling at him. But she had just confessed to him the night before about a time she was nearly raped, a time that had left her traumatized. She very well could think he was the same as the men that tried to rape her, and he wouldn't blame her. He had lost control.

"Cade," she whispered, and he closed his eyes, afraid of what she was going to say next to him. "Cade, please don't stop."

His eyes snapped open and he searched her face. The desire all over it made his heart race. No longer afraid to share with her the passion she was creating within him, he pulled her body tightly against his and slanted his mouth over hers aggressively, his lips pressing urgently against hers and she responded with the same eagerness.

He moved his fingers rapidly over the laces and hooks of her dress until he had slid it down to her waist and he paused, pulling back to look at her. She blushed as his eyes roved over her, and he drank in the sight of the woman that had tormented his thoughts and his dreams for the last several days.

She was slender, yet she wasn't too thin. Her collarbone was visible, and he pressed kisses across her, tasting the sweet, delicate flavor of her skin. Then he pulled back, his eyes continuing down her body.

Her chest was moving rapidly as she tried to breathe evenly, but it made her full breasts quiver. With the flame from the hearth the only source of light, her breasts seemed to move to their own rhythm. They were full and round and her areoles were a smooth maroon, the tips puckered tightly into two stiff peaks.

He dipped his head and kissed her breast gently, slowly circling the nipple and she arched again.

"Cade, what are you doing to me?" She gasped, her fingers tugging on his hair.

He smiled as he continued to torture her with kisses. "Seducing you, I hope," he murmured against her skin.

His kisses tightened the circle until he was breathing warmly over her nipple. She was tugging on his head with her fingers, urging him to place his lips on the tip that had become painfully taut.

She gasped and her fingers flexed against his scalp as he slowly ran his tongue around the stiff peak, slipping it into his warm mouth.

"Oh, God," Olivia whimpered as his mouth closed over her, his lips suckling at her breast, his hand massaging the other one and plucking lightly at the other aching peak.

Her hips flexed, and it was his turn to groan as her body moved against his stiff erection. He couldn't remember the last time he'd been this hungry for a woman.

"Olivia," he whispered, reluctantly releasing her breast from his mouth and focusing on her intently. "I want you."

She was watching him with her wide hazel eyes, the desire in them something he had never imagined to see. Not from her, at least. Which made it that much more of an aphrodisiac. She licked her lips, and he could see the pulse throbbing in the base of her neck.

He attempted to move quickly, having worked her skirts up around her waist, and attempted to mount her, anticipating the sweet, wet warmth that would welcome him. Yet, instead, white sharp pain exploded in his head and he couldn't seem to think straight. He heard his own angry moan of pain, but it sounded like it was far away.

And then he heard Olivia's voice, calm and soothing, her cool hands easing him back against the pillows. Everything seemed to fade in and out, going from light to darkness, but he clung to her voice. *What had happened?* His mind demanded to know. One moment he had been about to sheath himself in Olivia's welcoming body, and the next he was desperately trying to catch his breath and not pass out.

Olivia was moving around him, and he noticed that her gown was still open to her waist and her breasts swayed with her movements. He closed his eyes as pain burst forth again. Maybe this was a punishment of some sort. To crave and desire someone as beautiful and exquisite as Olivia might come with a steep payment.

Cade shook his head at himself. Now he was just thinking gibberish. Slowly, the pain began to ease, extremely slowly. As his breathing calmed, the room stopped spinning and everything began to come into focus instead of fading in and out. He felt cold and hot at the same time. He didn't understand what was happening. All he could do was watch Olivia, who was moving quickly around him.

She had pulled her gown partway closed, though he could still see the shining globes of her breasts in the firelight. But she was no longer smiling, and her face was no longer flushed with passion. Instead, everything about the expressions she had indicated worry and concern.

"My sweet angel," Cade whispered, reaching a hand out to caress her cheek and her eyes jumped to his. "I'm so sorry. All I could think of was… well, I think you know all I could think of. I completely forgot about my injuries. Now I've ruined a special moment we had together."

At first he was afraid she would pull away. Perhaps it had all been a magic spell that had been cast over both of them that had allowed them to touch and explore each other's bodies, to feel ecstasy and pleasure together. Perhaps the spell was broken, now, and he had no way of getting her back.

To his surprise, she caught his hand and held it to her

face, kissing his knuckles. "Cade, you haven't ruined any-thing. What you did… the way you held me… Thank you. You made me feel like a true woman."

She was *thanking* him? He hadn't brought her the satis-faction she deserved, and yet she was thanking him? And why was she doing it in such a way as though it seemed it would never happen again?

She continued talking, and he tried to focus on her words, as a fog seemed to be slowly creeping into his mind. "Your leg is infected again, Cade." She gave him a halfheart-ed smile. "I wouldn't have known if you hadn't split your cut just now when you tried to… well, when you moved so abruptly." She looked away from him, her eyes returning to his cut. "I have to treat it, Cade, and you know how much it is going to hurt."

Cade looked at her for several moments, trying to gather his wits about him. He hadn't been able to feel a lover's embrace with her because of his damned *leg*? That was what had stopped him from enjoying her sweet, sweet nectar? He wished he had the strength to throw a chair across the room.

"I'm sorry, Olivia. You deserved so much more. So much more. I've let you down."

She pressed a hand to his forehead and frowned. "You're burning with fever. I don't know how I didn't notice it before. It certainly explains a lot." Her eyes moved back up to his. "I've got to clean your wound, and this time I'm going to cauterize it instead of just using the alcohol. It should help prevent the infection from coming back."

Cade closed his eyes and nodded. The room was starting

to spin again. Her touch was, as always, gentle on him as she cleaned his wound. The pain had him grinding his teeth and his fists clutching the blanket that had been set to the side. He was covered in sweat and yet shivering. He wished he could travel back in time to just thirty minutes ago when he had been exploring Olivia's exquisite body.

It took her a long time to clean out the infection. And he could tell by the frown on her face she didn't like what she was seeing. But the worst was yet to come. She took the fire poker out of the hearth and approached him, the tip of the poker glowing red hot.

"Do you want a piece of leather to bite down on?" she asked, hesitating before she placed the poker on him.

Sweat rolled down his face and he shook his head no. He didn't need leather, he needed divine mercy. Sighing heavily, her jaw clenched, she pressed the poker to his wound. He heard a low, guttural groan that sounded like it came from far, far away and the room spun rapidly around him before he fell into a terribly dark and painful hole.

Chapter Ten

OLIVIA GAVE UP on preparing a delicious breakfast for Cade. Instead, she was focused on making sure he was still alive at the end of the day.

She hadn't slept all night as she sat at his bedside, pressing cool cloths to his fevered forehead. He moved restlessly and muttered in his sleep, but she couldn't make out anything that he said. The fever was worse than it had been before and, from what she could tell from the infection, he was in for one hell of a ride.

How could she have missed it? She had been tending to him for days now, and there was no excuse for her to have let this slip past her attention. If he died, it was purely her fault.

She surmised that he had developed the fever gradually and the journey had only made it worse faster. The infection had developed under a thin layer of skin that had begun to grow back. She was grateful that he passed out, because she had to cut away that layer of skin to give exposure to his infection and wound. One pass with the poker had not been enough. She had discovered further infection once she removed the skin, and as soon as she was finished she placed the hot iron poker into his flesh, cauterizing the wound.

He had moaned in his sleep, but otherwise seemed oblivious to all that she was doing. As he slept, she made a poultice using some of the herbs that Angie had made sure to pack for her and she smoothed it over his wound, then carefully wrapped it snuggly, hoping the skin would begin to grow together again, but this time without the infection.

The rest of the night she sat with him, fussing over him, and worrying. She wouldn't let him die. She couldn't let him die. And as she sat with him, her own face flamed as she remembered the way she had let him touch her, the things he had made her feel. She had never imagined such things could be done, or that such sensations could be created from a simple caress.

As morning began to dawn, Cade began to mutter loudly and became even more restless. "Bella!" he cried out suddenly, making Olivia jump. "No. No. No!" He began to thrash on the bed and Olivia tried to hold him still, afraid that he would undo the bandage around his leg.

"Cade," she said calmly, then more firmly, "Cade!"

His movements slowed, but he continued to mutter, and repeated the name Bella several times. Then his motions calmed altogether and he fell back to into a restless sleep, his breathing ragged.

Olivia was shaking as she pulled away from him. Her mind was racing with questions. Who was Bella? Obviously someone very important to him. Had she completely misjudged him? Had she just lay in bed with a married man?

AFTER TWO DAYS of battling Cade's fever and the infection, Olivia was completely exhausted. She had dozed lightly off and on, but true sleep had eluded her as she tended to Cade. And, she couldn't lie to herself, she had been distraught about the woman's name he had called out so urgently. He had continued to whisper her name from time to time and, each time he did, Olivia's heart clenched.

Bella had to be his wife, or his lover. She was obviously very important for him to dream of her so much. Which meant her actions with him were beyond inappropriate. She had nearly made love to a man whose heart already belonged to someone else.

What would it be like to be loved that intensely? She had witnessed the love and joy that Angie shared with Lorenzo. The two of them could look each other in the eye and know exactly what the other was thinking. Whenever they had the chance, they would touch, even if it was as simple as his hand brushing against hers as they passed each other.

It was something Olivia would never have. She knew without a doubt that she was going to die an old maid—she had already resigned herself to the fact. She was too afraid she would marry a man that turned out to be as vicious as the boys that had abused her. She had thought she was in love with the officer's nephew. And it all had been a ruse to humiliate her and disgrace her. She couldn't allow herself to be open to that kind of pain again.

The feel of his knuckles gently caressing her face jolted her out of the light doze she had drifted into while sitting at his bedside. Her eyes snapped open and he gazed back at her, his eyes free of fever. Without thinking, she caught his hand and held it to her cheek, then slowly released it as she remembered she wasn't the woman in his life that he needed and wanted.

"Here." She held a glass of water to his lips and cradled his head gently as he took several long sips from the glass. When she pulled it away from him, his eyes were watching her intently, his gaze so strong she felt he could see right through her, all the way to her aching soul.

"I don't remember much." He spoke softly, as though disturbing the sound of the hiss and crack of the fire was too intrusive. "What I do remember surely must have been a dream."

Olivia pulled her eyes away from his with difficulty and focused on smoothing her apron that she had donned earlier. "The infection returned to your leg," she spoke just as softly.

"Yes, but before that. What we had... what we did... was that real? Or was it a creation of my fever?"

Olivia could feel blood rushing to her face, and she wanted to cover it with her apron and sob into it. Yes, it had been real. To her. But to him she had been a convenient woman to use to soothe his desires. And, once she had healed him, he would leave her for Bella.

"Yes, what you remember did happen," she said stiffly, still avoiding eye contact. "But it was a complete mistake. I regret my actions greatly."

One of his eyebrows arched in question. "Did I hurt you? Did I frighten you?"

Olivia remembered his hands on her flesh, one hand sliding over the delicate skin of her thigh, touching her as though he had never touched a woman's flesh. And the other hand had been gently massaging her breast, then plucking her nipples until the ache within her had been nearly painful.

Deep inside her lower stomach, her muscles clenched, and her nipples hardened, craving his touch once again. A sweet ache burned within her, and it was everything she could do not to breathe rapidly with the desire washing over her.

She stood suddenly and went to the hearth, prepping the area to make him some tortillas. She couldn't be near him. Not when she was reminded of things she had never thought could happen between a man and a woman. She had to collect her wits and stop behaving so foolish around him.

"You didn't answer my question, Olivia." While his tone was soft, it left no doubt that he expected an answer.

"It was highly inappropriate. It-it..." Her mind searched for words but nothing could come to mind.

How could something feel so right and be so wrong? *Because he is devoted to another woman! You are not going to have an affair with a potentially married man!*

"It was incredible," he said, "and I wouldn't have done anything different."

His words pulled at her, and she so desperately wanted to believe in him. But she couldn't get Bella out of her mind. She pictured a gorgeous full-bodied young woman with long, softly curled black hair. Subconsciously she touched her own hair that was pulled back into the severe bun at the nape of her neck, then brushed her hand over her collarbone. She was thin, though not without soft curves. But his hands were made to hold the body of a woman with abundance to offer.

She remembered his hand in her hair, remembered his strong fingers caressing her scalp as he pulled her closer to him. She shook her head at herself and fought back the tears. She had been an absolute fool. She had wanted to think he desired and craved her. Yet he craved another, and she was just a poor substitute to take her place until he could get back to his beloved Bella.

She flipped the tortillas on the griddle over the fire. "Yes," she agreed reluctantly, knowing he wouldn't let the issue go until he had an answer from her. "It was incredible."

She turned to face him, holding the hot tortillas on a plate and slowly walked towards him. "I've never experienced anything like that in my life. You made me feel..." She hesitated as she tried to find the words. Finally, she just shrugged her shoulders. "You made me feel. I have felt nothing—empty—worthless, for a very, very long time. And you changed that for me for those moments we were together, Mr. Cade, and I am grateful to you."

CADE WATCHED HER facial expressions closely. He felt as weak as a newborn, but he could still sense something was wrong. Something had changed, and she seemed more aloof now than she had been the night he had come into their home, very close to death. She had saved his life twice now, and he wondered how he would ever repay the debt. But he got the feeling she didn't want anything to do with him anymore.

"What happened?" he asked as she drew closer to him.

She sat down in the chair near the bed, her back ramrod straight, and began to tear the tortillas into smaller pieces for him to eat.

Her eyes darted to his. "Surely you remember what we… how we—"

"I remember holding an incredibly beautiful and sensual woman in my arms. And I remember that, despite the nightmares she has gone through in life, I was able to touch her body, to make her sigh with desire, to draw her against my body, and to have her sweet caress over my body to the point that I didn't know if I would last long enough to please her. And I wanted—want—to please this beautiful woman."

He held her eyes with his intense stare, hoping to understand what he was trying to convey to her. Had he been too bold? Should she be offended by the things he had just said?

Finally, she tore her gaze away from his and held a piece of tortilla to his mouth. He took it from her, but continued to watch her as he chewed slowly, waiting for some type of response from her. Finally, he reached out and caught her hand, and he watched her visibly fight the flood of emotions that filled her. What had he done to make her feel this way? Had he lost everything he had gained with her?

"Why have you ever felt worthless, angel? How can you not see the treasure that you are, the beautiful woman that graces anyone with her presence?"

She tugged slightly at her hand, but he would not release

her. As her eyes stared at his, she couldn't hide the shimmering of unshed tears. "Talk to me, angel," he whispered.

"I have never had a man want me," she whispered, matching his hushed tones. "And you have been incredibly ill and unable to think with a clear mind. You see a woman that doesn't exist. You see a woman that will make do until you can return to the one who holds your heart."

A thousand questions swirled through Cade's mind and he released her hand so he could reach up and cup her face and swipe away the tear that had slipped down her cheek. "My mind is completely clear now, Olivia. And I crave you now more than ever. You are a temptation unlike anything I have ever faced. I know exactly what I see when I look at you, and you are blind not to see it yourself."

She closed her eyes briefly and leaned into his hand, allowing him to caress her cheek, but then pulled away, focusing on the tortillas. "You must eat," she said, her voice thick with unshed tears. "You need to regain your strength."

He refused to take the next piece of tortilla that she held to his mouth. "There is no woman in my life, Olivia. What makes you think there is a woman I crave to return to, that I crave more than you?"

Olivia shook her head. "It isn't important. What happened between us was a mistake. And when you have fully healed, you will feel the same."

He caught her wrist and could feel her pulse racing. "Why? Answer me. Why?"

Another tear slipped down her cheek and she pulled her wrist free of his grasp. "You-you spoke as your fever held you. I know there is a woman that holds your heart. I know there is a woman you wish to be with far more than you ever wish to be with me. And—and I know it has been a long time for most of the Texians to be with their women, and that even someone like me will satisfy your ache temporarily until you can go home to the one you truly want."

Cade stared at her in absolute confusion. What the hell was she talking about? "I have no home to return to," he said, his voice firm even though emotions raged within him, threatening to break him. "The Mexican Army saw to that. They made certain my home was burnt to the ground, burnt to ashes, and made me watch the destruction."

Olivia's eyes darted to his in surprise and sympathy. "I am so very sorry, Cade. I did not know... I wouldn't have..." Her voice trailed off. Then, hesitantly, "And your wife? Did they take her prisoner? Or did they... did they—"

"My wife died a little over two years ago giving birth to my baby girl. She and I were close, but she resented me for taking her from Virginia, from all of her friends and all of the things she knew and cherished. We grew apart, and the conception of my daughter was a complete shock to both of us. We were not, uh, intimate very often."

"Cade, I did not mean to remind you of such terrible things. Please, just eat a little more and rest. You need to heal and get stronger."

"No, you deserve to know the truth. You deserve to know what kind of man you have saved. And, if after you hear my story, you choose to stay as far from me as possible while I heal, I will understand."

She withdrew the piece of tortilla she had been holding close to his face and sat back, her expression pensive. He could tell she didn't know if she wanted to hear the rest of what he was going to tell her. But he owed it to her...she deserved to know why the Mexican Army hunted him, deserved to know why he wanted to heal and be on his way.

"I moved my wife and son from Virginia to Texas six years ago. I was a successful banker and we lived a very comfortable life. But when I heard about the opportunities available in Texas, the idea of leaving the confines of the city and starting fresh in a new and unknown territory appealed to me deeply. My wife was in support of it, too, until we got to Texas and she realized exactly how uncivilized the territory is. It took us an hour to ride to the closest general store, and there were very few women around for her to socialize. It became a nightmare for her.

"My son though..." A whimsical smile crossed his lips as he pictured his son riding his favorite horse, grinning at him with excitement every time they went to town, every time they went to check the crops they were growing and the cattle herd they were cultivating, every time they went hunting. "My son loved Texas. It was as though he had been born to live here."

"Sounds like he takes after his father."

Cade struggled to maintain his composure. "I became a Texian about three years ago as the military visited us, threatening us, demanding taxes, demanding that we give them whatever they wanted since we belonged to Mexico. They treated us as if we were their property, as if they owned us, and if we stepped out of line, they had no problem killing us."

Cade closed his eyes for several moments as images and smells flashed through his mind, things he hadn't wanted to remember ever again. But he needed to tell his story. He needed to purge it from his conscience. He opened his eyes to focus on Olivia, who had turned white as she had listened to him.

"I shared my Texian passion with a few other landowners around me, and together we gathered information and passed it through the chain to the Texian Army. We let them know where people were stationed, how many men they had at different points in our area. But I was a fool to trust the men around me. I was a fool to trust at all.

"I had gone to the general store for supplies when I saw the smoke on the horizon. I raced home as fast as I could, but there was nothing I could do. The Mexican Army waited for me there, along with one of my fellow landowners who was a spy for Mexico and had fooled us all. They-they brought my son out..." He paused and swallowed hard, but couldn't stop the tear that slid down the side of his face.

"He was just a boy. He had just turned ten only a few weeks earlier. He was just a boy," he whispered. He cleared his throat and continued, grateful that Olivia hadn't stopped him, grateful that she was letting him tell his story. "They beat me quite a bit in front of my son, and I'll never forget him yelling for them to stop, and the anger and fear on his face. They finally stopped and forced me to my knees in front of him. Then they asked me if helping the Texians was worth my son's life. I pleaded with them and told them I would join the Mexican Army if it meant they would spare him. And finally they agreed and let him go free and he ran into my arms.

"I held him as he cried, I soothed him that everything was going to be okay finally, and that the worst was over. And that was when they yanked him from my arms and slit his throat in front of me. His eyes widened in shock and unbelievable fear, and then slowly glazed over in death and they dropped him in front of me, leaving his body lying before me.

"I don't remember much that happened after that. I remember stroking his face. I remember crying to God in anger and in grief. And I remember his body slowly growing cold in my arms." Cade stopped talking for a few moments, allowing the tears to slide freely down his face.

He hadn't grieved the death of his son—he hadn't had the chance to. And now it was sinking in fully that he would never again see the energetic, happy young boy playing in the fields, racing his horse as the wind whipped at his blonde hair, so much like his own. He would never again receive one of those giant hugs that his son gave him when he least expected it. And he would never again get to kiss him on the forehead to say good night and whisper "I love you."

A choked sob escaped him, and instantly Olivia was there, holding him, cradling him and whispering softly in his ear. Her fingers wiped at the continuous flow of tears, and he could feel the warmth of her own tears striking his face. Gradually he began to hear what she was saying to him as the rush of the sound of his heartbeat in his ears faded.

"He's riding a beautiful horse in Heaven, racing through the clouds. He is watching you, still looking up to you, still admiring you as his father. Where he is now, is safe and bright and beautiful. He is happy, Cade. I believe it with all my heart. He is happy."

Cade felt his tears slowing and he pulled Olivia back far enough that he was able to see her face, see the tears that rolled down her cheeks. Just as she had done for him, he wiped them away with his fingers. "God, you are an amazing woman," he whispered, and pulled her back to him, pressing his lips to hers gently, softly.

Reluctantly, he pulled back. "After what seemed to be hours, and at the same time felt like only seconds, they yanked me away from my son and drug his body away. I yelled and I screamed, but it only earned me more punches and kicks from the men around me, including the man I had once thought was my ally, my friend."

Cade shook his head. "The man has a black heart. There is something so cold and so harsh within him, he takes pleasure in seeing others in pain and suffering. And it was as he smiled at me I remembered my sweet baby girl. I screamed for her and the men laughed at me. They pointed to the burning house and said she was already turning to ash with the house. My vision turned red. I launched at one of them and brought him down with my fists, then took his pistol and shot the next soldier that came near me. But I was outnumbered."

"Cade," Olivia whispered, "I'm so sorry. I didn't mean to

make you tell me this. I'm so, so sorry."

"No," Cade shook his head. "I needed to tell you. You deserve to know. The face of the colonel is branded in my mind forever. He was just as cold and ruthless as my former ally, Devon. He may have even been worse than Devon. He was the one that had slit my son's throat. He was the one that had given the orders to burn my house down with my sweet little girl inside."

Cade focused his eyes on Olivia, and they were cold and angry, no longer grieving. "I will stop at nothing to see those two men dead. They deserve to die—they are animals—they aren't even human."

Olivia ran her fingers through his hair, smoothing it out of his face. "They will face their punishment, one way or another. You can't risk losing your life to kill them."

"Yes. I can. And I will. Because I found out something, something they didn't want me to know."

Olivia looked at him quizzically, her fingers still in his hair, her face close to his.

"My daughter is alive."

Chapter Eleven

OLIVIA PULLED BACK slightly, shaking her head. Was he still feverish? Was he wishing for the impossible? "No, Cade, they told you. She burned in the fire. She's dead. There is nothing you can do."

Cade stared back at her, his eyes determined. "They took me prisoner. I don't remember much of the journey, because they took turns beating me every time we paused in our travel. But soon we were right outside of San Antonio, and they were setting up camp. They dumped me in one of the tents, my feet and wrists tied. I think I was in shock, because nothing felt real. I didn't even feel the pain in my body from all of the beatings.

"But then, late one night, one of the soldiers snuck into the tent and cut me free of my bonds. I had given up, though. I didn't have any fight left in me. They had killed my children, everything I lived for. What was the point in fighting them? But he forced me to my feet, forced me to pay attention. He grabbed my upper arms and yanked me forward until I was only inches from his face. That was when he told me...He was a spy for the Texians. He had been there at the very beginning when they raided my home.

"He told me how brave my son had been, how he had done everything possible to protect my daughter. But they took her. They took her prisoner with the hopes they could use her as bait or a trap for the Texians in the future. He shook me by my shoulders so hard my head snapped back and forth and he spoke softly but harshly and told me my sweet Isabella is alive. That they hold her prisoner some-where among the camp. He said I needed to escape, and then come back for my Bella.

"It was as if he had dumped cold water on me. She was alive. That was what I clung to, and that is what gave me the strength to get to your home. Unfortunately, as I escaped, I encountered the colonel, and he almost looked happy that he had found me loose within the camp. I think he relished the idea of killing me. But I fought like a man possessed. He sliced my leg with his sword, and that was nearly my undo-ing...until you."

Olivia was shaking as she pulled away from him slowly, her eyes closed, and tears slipped from underneath her eyelashes. When she opened her eyes finally, they were full of hope and determination. "She's alive," she whispered. "Your baby is alive, Cade. We must find her."

Cade shook his head slowly, his hand cupping her face. "This isn't your fight, Olivia. I cannot risk you getting hurt because you try to help me. You've already helped me enough as it is. All I ask is for you to allow me to gather my strength, and then I will be gone. I won't burden you anymore."

Olivia didn't know what to say. But what she did know

was that there was no way possible she wasn't going to help him find his daughter and rescue her from the foul men who held her. She didn't care what it took for her to be successful—they were going to find and save Bella.

She suddenly remembered what had started their entire conversation in the first place and a blush touched her cheeks as she realized how wrong she had been. Bella wasn't his wife or his lover. But she was the woman, or girl to be factual, that held his heart.

"What is it?" he asked, and she realized he had been watching her intently. "I understand if you don't want to have anything to do with me. I plan on killing those men, even if it is in their sleep. And I know that doesn't set well with you. I can tend to myself if you want to leave."

Olivia shook her head. "I'd kill them myself if I knew who they were. My parents were executed by the Mexican Army. I understand very well the desire to set things right."

"Then what is it? There is something you are thinking that you aren't sharing with me."

Had they spent that much time together that he already knew her so well? She handed him another piece of tortilla, unable to meet his eyes. "I-I had thought... I mean, it's just that, in your sleep...you called out for Bella many times. And I thought-I thought—"

"You thought she was my lover." A corner of his mouth lifted and, for the first time since he had started telling her the horrid story of the past several weeks for him, his face relaxed. His hand reached around and pulled her head down and pressed a kiss to her forehead, then each cheek, then finally held her lips hovering over his. "Kiss me, angel," he whispered. "Kiss me."

Olivia couldn't resist him. All of her reservations seemed to have flown away and she dipped her head, tentatively moving her lips over his and he moaned softly in appreciation. Empowered, she moved her lips more urgently, and tentatively licked his lower lip to taste him. He inhaled deeply and his hand cupped the back of her head and he crushed her to him, his lips moving just as urgently over hers, and soon they were tasting each other, their tongues lightly skimming each other's lips, then sliding together, almost as if dancing together as they tried to get closer and closer to each other.

When they pulled apart, they were both panting, and Olivia felt as though her heart was going to burst out of her chest. "Is it always like this?" she asked him, her voice quivering with passion.

"No, angel. No. It is never like this." And he pulled her back down to his lips that no longer craved anything except the taste of her.

"MOVE SLOWLY, AND lean on me. Don't worry about putting too much weight on me. I'm stronger than you think."

Cade sat perched on the edge of the bed and looked up at Olivia with a slight smile on his lips, but it didn't reach his eyes. "You've already shown me how strong you are." He noted, then drew a deep breath and returned his eyes to the floor.

His leg throbbed as if in anticipation of what was to come. But he would never get Bella if he didn't start rebuilding his strength, and he couldn't do that without pain. Clenching one hand into a fist, he wrapped his arm around Olivia's shoulders, and slowly they began to stand.

He held back the curse words burning the back of his throat as he tentatively put pressure on his leg. God, it hurt. He had known it would hurt, but for several heart pounding seconds he felt as if he would fall, taking Olivia with him. But she had spoken the truth, and she stood like a rock at his side, bracing him.

Gradually the black dots floating in front of his eyes faded away, and he saw the room clearly. He looked down at Olivia and she was looking up at him. "Do you need to sit down again?" Her voice was worried, and strained from the strength it was taking for her to help hold him upright.

Slowly he took some of his weight off of her and placed it on his injured leg and cringed at the pain, but he knew he could tolerate it. He would go through hell and back to get his Bella, and at the moment it felt like that was exactly what he was doing. "No, no," he said, belatedly replying to Olivia's question. "I can stand. I want to try to walk to the door and back. And that will be it. I won't push it any more than that."

"Cade, are you sure…"

Cade nodded curtly, and together they turned and began towards the door. His limp was drastic, and he had to rely on her more than he wanted. But they made it to the door and finally paused for him to catch his breath.

"How do you feel?" Olivia asked, staring up at him with concern.

"I won't lie to you, angel. It hurts. It hurts a lot. But it isn't bad enough that I can't tolerate it, if only a little at a time right now." He tried to shift some more of his weight onto his leg, but his body protested violently, and he reluctantly returned the weight to Olivia's shoulders.

"Don't push yourself too quickly," she said softly. "I know how fast you want to go, and I'd gladly give you all of my strength to make it even remotely possible. But you'll be no help to her until you are fully ready to rescue her."

He looked down at her and smiled, though it was hard for him to do anything other than scowl at the pain that burned through his thigh. His other injuries had begun to heal nicely. But this deep gash in his leg was the most severe, and the most damning to his need to get to Bella.

Drawing a deep breath, he took a wavering step towards the bed and nearly went down. Olivia braced him, though, and he was soon standing firm once more. He drew in his breath as slowly and easily as he could until he was no longer panting with pain and frustration. Olivia was watching him closely, though the look on her face was one of determination, not one of concern.

"A simple misstep," she said lightly. "Let's give it another go."

God, this woman was incredible. How had he been so fortunate to have been sent to her home the night after he had escaped the Mexican Army? There seemed to be only one plausible answer—God was watching over him. And he had been delivered to a woman who was soothing his physical pain and helping him find peace with his emotional distress as well.

They moved slowly back towards the bed, though he made sure each step was deliberate and used the muscles that had been so badly damaged. He would be strong again. Nothing would stop him until he held his precious little girl in his arms.

When he was finally sitting on the edge of the bed once more, he was breathing heavily and his face was covered in perspiration. The black dots threatened to invade his vision, but he fought them back and instead focused on Olivia, who was propping the pillows correctly and preparing the bed for him.

When she turned back to him she smiled and moved to help him reposition into the bed. He shook his head at her. "I can do it myself," he said softly, and she hesitated, gnawing on her lower lip. He forced a smile to his face, hoping it reassured her, because it sure as hell didn't reassure him. Focusing entirely on what he needed to do, he swung his legs up and over and shifted his body weight until he was propped against the pillows.

The feeling of a cool, damp cloth wiping at his face startled him and his eyes flew open. Olivia wiped at his face, her gentle smile a balm to his soul. "You did it," she said softly. "You're fever barely broke a few days ago and you are up walking today. You are amazing."

He shook his head and caught her hand against his cheek. "I wouldn't even be here if it wasn't for you."

Olivia's smile broadened, but she shook her head. "I suspect you would have found a way with or without me."

He held her hand to his cheek a few moments longer, then kissed her palm and leaned back against the pillows. "I have so much to overcome. And every day she slips further away. Where could she be, angel? They've won San Antonio. What will they do to a small two-year-old girl?"

Olivia shook her head. "I don't know. But I suspect they will keep her with them. They see her as a prisoner they can leverage. The Texians won't be willing to watch the death of a young girl, and this is a weakness they must plan to exploit somehow."

"We need to know what is happening with the war," Cade said firmly. "We must find out where they are headed now, and any other clues we can find out about their activities. She's with the main camp. I wouldn't be surprised if she isn't with Santa Anna directly." He laid his head back and stared at the ceiling. Then his eyes refocused on Olivia. "How long has it been since I came to you that night? How many days has it been?"

"It—well, it has been a while. Nearly a fortnight."

Cade clenched and unclenched his hands into fists, his stomach churning. Olivia stood and walked around the bed until she was on the opposite side. She climbed into the bed beside him and placed one hand alongside his face while the other smoothed back his hair. "She will be okay. And we will find her soon."

The roar of his blood rushing through his veins slowly faded, and he focused on the woman that lay near him. Slowly he realized she was talking to him again as he watched her full, pink lips, remembering what they had been like on his own and instantly craved to touch her again.

"...need to examine the wrappings to make sure your excursion didn't do anything to reopen the wound." She reached for his dressings, and he was relieved that she had fashioned a loincloth for him to wear. While it served the obvious purpose, it also served to prevent him from exposing to her just how much her touch impacted him.

Her hands moved quickly and efficiently, and he heard her sigh of relief as she looked down at his leg. "It is still healing nicely. We can continue your exercise tomorrow. It shouldn't take you long to build up your strength."

"How long?" he asked, his voice more urgent than he had intended. But he couldn't keep the hope from his voice at the same time.

"It's-it's hard to estimate, Cade. We can't rush this. If we do, you'll be no help to Bella at all. It will take time for you to be able to walk on your own again, and then even longer for you to gain the strength to ride a horse."

Cade shook his head and shut his eyes. "Too long. Far too long."

"If we rush it, then you may not be able to rescue Bella. We can't take any risks."

"It is a risk every day that I'm not out there looking for her that she is slipping further and further from my grasp. She's just a child, Olivia. She doesn't belong in the middle of a war."

Olivia's eyes searched his face. "I know," she whispered. "Let me go and get her."

A new fear suddenly clawed at Cade. Olivia was just stubborn enough to do such a thing, and the outcome for her was guaranteed. The soldiers would use her as their own plaything until they had beaten her physically, emotionally, and spiritually. And then they would either kill her or leave her to die. No matter how many ways he looked at it, the outcome for Olivia was horrific.

He caught her hand and gripped it tightly. "I can't let you do that, Olivia. I can't. There is no way you would make it through alive, and I would never be able to live with myself, even if by some miracle Bella was returned to me."

Olivia pulled back from him slightly. "Cade, you don't know me. You don't know all that I am capable of. I've been a spy for the Texians for many years now. And I've come through some dangerous situations where I should have died." Images suddenly floated before her eyes. Images and smells, and the overwhelming feeling of loss and victory at the same time. "I know how I can help. I know what I can do."

Cade had seen the emotions crossing her face, and knew she had seen and done things that no person should ever have to be challenged with, yet she still pressed on. And even now, when it wasn't her battle to fight, she was ready to step in and help him.

"No, no. If something happened to you..." His voice trailed off. He couldn't finish the thought. If something happened to her, he would never be able to forgive himself. "Bella is safe for now, as you said. But we must know what is going on in the war. Are they all still stationed in San Antonio? Or are they on the move? We need information. And since you are a spy…" His voice halted abruptly and he turned a hard gaze on her. "You're a spy? Do you realize the danger you put yourself in? Do you realize everything that could happen—"

"I'm very aware. And I have good resources. I need to travel to town tomorrow to get some supplies and check in at the *cocina*. I'll be able to get an update on the troops movements then." She adjusted the pillows around him. "In the meantime, rest. Gather your strength. We'll exercise again in the morning and then I'll leave."

Cade wanted to argue with her. He didn't want her doing these things, taking these risks, she was taking for him, but he had no choice. She was his best hope at saving Bella, even though it made the hair on the back of his neck stand up in warning. But before he could voice his concerns, the lull of healing sleep was too strong and he couldn't resist it any longer.

Chapter Twelve

WHEN OLIVIA PULLED up to the *cocina*, she couldn't have been more thrilled. It appeared they were thriving with business. Until she realized it was all of the soldiers that had come and fought to take the Alamo.

Their uniforms were not the standard they had become so familiar with. Instead they were ragtag white uniforms with patches and torn fabric, and many of the men were even without footwear. These were far different soldiers than they had served in the past.

These men were hard and had expressed barely any emotion as they ate the food in front of them. They had witnessed the most brutal and violent exchanges in their life and, from the faded brown stains of blood on many of them, they had been in direct contact with the men in the Alamo.

She swept inside the back entrance as if she hadn't been gone for several days and immediately grabbed an apron that was hanging near the door. She had it on and was already rolling out tortillas before Angie came into the kitchen, balancing dirty plates on her arm. They nearly all crashed to the floor when she saw Olivia as a startled expression and then excitement flashed across her face.

Olivia hurried forward and helped her with the plates, then turned and embraced her sister, holding her tightly and fighting back tears. She hadn't realized how much she had missed her family, and her already raw emotions were struggling to maintain her composure.

She leaned back and smoothed her hands over Angie's hair, as usual coming free of the loose bun on the top of her head. "How have you been?"

Angie shook her head. "You don't know how happy I am to see you, Vi. I've missed you so terribly much, something I never thought I would say."

Olivia laughed and wiped some flour off of Angie's cheek. "And it is something I never thought I would hear. How are *Abuela* and *Abuelo*? They aren't working too hard, are they?"

Angie began to move around the kitchen, preparing plates for the customers that waited on the other side of the wall. "They are working hard, but it isn't anything more than what we've faced in the past." Her smile faltered slightly and she looked away from Olivia. "There hasn't been any word."

Olivia closed her eyes briefly and said a silent prayer. Angie's husband had been in the Alamo. And none of the Texian fighters had been spared. Yet her sister still clung to the hope that he was alive, that somehow he had escaped Santa Anna's merciless slaughter of all of the Texians.

Olivia smoothed her hands on her apron and returned to rolling out the dough for the tortillas. "So is Santa Anna still here? Or is he returning to Mexico?"

Angie's smile returned. "We're not giving up. We won't let them win. Santa Anna is still here, but he has sent his other forces to the East. Houston is pulling back... I think to gather more men. Santa Anna knows that the war will never end unless Houston admits defeat, and that will never happen."

Olivia's heart was pounding. The Mexican Army was on the move, which meant little Bella could be on the move, too. "Angie, I need your help."

Angie stopped pouring *chile* sauce over enchiladas and looked at Olivia with concern. "What is it? Are you alright? *Por Dios*, I didn't even ask you how things are going tending to your Texian. What has happened?"

Olivia smiled at her and helped her finish the next two plates. "Let's get this food out to the hungry men and then we will talk. Don't worry—I am safe. But our Texian isn't. And I need your help to make sure he doesn't lose everything in his life."

⚜

BELLA WAS BEING treated with the type of behavior to be expected from a dictator who enjoyed using people for his own benefit. The stories of Santa Anna's generals having a small girl with them had filtered through over the past few days, and the soldiers had laughed as they had described how gullible the foolish people were that had tried to come and take over their beloved Mexico.

"When they arrive at a town, they drag her out for everyone to see her. And then a general will order one of the men to cut her throat if no one steps forward and gives him information about Houston. Inevitably, someone steps forward, sometimes even more than one person because they can't bear the thought of that sweet baby dying because they held their tongues."

Olivia wiped a hand down her face, wishing she could hold a knife to Santa Anna's throat. She was exhausted, and needed to return to Cade as soon as possible. She had already been to the market and the small wagon and mule waited at the side of the house. But getting the information on Bella was the most important thing at the moment. Now, knowing that Bella was even further out of their grasp than she had anticipated, her whole body was engulfed in weariness and despair. She felt drained, hollow... lifeless.

"Do you know where they are now?" she asked, clinging to hope.

Angie shook her head. "Not precisely. I know they are drawing close to the Colorado River. Whether they plan to cross it or not, I don't know. It may be where Houston stops to fight them."

Fear prickled down Olivia's spine. If they battled, the chance of Bella surviving was very slim. They had to get to her soon. But Cade was in no condition.

Angie reached out and grasped Olivia's hand. "You haven't heard, yet, have you?"

Olivia's eyes searched her sister's. "Heard what?" Her heart was racing in her chest.

"There was a battle at Refugio." Angie's eyes shimmered

with tears. "They executed every single Texian, even those who surrendered."

"Dear God." Olivia gripped her sister's hand more tightly and fought off her own tears, knowing that she always had to be the strong one. "They are animals. We must stop them!"

"We will. I know we will. Houston is a good general. He will beat Santa Anna." Angie's face was firm in her conviction.

Olivia nodded, even though she knew deep in her heart that more Texians were going to die under the ruthless command of Santa Anna. She also knew Houston was their last hope in winning the war.

Olivia glanced outside and saw that the sun was beginning to set low in the trees. "I better head back before it gets dark," she murmured to herself, but Angie overheard her.

"Will you make it before it is dark? Maybe you should stay the night here. I'm certain your Texian will survive one night without you. There is no sense in putting yourself in danger."

Olivia plastered a smile on her face and shook her head. "I'll be just fine. As long as the mule doesn't slip and fall in the mud." She forced a laugh, but it didn't fool Angie.

"I've never seen you smile so much. This Texian must be good for you. But be careful, Vi. We miss you so much. It was a blessing having your help today. But you're going to wear yourself to nothing if you keep working so hard and taking care of this Texian. Why is he so special, Vi? Why are you doing so much for him?"

Olivia didn't hesitate in her answer. "He's a good man who has given up a great deal to support the revolution. The least we can do is help mend him and see him back protecting all of us."

Angie raised an eyebrow and Olivia felt a blush creeping up her neck. She turned quickly and headed to the rear door. She paused and turned, smiling at Angie, a genuine smile this time. "Thank you, Angie, for everything."

Angie rushed forward and gathered Olivia in a deep hug. "I love you, Vi."

Olivia had to hold back her tears. "I love you too," she whispered softly, then turned and was gone.

THE MUD MADE for an extremely difficult trek back to the house. The mule's feet slid as it sought solid ground to walk on, and the wagon lurched each time, making Olivia a little ill to her stomach.

But as she got further away from the mud tracks of town she was able to guide the mule onto an area that had some patches of grass and he could have better traction. Soon they were moving along smoothly, though not as fast as Olivia would have liked.

The sun was dipping lower and lower, and she had promised Cade she would be back before sundown. It was going to take a miracle to make that happen. She slapped the reins on the mule's rear and clucked to it, urging it to pick up the pace.

She was more than halfway there when she heard the sound. Beating almost in rhythm to her rapid heartbeat were the thundering of hooves. She didn't look behind her, she just moved forward at the same pace she had been. Ice cold fear slid down her back and her stomach clenched.

Suddenly, an officer riding a tall bay gelding rode up alongside her and reached down, grabbing the reins forcefully. "Whoa, *senorita*! Where are you going in such a hurry? Well, in a hurry with this little runt pulling you." He laughed at the mule.

As if it understood him, the mule flattened his ears and reached back and tried to bite the horse that stood next to him. The officer frowned slightly, then pulled his horse back enough that it was out of reach of the mule. Then he returned his gaze to Olivia.

"It isn't safe to be traveling these roads at night," he continued.

Olivia forced a smile to her face. "But, *senor*, it is not night yet. I still have plenty of light to carry me forward."

"And where are you headed?" She hadn't heard the other soldier that had ridden up on her right side and flinched when she heard his voice. "Ah, no reason to be afraid, *senorita*," he said, smiling to reveal slightly yellowed teeth and a gap where he had lost a tooth, either in battle or a barroom brawl. She didn't care.

"I'm traveling to my sister's home. She needs some supplies given the chaos that has occurred around here." She prayed her lie was convincing enough.

"You won't make it much further before it is dark, *seno-*

rita. Why don't we just help you make camp here." The officer's voice cut in again, and sweat began to build in the palms of her hands.

She turned back to him, trying to plant the sweetest smile possible on her face. "That is so kind and generous of you, sir. But I must decline. I intend on getting to my sister tonight. The moon will be out soon enough to guide my way."

Before she realized it another soldier appeared at her elbow, having dismounted his horse. "Now that isn't a very cordial way to behave, *senorita.*" He spoke in a low voice, but the intentions in his eyes were obvious.

Olivia turned and tried to jerk the reins free from the officer and smacked the mule's rear hard, but he wasn't fast enough. He only made a few steps before the officer leaned down again and jerked her to a stop.

When she looked up at him, her heart raced in fear. This man had nothing but ice for a soul. "That wasn't a very nice thing to do, *senorita,*" he said softly, his eyes holding malice and something else. Anticipation?

The soldier standing near her grabbed her arm and held it in a tight grip as he began to pull her from her seat. She grasped the wood on the seat tightly with her other hand and pulled hard to free herself from his grip, but he was far stronger than her. And it didn't help when the officer on the horse next to her grabbed her by her hair and pulled her towards the soldier.

It hurt, but she wouldn't give him the satisfaction of seeing her pain. But she could no longer maintain her grip on the seat and tumbled off, landing on her hands and knees in the mud. The men laughed at her, and she grabbed the wagon to pull herself upright.

The officer had already dismounted and grabbed her by her hair once again, hauling her up to face him. He was a good head taller than she was, but she refused to lift her eyes to his face. He chuckled and she could smell the stench of tobacco and whiskey. He put a finger underneath her chin and lifted it, but she still refused to make eye contact with him.

"Look at me, *senorita*," he said calmly. When she didn't comply, he yelled, "Look at me!"

She couldn't stop her flinch and the men all laughed again. Slowly, she raised her eyes to meet those of the officer, and she saw a man who had lost his soul altogether. Whether he had lost it in the battle of the Alamo or never had one to begin with, she didn't care. A man with no soul was dangerous. Because, for him, the only source of joy was witnessing and inflicting pain upon others.

She needed to get one of her shotguns. She had one on the other side of the wagon that she should have grabbed when they had approached her, and she had another at the back of the wagon, underneath the tarp. Grandfather had always driven home the point that it was better to be over prepared than under. But at that moment, neither option was going to help her.

The officer smiled at her and released his tight grip on her hair and instead pinned her against the wagon with his body, holding her firmly in place. "It is very dangerous out her for a beautiful woman such as yourself. We will protect you on your journey," he said, still smiling and glanced at his other two comrades. "Won't we, *hombres*? We will protect you as long as pay us a small fee."

Olivia was trying to control the tremors that were starting to take over her body. "I am poor, *senor*. I do not have any money."

"Then we will make arrangements for you to pay in another way." His voice was so repulsive she nearly threw up.

Suddenly his hands were on her breasts and he buried his face against her neck, mumbling about his approval of what he held. Olivia had to take action and save herself. She drew her knee up hard and fast and the officer cried out in pain, stepping away from her. She turned on the guard next to him and before he knew what had happened, she planted a solid blow to his chin with her right fist, and he stumbled backwards, stunned.

She raced to the rear of the wagon where she was brought up short by a hand striking her hard across the face. She had forgotten about the third soldier. But he clearly hadn't forgotten about her. He yanked her back up and struck her again, and this time she tasted blood in her mouth. When he held her upright and sneered at her, she felt dazed and disoriented from all the strikes to her head and face. He had a sharp, angular face, making him appear even more frightening than he already was.

"You just made a big mistake, *senorita*," he said, his accent heavy.

He slammed her against the back of the wagon and began ripping at her dress, the buttons popping all around them. Olivia was too proud to beg, and she knew it would do no good. These men were intent on violating her, and only sheer force—or a miracle—was going to save her now. She twisted and clawed, trying to free herself from the soldier whose smell assaulted her nose and his filthy hands grabbed at her clothing. Finally, she was able to rake her nails down his face and he yelped in pain, stepping back from her.

The other guard had recovered from her punch, unfortunately, and he quickly took the place of his comrade. She heard her dress rip and felt the cold air on her skin and fought even harder. She wasn't going to let this happen. She refused to let it happen!

Out of the corner of her eye, she saw the officer step around the back of the wagon, having regained his composure. He pulled away the guard and held her at arm's length, his hard, large hands keeping hers at her side. His grip on her wrists was punishing, and she slowly came to realize that she would not be able to defeat this man. Not without her shotgun.

"You are very pretty, *senorita*. It pains me to see you in such distress." She gasped in surprise as he flipped her around and bent her over the back of the wagon. "So I just won't look at you." He laughed, and the guards joined in his laughter as he began tossing her skirts over her head.

Oh, dear God. Not like this. Please, not like this. That was when her mind suddenly kicked in and she remembered her shotgun. With her skirts over her head, her movements were concealed and she began to reach under the tarp.

Whack!

The sharp slap to her bare behind was not only painful, it was horribly mortifying, and she fought against the sting of tears. She would not let these men win.

Whack!

The second smack helped jerk her body forward slightly and she could feel the butt of the gun with her fingertips. She just needed him to continue his current line of torture a little longer…

Whack!

"See, *hombres*, she just needs to be tamed, that's all. Now she will take me gladly, and you'll thank me afterwards, *senorita*. Because you've never had it as good—"

Olivia whirled and aimed the shotgun directly at his most vulnerable spot. "I'd be very careful with what you do next, soldier." She spoke calmly, even though her heart was racing.

The officer backed away from her, but then his eyes narrowed. "You wouldn't shoot me. I'm an officer. There would be dire consequences for you and your entire family." He began to move towards her again, a hesitant light in his eyes, but still soulless.

She cocked the gun. "Do you want to find out the answer the hard way?" she demanded.

The other two soldiers, seeming to have finally caught on to what was happening, reached for their pistols. "Tell your men to stand down or I will make you a eunuch, do you understand me?"

The officer waved his hands at the two soldiers, motioning for them to stop. "Good," Olivia said, praising him as if he were a small child. "Now, I want all of your guns loaded in the wagon. I said now!"

The officer glowered at her for several long moments, and Olivia feared that he was going to try to order his men to move on her even if it cost one of them his life. He was so angry at her that he might be willing to make that sacrifice. But as long as his manhood was at stake, perhaps he wouldn't take the risk.

Finally, he nodded and his men stepped forward and tossed the guns into the back of the wagon. Olivia was doing her best to hide her shakes by steading the shotgun with both hands. Slowly, she moved around the wagon and walked backwards towards the front.

"All three of you, turn around and get on your knees," she ordered, as she quickly gathered the reins of the three horses they had been riding. She couldn't take the chance they would follow her. She swiftly tied the reins to the wagon as the men got on their knees, cursing her with every foul name she had ever heard, and some new ones she hadn't.

Carefully, she climbed into the wagon, keeping her gun leveled at them. "You stay on your knees and don't get up until you no longer hear my wagon. Or I will shoot you."

"You little bitch." The officer growled and he began to stand.

With a calmness she couldn't explain, she fired the shotgun quickly, and buckshot whizzed just over his head, knocking his hat off his head. He ducked down quickly and resumed to kneeling, his hands searching his head to be certain he hadn't been struck. "I will find you and make you pay for this, whore!" He screeched at her.

Sitting twisted in the seat so she could keep her eyes, and her gun, on the men, she smacked the reins hard on the mule's rear and it leapt forward with a jerk, already spooked from the gunshot. None of the men turned around, but she waited, watching them, as the mule moved faster than she could ever remember.

When they were several hundred feet from the men, she quickly turned the mule and headed into the dense wooded area for concealment. There was barely enough room for the wagon to fit between the trees, but she knew it thinned out only a short way ahead and she would follow that path to get to Angie's house instead of staying on the original trail where they could watch her.

She didn't think the officer would actually come looking for her. But there was a small possibility he would, and she could leave nothing to chance.

A sense of calm purpose was all that Olivia felt as she continued on the route she had chosen. When she reached the area that thinned out, she stopped the wagon just long enough that she could untie the horses and slap them on the rear, spurring them to run. Whether they ran back to their masters or to graze in the wild, she didn't care. She couldn't have three horses staying at the home in case a soldier might come by to inspect their area.

As she climbed back up into the wagon, the clouds that had been gathering turned into loud thunderstorms, as lightening arced through the dark sky and rain began to pour down. Olivia was both miserable and grateful for the rain. It made the travel that much more difficult, but at least it would wash away her trail and, should those soldiers seek revenge, they wouldn't be able to track her. And, best of all, it would wash their horrible scent from her body. At least she prayed it would. But it could not erase it from her memory.

With the feeling of cold water dripping on her chest she looked down and realized her bodice had been ripped open. As if in a trance, she tried to gather the material together as best she could to cover her nudity. It was as she did so that she noticed the bruises on her wrists and forearms. She couldn't remember how she had gotten them. She knew why it hurt so much to sit—that memory was very clear in her mind.

And, yet, she still felt nothing. She needed to get to the house where she would be safe with Cade. She looked at the sky again. It was way past dark, and he would be angry she hadn't held to her word. With determination, she clucked to the mule and slapped the reins, and he took off at a bone-jarring trot where each bounce reminded her of the degrading humiliation she had just endured.

Chapter Thirteen

WHERE WAS SHE? "I'll be home before dark," she had said. It was now far past sunset, and the rain was pouring down in buckets. The only way he could see anything outside was when the giant streaks of lightening lit up the sky.

Perhaps she had seen the dark clouds and decided to stay in town with her sisters. It would be the smart thing to do. But deep inside he knew she wouldn't have made that decision, no matter how sensible she was being. She was a woman of her word, and if she said she would come back to him, by God, she would find a way to come back to him.

A thousand different scenarios were playing through his mind, and none of them were good. Unable to take the restless wanderings of his mind, he slid to the edge of the bed and grabbed the makeshift crutch he had built for himself. Taking several deep breaths, he stood with a groan, slowly putting weight on his injured leg.

He leaned heavily on the crutch, trying to catch his breath as he fought through the pain. Gradually it eased, and he stood fully upright and began to hobble his way to one of the windows. His leg protested every step, but he blocked out the pain in his mind. What if Olivia was out there and needed help? It was insane for a woman to travel alone during these uncertain times, especially in the dark!

Something caught his eye, a glint of some sort. He watched it as it moved closer and closer, and he could finally see the harness on the mule clearly with Olivia driving the wagon forward, urging the mule to pick up the pace. Relief washed over him, but was quickly replaced by anger. How could she be so foolish? Didn't she realize the danger she had put herself in?

She pulled the mule into the shed, getting the wagon under cover from the rain, then got down and began to quickly unhitch the mule and put him in his stall. Then she hurried to the back of the wagon, tossed the tarp back, and grabbed a giant bag of something.

He opened the door for her before she could try to do it on her own. She hesitated a moment before stepping inside, then moved in and looked at him with startled eyes. "What are you doing out of bed?"

"What are you doing out in the dark?" he demanded, his jaw clenching and unclenching with his anger.

"Oh," she said, and moved past him to the small pantry where she placed the bag. "I was held up longer than I planned. I'm sorry I wasn't back sooner."

She emerged from the pantry with an apron on, something Cade thought odd, but he didn't give it much thought as he still had the anger bubbling inside of him for taking the huge risk she took. Before he could say anything, though, she was already past him and going back out to gather more items from the wagon.

Realizing that a conversation with her at this point was going to be futile, he held the door for her as she continued bringing in the supplies.

She smiled at him when she had finished. "Thank you. Now, let's get you back to bed. You already exercised earlier today and we don't want to put too much strain on your leg."

Now he could talk. And that was exactly what he was going to do. "Do you realize the danger you put yourself in? Do you even comprehend how dangerous it is for a woman to travel alone, much less alone at night? What were you thinking?"

"Time got away from me," she said, her voice quivering slightly.

"You're chilled to the bone. I can get to the bed on my own. You need to get warmed up."

Olivia nodded at him, but didn't speak. Cade took a long hard look at her and could see—nothing. Her face was blank and vacant, devoid of all emotions. In the flickering firelight it was hard to see much of anything, but he felt he couldn't leave her to go to the bed. "Olivia? What has happened? Did you get some news?"

His heart was thundering. What if she had found out that his dear sweet Bella was dead? Dear God, what had she discovered?

With fear gripping his heart, he reached out and grabbed Olivia's arm and she flinched hard. Why was she afraid of him again? He thought they had resolved all of this and they were in a better place.

He let go of her arm and stared at her with both fear and concern. "What did you learn today?"

Olivia shook her head and touched his arm, as though to reassure him. "Bella is safe. They are using her to get the cooperation of Texian sympathizers. They threaten that they will kill her if someone doesn't come forward with information. Inevitably someone always does. It is a clever ruse. From what my sister has heard, Bella is treated very well as long as she plays her part."

Relief rushed over Cade so intense he nearly fell. Olivia's hands reached out to grab him and steady him. "You must get into bed."

He nodded and turned towards the bed, then turned back to Olivia. "So she is no longer in San Antonio?"

"No. They've headed East. They are trying to get close to General Houston to engage battle."

"She cannot be in the middle of a battle! It is no place for anyone, much less a child!" Cade's fear had mounted again.

"I know, I know," Olivia said soothingly. "But Houston is a very shrewd man. They will not get close enough to him."

Cade's eyes searched Olivia's. "Then what is it? Tell me. What is it that has you so disturbed tonight?"

She shook her head but wouldn't make eye contact with him. "I'm not disturbed, but thank you for your consideration. Now, to the bed."

"No, now, you out of those wet clothes."

Before she could protest or stop him, he had unfastened

the tie around her waist and lifted the apron off of her. "No, please, stop!" She tried to grab the apron, but he was too fast. And she stood before him with her ripped bodice, her breasts bared to see.

Cade's felt the blood drain from his face, then slowly flushed with anger. "What happened to you? Who did this? Who did this?"

Olivia appeared on the verge of tears. He could only imagine what she felt, and she had been carrying the burden on her shoulders the entire time she unloaded the wagon, when instead, he should have been tending to her. But he had no way of knowing.

"Please, Cade, just go back to bed. I'll change."

"Are you hurt? What happened?"

With a strength that surprised even him, he guided her to the bed so he could sit down and take the ache away from his leg.

He sat on the edge of the bed and reached for her and noticed his hands were trembling. Whether it was his rage, his fear of what had been done to her, or both, he didn't know. He briefly clenched his hands into fists, then reached for her again. Slowly he began to unhook the rest of her bodice and her hands covered his dark, calloused ones.

He took a steadying breath, ready for her to push him away as he looked up at her. But instead, silent tears of gratitude slid down her cheeks and she smiled lightly at him. He returned the smile, though it was difficult. The entire reason she was in this position was because of him.

He returned his focus to his hands, but she didn't remove hers, just let them move with him as he slipped her wet dress off of her, then gradually every single other layer until she stood before him naked.

His heart was thundering in his ears as he looked at her standing before him in the firelight, her glorious body his to admire. But she had just gone through hell, and he couldn't look at her with the passion he normally did. Instead he looked at her as a man that wanted to know what had been done to his sweet angel.

There were multiple bruises, all over her breasts, bruises made by a man squeezing hard enough to the point of pain. And the bruises didn't stop there. She had several more on her collarbone and all up and down her arms, especially her upper arms and wrists.

"Where else?" he asked hoarsely. "Where else did this filth touch you?"

He was already turning her around before she could get a protest out, and he sucked in a deep breath. The welts on her backside, clearly displaying a large handprint made him so angry he nearly smashed the nightstand near the bed.

He turned her back to face him when he'd finished his inspection of her and she had silent tears slipping down her cheeks. "Who did this to you, angel? Who did this?"

She kneeled down on the floor next to him on the bed and looked up at him, shaking her head. "I don't know. It was three from the Mexican Army. One of them was an officer."

Cade felt helpless. What could he do to make her feel better? What would be the appropriate thing to say to her?

She glanced up at him and shook her head. "Please, the last thing I need is pity. Save that for someone else." She stood quickly and went to the nicely carved dresser and pulled out a simple white sleeping gown. She pulled it over her head quickly.

"Are you hungry?" Her voice wobbled, and she swallowed hard.

"No," he replied softly. She stood near the bed, and he reached out and caught her hand. "You have no reason to be embarrassed in front of me, Olivia. You have experienced more than I could ever imagine. All that we've both been through the last few weeks should more than tell you that you can be true to yourself around me."

"It was nothing. Truly, I don't wish to dwell on it any further." She spoke quickly, her words nearly tripping over themselves.

Cade sighed heavily, and slowly released her hand. "I only want to help you, angel. You've helped me with so much."

"I could use some brandy," Olivia proclaimed, surprising Cade. "Could you?"

"Yes, I could certainly use some."

Olivia went to the pantry and pulled out a bottle of brandy and searched the cupboards for glasses. Soon a large dosage of the liquor was handed over to Cade in a glass that threatened to slosh over. She went to the other side of the bed and carefully climbed in, telling Cade how sensitive her rear must be at that moment, and his anger flared again.

She poured herself a large portion of brandy, then set the bottle on the floor. She stared into her drink for several long moments before suddenly chugging it back in two large gulps. She squeezed her eyes tight and sucked in her cheeks, before letting out a soft gasp and reaching for the bottle.

She had chugged back another before Cade had even finished half of his. She was beginning to pour her third when he pulled the bottle away from her and set it down on his side of the bed. She frowned deeply at him.

"I'll have you know I can drink more than most grown men," she said with determination. "So you can give me back that bottle."

"Not until you tell me what happened to you tonight," he said, ignoring the perturbed expression on her face.

"I don't want to think about it, Cade. I don't want to remember it. So, please… give me the damned bottle."

He could tell she was barely keeping herself together. But he wouldn't let her drink herself to oblivion in order to forget what had happened to her. He had tried to do that when he had been at her home, and it had done nothing but increase his anger and his sorrow.

"You need to talk about it, angel. If you don't, it will eat you from the inside. Believe me, I know."

Olivia shook her head in disagreement and for several long moments she stared blankly into her empty glass. Cade was patient, though, knowing she would say something soon enough. She had to. He didn't want to think of the way she would be if she kept it bottled up inside. She would become even more of a recluse, even more cold, same as she had when she was nearly raped at the age of fifteen. She would build an even stronger wall around her heart.

It was after a long silence, punctuated only by the sound of the logs in the fire popping and crackling, that she finally spoke. "They were too fast for the mule to outrun them. I could hear the hoofbeats of one soldier riding up behind me. I had no idea there were three of them." She shook her head again, still staring into the glass as if it held answers to questions only she knew. "I suddenly felt like I had when I was fifteen—helpless and scared."

Cade reached over and smoothed a piece of her hair out of her face. He wanted her to know he was there to comfort her, to support her, and in no way would he judge her. She still wouldn't look at him, though. She continued staring into her empty glass, her eyes vacant as she remembered.

"There were three of them. The officer was the one that came up and forced the wagon to stop, and then another soldier grabbed me from the wagon." She frowned and touched the top of her head and winced. "And someone was pulling my hair. I don't know who it was—probably the officer, but everything was happening so fast."

She fell silent again for several long moments, but Cade was patient. But he wasn't sure if he wanted to hear the rest. From the marks on her body, he was quite certain she had been raped. And if she confirmed that as being true... Rage already filled him and he felt completely inept. He was tired of innocent lives being hurt because of him.

"I tried to get away. And I was partly successful." She looked down at her hand and Cade saw there were bruises on her knuckles and smiled to himself. She probably didn't pack much of a wallop, but she had tried, and somehow that made him proud.

"I had forgotten about the third man, and he stopped me." This time her fingers lightly touched her jaw and she flinched and he could see the bruises that were starting to show up on her beautiful skin. He clenched his hand into a fist, but he said nothing.

"That's when they decided they'd played long enough and, well…" She cleared her throat, and he could tell it was coming to the point she didn't want to talk about. His stomach clenched with fear as she continued to speak.

"The officer flipped me over the back of the wagon and began to spank me so hard. It was humiliating and painful. But what was worse was that I could hear the other men unfastening their britches. I knew what was about to come.

"But his vicious spanking was actually a good thing. Because his actions were so rough, he pushed me further into the wagon. Far enough that I was able to grab my shotgun."

Cade's mind was suddenly trying to process this new information. She took a deep breath and glanced over at him. "I could use another shot of brandy, if you don't mind."

He was still trying to comprehend what she was telling him as he poured a shot of brandy into her glass. She had tossed it back and finished it before he had even set the bottle back down. Again, only staring at the empty glass, she continued.

"I turned on the officer with the shotgun aimed at his—his most prized possession, I guess you could say. At first he was going to try and call my bluff, but when I cocked the shotgun, all of them became real serious. I took their guns and their horses and left. I had to fire the gun once when the officer tried to stand up, but he didn't make that mistake again."

For the first time since she had started her story, she looked at Cade. "I was so scared. They were so strong, and they showed that they didn't care what they had to do to get at me."

Relief had washed over Cade so strongly his world spun for a few moments. They hadn't raped her. She hadn't gone through the violent attack on her innocence.

"You defeated three Mexican soldiers entirely on your own, Olivia. I don't know of other women who could say the same."

She returned her stare into the empty glass, and he didn't know what thoughts were running through her head.

Finally, she turned to look at him, tears in her eyes and a wobbly smile. "I did defeat three soldiers, didn't I?"

Cade reached for her and smoothed the tears from her eyes. "I know they scared you. And I know what they did to you... the way they touched you..." Anger began to build in him once again and he drew a deep breath. "In spite of all that, in spite of your terror from when you were so young, you were able to stay calm enough to stop them. Don't you realize how amazing you are? But this has to stop. I can't stand by and have you at this risk anymore. I'll go to town with you from now on."

"How can you? You'll be recognized by the army right away. You must stay hidden."

"I have to help you, Olivia."

Olivia lowered her lashes and her hands caught his. Slowly she looked up at him and smiled weakly. "I didn't think I was going to survive. I've heard what they do to some of their female captives. That makes me far from amazing—I was terrified."

"You fought. Even though you were scared—you fought. That makes you brave and amazing in my book."

Her eyes searched his. "I've never—You are the only man who has ever seen me naked. And yet it felt so right. I didn't even hesitate. I've lived my life by such strict rules and guides for so long—why am I changing? Why am I suddenly comfortable sleeping next to a man I barely know? Why am I comfortable with you touching me in ways I never imagined?"

Cade didn't know how to answer her. He had noticed the way she had been gradually relaxing around him, the way she was becoming more comfortable with him. But it had been a huge step for her to stand before him as he had disrobed her and gazed upon her nude body.

"I don't know," he replied honestly. "You know I will never hurt you or make you do something you don't want. Perhaps that is why? Dear God, Olivia, I'm just so grateful..." He gathered her to him, holding her gently. "I was so very afraid they had raped you. Or worse. Before you arrived, I feared I might not ever see you again." Her fresh linen nightgown mingled with the aroma of her rain-washed body, and it was a scent that was pure Olivia—the smell of a new spring morning with dew still clinging to the ground. It was the most intoxicating scent he had ever smelled.

OLIVIA SANK INTO Cade's embrace gratefully. His warmth touched her all over, even inside, and her heart thundered. What was it about this man's touch that caused such feelings? She never wanted to be out of his arms. She never wanted to be anywhere other than with him. Which was a foolish notion, because he would leave her as soon as he was healed. But she vowed to enjoy every moment until then.

And it was in those moments, being held in his warm, caring arms, that a plan began to hatch in her mind, a plan that would most likely get her killed. But it could be the only way Cade would ever be united with his daughter again.

Chapter Fourteen

THE SOUNDS OF gunfire and men screaming in pain were all around her. She couldn't get her bearing through all of the smoke that clung to the air. She spun around as different sounds exploded around her.

The smoke finally cleared slightly, and she could finally see around her, though not far. But it was far enough that she could see the Mexican soldiers advancing rapidly. She suddenly realized she held a shotgun in her hands, and she fired, the jolt of the butt of the gun kicking into her shoulder painfully hard.

She saw a man fall, clutching at his gut as blood spewed forth, but she couldn't tell if that was her gunshot or one of the soldiers around her that had given him a death blow. She checked her gun and was relieved to see that she had one more shot left and she squared off again, facing the enemy as they advanced.

But before she could get a shot off, a cannon exploded nearby and she went flying through the air, landing hard on the cold, icy ground. She gasped for air as the wind had been knocked out of her, but everything else seemed to be intact.

She began to sit up when she saw him. The enemy was

charging towards her, his bayonet held at just the right angle to pierce through her heart. As if it had suddenly become natural for her, she lifted her shotgun and fired, paying no attention to the pain in her shoulder this time. The man crumbled, his white soldier's uniform turning crimson at the chest, his eyes staring at her in surprise, before falling face-first to the ground.

She was proud of herself, yet at the same time wanted to throw up. She had just taken a man's life. But if she hadn't taken his, he would have taken hers. As if viewing herself from a distance, she reloaded quickly, aimed, fired, and went through the motions all over again for several minutes.

But the enemy was good. And they had so many more men. She was reloading as one of them charged her, and she fumbled to get the gun locked and cocked. The soldier lunged towards her with his bayonet just as she fired her shotgun.

He fell forward on top of her, and she saw his face, smudged with gun powder. But that didn't hide the fact that he was practically still a child, probably no more than fifteen years of age, if that.

He looked at her quizzically as his blood drained out of him. "Why?" he rasped, and blood began to drip from his lips. "Why does it hurt so much?"

Oh, dear God! She had to help him. She had to ease his pain somehow, even if he was the enemy. But suddenly there seemed to be blood everywhere, and the harder she tried to get away from it, the more there was, until she was covered in blood, completely soaked. And the boy's face, now so pale his skin looked translucent, still hovered above her, his eyes probing into hers, as he again whispered, "Why?"

"I'm sorry. I'm so sorry. Please, God, oh, please…"

"Olivia." The deep, warm voice was soothing, and she wondered if God had heard her desperate plea. But the boy was still there, but now it was obvious he was dead, his body becoming completely lifeless, and yet his eyes still stared down at her.

"Olivia." The voice called again, but she didn't want to hear it.

She needed to hide; she had to get away from the battle. She felt the shotgun in her hands and wondered if she'd ever be able to use it again.

"Olivia!" This time the voice was insistent, and the images surrounding her began to fade slowly. "Olivia!" The blood and the dead boy disappeared, and she was suddenly warm and clear of blood… and awake.

She opened her eyes slowly, realizing gradually that she was shaking violently, and gripped the blankets covering her tightly. As the dream lost its hold on her, she suddenly realized Cade hovered over her, his eyebrows pulled together in confusion and concern.

She felt as though she had a scream trapped in her throat, and she tried desperately to compose herself. Subconsciously, she smoothed her hair over her damaged ear that throbbed and ached, reminding her that the dream wasn't just a dream.

"Cade… what is it? Is it your leg?"

He frowned at her. "You know damned well it isn't my

leg. You were having a nightmare, Olivia. A terrible one from the way you were acting."

"Oh," Olivia fumbled for words. "I-I don't usually dream. That's very odd. I'm sorry to have woken you. Please, go back to sleep."

She was still shaking, but it wasn't as violent as it had been when she first woke up. And she was gradually becoming aware of her immediate surroundings. Cade had moved from his designated side of the bed, something they had agreed upon in order for her to feel comfortable enough to sleep in the same bed as a man. Now he was on her side of the bed, his body pressed alongside hers and he was propped up with an arm on each side of her, leaning over her.

He lifted one of his hands and smoothed her hair back away from her forehead. "Tell me about it, angel. A dream that violent is agonizing to live with."

Olivia realized her hair had come free of the braid she had tied, and it was only a matter of time before he saw her ear. But something he said grabbed her attention. "How do you know it was violent?"

He gave her a soft smile. "Because you were fighting me in your sleep. I tried to hold your arms down so you wouldn't hurt yourself or me, and you tossed around so hard that I could barely hold you still."

"Oh," she said softly, suddenly embarrassed.

She didn't want anyone to see her in such condition, especially this man that was so strong and brave and would probably laugh at her foolish nightmare. But it was a torment to her, to have to relive those horrific moments over and over in her dreams, leading to many nights where she was afraid to even fall asleep.

"I'm fine now, really. Thank you for tending to me, but you need to get your rest, and I am tired as well. I'd like to go back to sleep, too."

"And return to your nightmare? Or are you going to stay awake as long as you can, resisting the urge to sleep because you don't want to risk falling into that nightmare again?"

Olivia felt frustration and desperation clawing at her. "How do you know so much about what it is like to have violent dreams?" she demanded.

He sighed heavily and his thumb rubbed her cheek. "I used to relive the death of my son almost every night. The dream wasn't always the same. Sometimes it started with me racing towards the smoke on the horizon, sometimes it started with the man I once thought my friend betraying me. But they all ended with my son dying in front of me."

Olivia closed her eyes briefly, wishing she hadn't asked the question. His eyes were haunted with the memory of his child's death.

When she opened her eyes, he was watching her intently. "How-how did you get past it?" she asked hesitantly.

He gave her a tender smile. "I told an angel all about my terrible past. And she comforted me instead of condemning me for what had happened."

Olivia's eyes lifted to his and she saw warmth and caring. "It-it isn't something I've ever told anyone," she said softly. Again she smoothed her hair over her ear. Every time she had the nightmare, her ear would ache painfully, serving as a constant reminder of her past. "I don't even know if I can put it in words."

He leaned down and pressed a kiss to her forehead, then trailed kisses down the side of her face. "I will listen to anything you want to say. And if you don't want to tell me anything, I'm okay with that, too."

Olivia drew in a shaky breath. "It was during the battle for the Texians to claim the Alamo this past winter. If only we had known it would bring such wrath from Santa Anna, maybe we would have chosen a different plan to gain leverage in the war."

She paused for several long seconds, her eyes seeing the past. "The Texians stormed San Antonio in a rush. In no time we had trenches in the streets for the soldiers to find security from the nonstop barrage of gunfire from the Mexican Army. I sent my family to safety, but I chose to fight."

"You did what?" His face was incredulous, on the border of being angry. "Do you realize—"

"Of course I realize! I was there. I was in the middle of all of it!" Olivia hadn't realized how strongly she felt about the experience until she heard her own words. She softened the tone of her voice. "I knew the risk I was taking, but it was worth it."

One of his eyebrows lifted. "Why? Why are you so determined to fight Mexico? You've been raised by a Mexican family, lived here under Mexican rule your entire life... why?"

Olivia ran a hand down her face and drew in a deep

breath. "My entire life I was raised to respect the Mexican leadership. There was never a question about living as we should, according to the laws. As I grew older, though, I began to resent the dictatorship we lived under. But I had no idea that my parents felt the same way. And they had taken it a step forward... they became spies for the Texians.

"And... well, and then, they were assassinated by the Mexican Army. I took up their mission, and became even more passionate about it as soon as I became involved. The Texians must win. We cannot fail—there is more at stake than the freedom of Texians. It is our dignity, our lifestyle, our ability to do and be whatever or whoever we want to be. We are going to win!"

Cade nodded at her solemnly. "I understand. Believe me, I do. Is that what spurs your nightmares? The death of your parents?"

Olivia lowered her eyes, then lifted them back to his. "No. My nightmare stems from my own sins."

Cade tilted his head to the side and his fingers moved from her face to her head and began to gently massage her scalp. "I doubt you have sins that will shock me. Though I still haven't forgotten that you risked your life to join in the battle in December."

"And that is where my sins begin. Cade, I got into the trenches with the soldiers and I had my father's shotgun and his rifle. I fired blindly at first. But then I started to get comfortable with the guns, and braver. I begin to peek over the trench and take aim and shoot. There were so many men that fell from my shots. I don't know how many men I killed.

"I felt this odd numbness, as if I wasn't really there… as if I was watching everything happen from a distance. But then, Lorenzo, Angie's husband, found me. He was furious to find me out there."

"As well he should be."

Olivia frowned at him before returning to her story. "He told me to get to the barn on the outskirts of town that belonged to a church. But I wouldn't listen to him. While we were arguing there was this terrible noise, and before I knew it, Lorenzo threw me as far as he could and was running towards me when the cannon exploded behind him. I was lost in the cloud of dirt and falling debris, and I couldn't find Lorenzo anywhere."

She hesitated and drew in a shaky breath. She closed her eyes for several seconds, and she could almost smell the gun smoke, hear the cries of the wounded, hear the yells of the men fighting, and feel her own heart racing in her chest. When she opened her eyes, Cade was watching her with concern. She had to finish telling him what happened.

"There was a clearing in the smoke and some Mexican soldiers were advancing nearby. One of them spotted me and immediately charged in my direction. My gun had been tossed to the side when Lorenzo had thrown me, and I scrambled to grab it. The soldier was almost right on top of me when I grabbed the gun and fired." Tears burned her eyes, but she refused to let them fall.

"He pitched forward on top of me, bleeding to death slowly. And that was the first time I really looked at him. He was just a boy. Probably only fourteen, fifteen at most. The shock and fear in his eyes as his life slipped away... there was nothing I could do. I had been so determined with my fight for the Texians that I hadn't paused to think that I was actually killing people, killing children! What kind of person am I? What kind of monster have I become?"

Cade sighed heavily and lowered his forehead to hers and stayed that way for a few minutes, and Olivia found it strangely comforting, as if he was sharing in her grief and torment. When he pulled back, his eyes searched her face and he shook his head.

"You aren't a monster, Olivia. It's war. Both sides know what they are facing and that they risk death. But you should have never been there. You should never have been exposed to such horrors."

"It was my decision to make. I supported the Texians—it only seemed right that I fight alongside them. But to see a child die by my hands... to hold the enemy as he took his last shuddering breaths... I had gone into the battle naïve. I did not leave it with the same blissful ignorance."

"Is that how this happened?" Cade asked, pulling back her hair that covered her disfigured ear.

She gasped and pulled away from him, her hand instantly flying up to cover her ear from his view. "How did you— No one knows about this! How did you find out?"

"Several times I've tried to talk to you when I'm on your left side. Especially at night when we lie here in bed. When you wouldn't respond, I thought at first that you just didn't want to talk about the topic. But as it continued to happen, I began to realize you couldn't hear me. In your sleep the other night I pulled your hair back and saw your ear. Did it happen in the battle?"

Olivia kept a hand over her ear and stared at him in shock. "You—you have seen it? And you aren't repulsed?"

He reached for her but she flinched, and he lowered his hand slowly. "Olivia... nothing about you could ever repulse me. I wish that you hadn't gone through such a horrible experience, but I don't understand your desire to hide it."

"It is hideous. And it is a weakness that I don't want anyone to know about. No one should know that I can't hear out of it." She lay staring up at him in frustration and outrage.

"I know. And I also know you are one of the most beautiful women I've ever known in my entire life, and your ear doesn't change any of that. You are strong, Olivia. Even without the hearing in that one ear."

Slowly she lowered her hand from where it protected her ear, watching him intently. "I've never been called beautiful before you," she said softly. "I'm the *fria* sister of the family. The cold one. No man has ever wanted to be near me. Except you."

He reached for her again and this time she didn't flinch away from him. His hand slid gently around her head and he lifted her to him, placing his lips against hers, softly and undemanding. His kiss was long and slow, leaving her hungry for more, but he pulled back, releasing her so that she lay on her pillow once again.

"Does it hurt?" he asked, his fingers running through her

hair, exposing her ear completely.

Olivia's head was spinning from the sweet kiss he had just given her, and she tried to understand what he had just asked her. "Oh," she murmured as her wits returned. "Not all the time. When I have one of my nightmares it hurts fiercely. Other times it comes and goes, just reminding me of what happened. I suppose it is the penance I must pay."

Cade shifted slightly, and Olivia suddenly realized how close they were to each other, and that he leaned over her with his chest bare, showing the blonde hair that lay against a bronzed body, tapering all the way down to the loin cloth she had made, a loin cloth that suddenly seemed to be far too little fabric for the man.

She jerked her eyes back up to his face and expected to see a smug grin. Instead, he watched her with darkened eyes, his face a mask as to what he was thinking. Olivia was finding it hard to breathe with him hovering over her, the warmth of his body seeping into hers.

"I'm-I'm sorry I awoke you with my nightmare. And I thank you for letting me tell you about it. Perhaps I'll be the same as you and no longer be tormented by the dream now that I've finally told someone what happened. But you must get your rest. You needn't worry about me." She hoped she had made a firm enough statement that he would move back to his side of the bed.

Instead, his eyes roved over her face and his thumb rubbed the lips he had just recently kissed. "You are unlike any woman I've ever known." His voice was hushed, heightening the intimacy of their position. "And so very, very beautiful, in every way."

He lowered his head and, against Olivia's better judgment, she eagerly met his lips for the kiss. Her hands shifted and she laid one upon the side of his face, feeling the stubble of his unshaven skin, and she laid the other hand upon his chest, enjoying the feel of his crisp, blonde curls against her palm.

Gradually he pulled away, but still stayed close enough to her that she didn't feel alone in the night, surrounded by her nightmares. "Get some sleep, angel. I'll protect you from any of your nightmares."

As ridiculous as it sounded, she believed him, and she drifted into a peaceful, healing sleep.

Chapter Fifteen

LIFE HAD SETTLED into a simple routine, with constant exercise to build Cade's strength, chores, and cooking. With more than a little reservation, Olivia had taken the lotion Serena had given Cade and began to massage it into his leg, focusing on his aching muscles.

It put them in another intimate situation and, surprisingly, neither of them seemed bothered by it. She still fought her personal demons that he didn't really desire her or see her as appealing, but his actions spoke otherwise.

He was getting better at moving around the house, and took advantage of every time he passed her pressing a kiss to her cheek or forehead, holding her close as they took advantage of watching the sun rise and set on the front and back porches.

His restlessness was obvious, though. He pushed himself to his physical limit every day, and every day he was growing stronger. He was able to chop firewood and bring stacks into the house. He was able to tend to the mule to make sure it was comfortable in the difficult conditions of the rain and unusual cold for the season. Overall, he was just more active with everything. She knew it was a matter of time before he was prepared to go after Bella. Which meant she had to get everything prepared for her plan to work as quickly as possible.

When, only a couple of weeks after her last journey to town, she informed him she needed to go to town again, he insisted that he would go with her. "I won't allow you to be exposed to that danger again."

"And I won't allow the healing that we've accomplished to be put in jeopardy by an unnecessary journey. I'll be fine, Cade. I'm only gathering a few items, and won't need the wagon this time, which will allow me to travel faster."

"What is so important that you have to go into town? Don't we have enough food and supplies to get by a few more weeks?"

Olivia shook her head but wouldn't look at him, instead focusing on the laundry she had just brought in off the lines. "Barely. And I won't make the mistake of traveling so late this time. Besides, I need to know how Angie is coming along with her pregnancy and the illness to her stomach. I need to know that Serena hasn't burned down half the town." She sighed heavily and finally made eye contact with him. "I need to see my family, Cade."

He couldn't argue with that. And so it was the next morning that she set out on the mule, riding at a brisk pace towards town. She had known it would be difficult, but she hadn't expected the churning of her stomach and the dampness in her hands to realize how afraid she really was. The officer that had attacked her had vowed to take his revenge out on her. She had no idea he would do exactly that if he saw her.

She kept a low profile, wearing a wide-brimmed hat and dressed in one of the few gowns she had remaining to her name. The mule moved more swiftly than usual, more than likely eager to be able to stretch out after being kept in the small stable yard for so long.

It was still fairly early in the morning when she reached the *cocina*, and her grandfather was just pulling *tripas* off of the grill outside. His face split into a wide grin at the sight of her, and he waved for her to hurry over as he set the pan down, putting the food on hold until he'd had a chance to hug his granddaughter.

Olivia scrambled off the mule and hastily tied it to the porch post before rushing into his open arms. She breathed in the scent of him, the smell of smoke from the pit, the musky lotion he used when he shaved and had used for years—the smell of home.

He pulled back and held her at arm's length, his eyes searching her from head to toe. "You look good, *hijita*. Is this man being respectful of you? You are still a pure lady?"

Olivia's face went bright red. "*Abuelo*! You know me well enough to know that I will keep a man in his place, no matter what the situation is."

His grin returned. "That's my girl. How is this cowboy of yours? How is his recovery?"

"Slow. But steady. He is able to walk around some now, but he still hasn't tried to ride the mule. He is still in a great deal of pain."

He sighed and shook his head. "He was badly injured.

But they seem to have given up the search for him. At least from what I've seen and the way the officers are acting. I wonder why they wanted to capture him so badly. Have you learned more from him?"

"Yes, and that's one of the reasons I'm here. But let's get this food inside before it gets cold, and then *Abuela* will be mad at you."

He chuckled slightly, then picked up the pan and followed Olivia inside. Her grandmother was already headed in their direction, more than likely to bark at her grandfather about the *tripas*, but was drawn up short when she saw Olivia.

"Olivia! Oh, my dear girl, how much I've missed you!"

"*We've* missed you." Her grandfather corrected her as he stepped through the door and placed the *tripas* on the counter.

Her grandmother just scowled at him, before turning back to Olivia and grabbing her in a tight embrace. "How have you been? Is the cowboy treating you well?"

"Yes, *Abuela*. He is a gentleman."

"Good. Now, we are busy this morning, so it is good that you have arrived. Grab your apron."

Olivia did so with a smile on her face and had barely turned around before she was grabbed in another tight hug. "Serena! Oh, Serena, I've missed you so much!"

Serena pulled back, a half grin teasing her lips. "Even all my antics?"

"Even all your antics," Olivia said, laughing softly. "I've missed all of you so very much."

After an equally excited greeting from Angie, they all turned to the breakfast service and a room full of hungry soldiers. Olivia was surprised as she watched her two sisters navigate the room. Serena was the most surprising of all.

The usually wild child was wearing a normal skirt and shirtwaist, although she had tied a bright scarf around her waist. Even her hair was slightly tamed, tied back with the same colored bright scarf. Where there were usually wild, crazy curls, she had combed it down some, and it wasn't full of any of her decorated beads, feathers, or other miscellaneous items she usually used.

And she was working the room quickly and efficiently, taking care of the hungry customers while flashing them polite smiles that Olivia doubted she'd ever seen before. Serena had changed in just the few weeks that Olivia been gone, and had matured in ways she had never expected.

Several hours later, they had finished cleaning the kitchen and gathered together in their small, private living area that they kept separate from the dining area of their customers. Olivia sat near Serena and ran her hand over the young girl's hair. "You've changed," she said softly.

Serena looked over at her with a smirk. "Some. But only as little as necessary."

Olivia smiled and pressed a kiss to her forehead. "Don't change too much. You are incredibly special as you are."

Serena's face lit up. "I miss you, too, Vi."

"We all do," Angie said, and collectively the family nodded. "Now all of us want to know how the *gringo* is. How is he recovering from his wounds?"

"Slower than he'd like, but faster than I expected. He pushes himself every day."

"And does he take care of you? Does he behave the way he should?" Serena was the one asking the questions this time, and Olivia's eyebrow lifted in surprise.

"Yes, he does. He's a gentleman." She didn't need to explain to them the many things they'd already overcome. "But there is much more to the man than we ever knew. And I need to help him, even though it is very dangerous."

She drew a deep breath and began to tell Cade's story, leading up to his arrival at their home a few weeks prior. Her family listened intently, respectfully holding back questions. Until Olivia began to describe her plan.

"Olivia, you can't. It is far too great of a risk!" Angie spoke emphatically.

Olivia turned to look at her younger sister with an eyebrow raised. "You are one to speak, Angie. You took far greater risks with Lorenzo..." Her voice died away as she saw Angie's face at the mention of Lorenzo. She reached out and squeezed her hand gently.

"Dear child, your plan puts you at the very heart of this war. I can't allow it!"

"*Abuelo*, I will move forward with this, with or without your approval. I am merely asking for your help."

"I can help." Serena's statement was the calm amongst the protest around them.

Olivia pivoted to face Serena, doing her best to hide her surprise. "Serena, I won't put you at risk."

"I know. And I know everything we need to do to get you ready."

OLIVIA HUMMED SOFTLY to herself as she rolled the tortilla dough into round spheres, ready to be rolled out and then tossed on the flat surface heating over the fire. Cade was enjoying the fresh morning air on the front porch, stretching his leg.

Time was growing short. He was improving with every day, and now that they had two horses, thanks to Serena, he would be able to attempt to ride soon. And there was nothing she could do to stop him, even if she wanted to.

But that was part of her problem. She wanted him to go after Bella. She wanted him to find her safely, and she wanted him to be happy once again. He deserved it after all that he had been through.

She gasped in surprise as strong arms suddenly circled around her waist, but her lips pulled into a smile and leaned back into Cade's warm embrace. "Aren't you supposed to be stretching your leg?"

"I'm able to stretch just fine standing here with you. And I find it far more enjoyable."

"If you want to have a fresh breakfast, it may help for you to find another location to stretch, because you are being very distracting right now."

"So I'm able to distract the extremely focused, highly serious Miss Torres? It can't be possible."

Olivia lay her head back on his shoulder and turned her face to his, her lips seeking a kiss. She was quickly rewarded as his arms tightened around her, and then his lips roved lower to her neck and she sighed softly. "You are a bad influence, you know that, don't you?"

He chuckled against her neck and his whiskers tickled her, prompting her to let loose a soft chuckle as well and he pulled back, his eyes staring down at her. "You should do that more often."

"Do what?" she asked, her head still resting on his shoulder, her eyes gazing up at him. She never wanted the moment to end.

"Laugh. I think this is the first time I've ever heard you laugh to be honest. It is a wonderful sound." His blue eyes were shining from the sunlight that was faintly streaming through the window, and she felt mesmerized.

"I can't remember the last time I laughed. Perhaps you aren't entirely a bad influence."

He smiled and planted another kiss on her lips. "Now, why don't you teach me something, angel?"

Olivia's eyes widened. "Exactly what do you have in mind?"

He chuckled again. "Don't worry, it isn't anything too complicated... at least I don't think it is. Teach me how to make these tortillas."

"You want to learn how to make tortillas?" she asked in disbelief.

"It will give me something new to teach Bella."

Olivia pressed him a solid kiss. "Something tells me that Bella will be a natural at this. But you may be all thumbs. So let's see how you do."

She grabbed one of the spheres and sprinkled flour onto

the board. "Now," she said, sliding her hands over his and gently pulling them away from her waist and placing them on the rolling pin, "we roll out the dough into a circle."

As they rolled out the dough, he distracted her by constantly nuzzling her neck, and by the time they had finished, the dough was terribly deformed and shaped nothing like the circle it was meant to be.

Olivia turned around within his arms and rubbed flour down his nose. "You, sir, are not meant to make tortillas."

He sighed heavily and feigned disappointment, then leaned in for another kiss. When he pulled back from her his eyes were serious. "Bella is going to love you."

The comment took Olivia completely by surprise. Her heart began to pound rapidly. "You are leaving for her soon, aren't you?"

"Thanks to your healing, I'll be ready to go within a few days. I just need to make sure I can ride safely. It won't do me any good to leave for her and not make it. She needs me, angel. And I need her."

Olivia forced a smile to her face and ran a hand through his hair. "Yes. But I'm giving you a shave and a haircut before you go anywhere. The way you look now you may scare her more than anything."

But inside her gut churned. He was almost healed. It was almost time for her to put her plan into action.

Chapter Sixteen

March 29ᵗʰ, 1836

THE COLD WINTER had turned into a soggy, muddy, messy spring. Which made it difficult to do anything outside, even though Olivia knew Cade craved to get out of the house. They enjoyed the time they had on the porch in the mornings and out back in the evenings as the sun set, but he yearned to move more. He was anxious to go after Bella.

The last information Olivia had learned from her family was that the Mexican Army had crossed the Colorado River and was continuing to move east. Given that she had learned this only days earlier, the information could have been at least a week old or more. The whole war could have been won or lost by now for all they knew. And then where did that leave Bella? What was happening to her?

CADE WORKED HIS way back and forth on the porch, listening to Olivia's sweet humming inside. God, what an amazing woman. He had never expected to find someone like her ever in his life. His marriage to his wife had been pleasant. But it was formal and structured, and she shied away from any true displays of affection.

Even in the bedroom, she had acted as though it was her responsibility as his wife to attend to his needs. It had seemed more of a chore to her than a thing of pleasure. But he had assumed that was the way it was supposed to be between a man and wife.

But Olivia taught him something very different. She responded to his touch in ways that were honest and pure and made him desire her with such a power just with his thoughts that he had to sit in the old rocking chair placed at the corner of the porch.

He took several deep breaths, trying to calm the passion that burned within him. She deserved so much more. She deserved a better man, a stronger man, and certainly not a man that came with an instant family. He had no doubt she would be good with Bella, but it was unfair of him to expect such a thing of any woman, let alone one as amazing as Olivia.

Yet, his passion for her had stirred passion within her body as well, and she had responded to him so quickly and easily. But he had held back from pushing the passion on her again. She had already dealt with so much—he couldn't try to seduce her. And he could never be the kind of man to lie with a woman and then leave her. That was not the man he was.

But the gentle kisses and touches and caresses they had shared over the past several days had been extremely pleasurable, and had caused the fire within him to burn hotter than ever. But he had to exercise restraint. She was an incredible woman who deserved so much. He could offer her an unknown future—no home, no plan, nothing but a two-year-old daughter that would only add to the difficulties of the relationship. In the back of his mind, though, a small voice said Olivia was a woman who would say yes to that life, even with all of the uncertainties.

She had lowered her inhibitions so much, and it felt as though they operated as one. Their days moved together seamlessly, and at night they stayed on each other's designated side of the bed, but inevitably, their bodies gravitated towards each other, and they woke wrapped in each other's arms.

But the haunts of his past were what truly stopped him. He didn't deserve a woman as pure and strong as Olivia. Everyone around him either died, or, in the case of his daughter, kidnapped by mad men with the ultimate end being death. His wife had died giving birth to *his* daughter. His son had died for *his* mistakes. And now his daughter's life was on the line because of *his* choices. Before being captured by the Mexican Army, he had done things that had upset many people. Serving as the sheriff earned him many enemies. Olivia didn't need to know about that. He feared it was his penance for hanging men who had murdered others. God hadn't wanted him to be that final judge. He prayed about it daily. Was that why he was cursed?

But he had come to enjoy his time with her far too much. He couldn't forget Bella was out there, her life in danger every day that passed. It was time for him to test his strength. It was time for him to go save his daughter.

OLIVIA STOOD BY anxiously as Cade tried to haul himself up and into the saddle on the horse's back. He used his upper body strength as much as possible, though he still had to rely on his legs to launch him up and swing his leg over the body of the mule.

He was covered in a light sweat by the time he settled into the saddle, and was breathing deeply, but he flashed a smile at her. "The hard part is over, at least. I shouldn't be gone longer than an hour."

She smiled at him in return. "That will be the perfect time for dinner." Her smile slipped slightly and she stepped towards him, awkwardly guiding his boot a bit further into the stirrup. "Be careful, please? Don't take any unnecessary risks, okay?

He smiled and nodded at her, before turning the horse and gently nudging it out from the stables and away from the house. "You worry too much, angel. I will see you soon."

Olivia watched until she couldn't see him anymore, then turned back to the house. It was only a matter of time now. If he felt comfortable enough to ride the horse, he would be ready to go in search of his daughter. And she still had so much to prepare before that happened.

She stepped into the house and began to work quickly, taking the blankets out to air in the spring breeze, and beginning to wash the laundry out back. She had so many chores to tend to before he returned if she was going to pull off her plan.

She was fastening the last of the laundry to the line to dry when she heard the sound of boots striking the porch. Had it already been an hour? No, she knew how long her dinner would take to cook. He must have returned early. She prayed it wasn't because of his leg.

"Cade? What happened? Are you alri—" Her words stuck in her throat and she stopped mid-step as the officer that had attacked, that had humiliated her, that had nearly raped her, came walking into the house, holding his riding gloves in one hand, slapping them against the palm of his other hand.

Dear God, she had no way to defend herself. The gun was too far away. Her only hope was to run. She turned and grabbed her skirts, lifting them above her knees as she forced her legs to propel her forward. The trees were dense enough that she should be able to find a hiding place quickly.

She could hear him behind her, could hear his heavy boots striking the earth as he ran closer and closer. She dodged around the trees, trying desperately to avoid the inevitable. This Officer was no fool. He anticipated her next moves and raced ahead, and before she could adjust her course, she slammed into his chest and fell backwards.

The mad man was laughing, enjoying her fear. She scrambled backwards, then back to her feet and turned to run but was drawn up short by his arm snaking around her waist. His breath blew hard against her cheek and she cringed at the aroma of cigars and whiskey.

"Look what I've found." He chuckled. "I knew I'd find you eventually. And I knew you had to be lying about that sister living south of here. No woman would make that trip in the dark, especially with the Comanche starting to act up again. So now I have you all to myself."

She twisted and turned against his hold, trying to break free. "Do you pride yourself on preying on people weaker than you? Is that what you get such perverted joy out of this?"

He whirled her around so that she was facing him and he began to rapidly pull on the strings of her dress, quickly working his way through her bodice. "No, my dear. I get joy out of this. Out of you squirming and writhing that sweet little body against me, of you crying for me to stop when you really want it."

Olivia shoved at him, but he was solid as a wall. "You're delusional! You are absolutely out of your mind!"

He had worked her bodice open and grabbed her breasts, rubbing and squeezing them. He shoved her back against a tree so hard her head snapped and hit the rough bark, and for a brief moment she was dazed.

When she had regained her senses, she realized he was frantically unfastening his trousers while still trying to fondle her breasts. Rage suddenly filled her. She would not be his victim. She would not allow him to violate her and she certainly wouldn't give him the satisfaction he sought.

She drew her leg up sharply and he hissed in pain, falling to his knees. She turned to run but he grabbed her skirts, holding her back.

"I won't let you get away from me again." He growled, though he was still huddled over.

She turned and slammed her elbows down on his back, right on his spine, and he yelped in pain, falling to his side, but not releasing his grip on her skirts. She took the advantage and kicked him hard in the chest and he grunted, but still wouldn't release his hold.

She raised her leg to kick him again and was shocked when he grabbed her foot and yanked, causing her to fall to the ground with him. Instantly she flipped over and tried to pull herself to a standing position, but he had her legs pinned under his body, and he snapped her back over as he crawled up the length of hers.

"Had I known you wanted it to be rough, I could have started it sooner." He sneered, and his hand suddenly smacked her hard across the face.

She looked back at him and smiled. "I should have expected something so weak from someone as pathetic as you."

The next crack across her face drew blood from the corner of her mouth and she could taste the coppery flavor inside her mouth as well. She took advantage of it and spit into his face.

Obviously repulsed, he wiped her spit from his face. "You have made a terrible, terrible mistake, *senorita*. I was going to simply make love to you—and you would have enjoyed it. But now, the only thing I desire is to watch you die as painfully as possible."

Olivia's heart was racing and her ears were ringing. She felt at a complete loss. How could she possibly defeat this man without a weapon?

He stood slowly and she tried to get to her feet, but everything spun around her. She could hear his laughter, but it seemed to be coming from a distance. Then, suddenly, he was dragging her by her hair, and she couldn't contain her cry of pain, even though she didn't want to give the man any satisfaction.

He propped her in a seated position against one of the trees and then straddled her, smiling in such an evil way Olivia wondered if she could actually be facing the devil.

"Do you want to know how I'm going to kill you?"

"You will die before I do," Olivia said with much more conviction in her voice than she truly felt. Her hands were searching the ground around them for anything she could use as a weapon—a rock, a large limb, anything.

He continued speaking as though she had said nothing. "I like for it to be very intimate when I kill people for fun. Oh, yes, my dear, you are hardly the first I've killed. Killing men in battle brings me some pleasure. But the real joy is when I get to watch their life drain from their eyes, watch them struggle to get in a gasp of air before their body quits on them. That is where I find real joy."

"You are insane. You are an absolute madman. What happened to you to make you so sick in the mind?"

A muscle in his eye twitched, but he said nothing as he pulled the strings for her bodice free and held them in both hands. And suddenly it dawned on her. He was going to strangle her.

She began to fight with him, shoving as hard as she could, but her strength was no match to his. And suddenly the ties were twisting around her neck, winding tighter and tighter. At first she clawed at them, trying to relieve the pressure, gasping desperately for air.

When that proved unsuccessful she began to claw at him, at his face, at his hands, even at his cursed red jacket. But he just laughed, a horrible, terrifying laugh that told her she was dying by the hands of this man.

She continued to claw at him and her fingers hit something hard within his jacket. She didn't bother wondering what it was, she just used her frantic movements to conceal that she was getting it. Black spots were beginning to appear before her eyes, and she knew she didn't have long. And he was still laughing. He truly did take pleasure out of watching the death of people.

It was a knife. It was a long, sharp knife. And she had no time to think about what she would do with it, as she could already feel herself sliding down a dark, black hole. Without another thought, she shoved as hard as she could into his neck.

The bindings suddenly released and she gasped for air and watched the officer grip the handle of the knife and pull it out. Blood ran down his neck rapidly, and he stared at her in absolute amazement, before pitching to the side and lying perfectly still.

Olivia continued gasping for breath, her hands rubbing at her neck where the laces had so recently been taking her life. Her laces. She needed those for her bodice. Oddly calm, she pulled the laces from the officer's lifeless hands and began to lace up her bodice and fasten her dress. Smoothing her hair away from her face she stood on trembling legs and headed back towards the house.

"Olivia? Olivia!"

The sound of Cade's voice was a balm to her soul. "I'm here." Her voice came out barely a whisper. She picked up her skirts and began running to the house. "I'm here, I'm here, I'm here!" She kept trying to scream, but only a squeak would occasionally escape.

She ran to the back door just as he came hobbling out. "Olivia." He gasped in relief, then saw the blood drenching her dress. "Dear God, Olivia, where are you hurt?"

She looked down at herself, having not been aware of the blood until she saw it.

She shook her head. "I'm fine. I'm fine," she whispered.

"Oh, thank God." He stepped forward and pulled her into a tight embrace, before pulling back and examining her. He stopped when he saw the deep lines around her throat. His fingers ran over the marks lightly, and his eyes snapped to hers. "What happened? Who did this to you?"

She shook her head again, fighting the tears that stung her eyes. "The officer..." she whispered. "The officer from a few weeks ago, the one—"

Dawning burst on Cade's face, quickly followed by rage. "Where is he? I'll kill the bastard." His eyes searched their surroundings, and he began to head towards the trees when Olivia grabbed his arm firmly. His eyes jerked back to hers in surprise.

"He's already dead." She gestured to her dress.

Upon seeing the dress soaked in blood, another person's blood, tears began to fall silently from her eyes. She hadn't ever wanted to kill someone again, but she had no choice. She had to save her own life.

WHEN SHE LOOKED up at him, tears streaming down her face, Cade felt as if he'd been punched in the gut. He wanted to protect her, he wanted to save her from any more heartache in her life. But it seemed her staying with him through his recovery had put her in far too great of a risk.

He buried his hands in her hair and pulled her to him, holding her against his chest, his eyes squeezed shut tightly. Her tears spilled against his chest, dampening his shirt and he kissed the top of her head, breathing in her scent as his mind raced about what to do.

He had to hide the body along with her bloody dress. Then, somehow, he had to convince her that tomorrow she needed to return to San Antonio. Once she was gone, he would leave for the east and find his sweet little Bella. Olivia would no longer be in danger, and he would begin piecing his life back together as soon as he had Bella.

And he would never see Olivia again.

The thought hit him like another punch in the gut. How could he get by without her? She was part of his daily life, part of every moment of his day. He needed her. But as he slowly looked down at her face and saw the streak of tears that trailed down, he came to the hard conclusion. He needed her, but she didn't need him.

OLIVIA SCRUBBED HER skin raw, determined to get every last drop of that terrible man's blood off of her. But no matter how much she scrubbed, it didn't erase the smell of his breath, the pain of her laces against her throat, and the smell of his blood as he died on top of her. Nor could the memory be erased of the look on his face when he realized he was dying.

After killing the boy soldier only a few months ago, she was determined to never kill again. To take another person's life was not something she wanted resting on her conscience for the remainder of her life. She was fairly certain she would be turned away at the gates of heaven for the crimes she had committed.

But this had been different. This wasn't war—this was a desperate attempt to save her own life. Yet, still, her heart weighed heavily with what she had done. The only thing that made it better was Cade's reassurance, his calm nature as he gently soothed her.

By the time Cade returned from burying the body and the dress, she had made a fresh, hot bath for him and was preparing their evening meal. He was silent as he came through the door, and she could tell his leg was paining him greatly. Such a physical burden was more than he should have endured.

Without saying a word, she went to him and began to unfasten his shirt. He hadn't worn clothes in so long as he recovered, she imagined it felt strange against his skin.

He watched her with dark eyes, but made no move to stop her. She slipped his shirt off and was faced with his strong chest, and her heart skipped a beat. When it came to this man, she felt no fear, only security and something else she tried to identify. Her fingers fumbled on the laces of his britches as she realized the feeling must be desire.

She had seen desire between Angie and Lorenzo, and had felt a twinge of jealousy given that she never expected to feel such a thing for herself. She was the cold and frigid sister out of the three of them. She was the one that men turned away from, or ignored her altogether. She had never done any-thing to appear attractive to men. Cade had been right—she had created the *fria* sister.

She always wore her shirtwaist buttoned to her neck, kept her hair back in a severe bun, and made sure to never show any expression on her face. If any man said anything inappropriate to her or tried to touch her, even if it was just her hand, she would slap him away and let him know his interest was completely unwelcome.

She had come to terms with the idea that she would be a lonely old maid, running the *cocina* until she could no longer physically handle the demands. But now she had tasted desire. She had tasted passion. She had felt attractive and beautiful. And she would lose all of that as soon as Cade found Bella and they moved on with their lives. She would return to being the frigid and cold woman that turned away all men.

She finished unlacing his britches and hesitated, her fin-gers trembling. She had seen him naked multiple times before. But that had been while he was ill. Now he stood before her as a man fully capable of fulfilling the passionate dreams she fought each night.

Drawing a deep breath, she reached for the fabric to pull it down, revealing what an incredible specimen of man he really was. Her hands were trembling slightly, and her gaze shot to his when his large hands covered hers.

He was watching her with eyes that spoke the same language of desire that she felt. "Kiss me, angel," he said softly, and she didn't pull back as he lowered his head. Instead she stood on tiptoe, rushing to meet his lips as his arms wrapped around her.

They let out soft moans of pleasure as their lips crushed together, urgent and insistent. Something deep inside Olivia clenched with the strength of her desire for this man, and her arms slid up around his shoulders, clinging to him, and she parted her mouth for him at his gentle nudging.

Cade's arms circled around her waist and pulled her closer as his mouth slanted over hers. He couldn't seem to get enough of her, making her even more light-headed, and with slow, cautious steps, he backed her up to the wall until she was pushed against it. His tongue swept into her mouth and her eager response seemed to only heighten his need for her.

She was alive. Only an hour ago her life had almost ended. But now she was alive, and in the arms of the man that had changed her—brought her joy and happiness. She didn't want the kiss to ever end. It reminded her that she was alive, and that he was, too.

Their intense kiss lasted for several minutes, though it

felt it had only been seconds. Finally, Olivia broke the kiss off with a gasp for air. "Your bath water is getting cold," she whispered, given that was the only thing that could come to mind at the moment.

Cade looked at her, studying her face and brushed her hair away from her face. "I almost lost you today," he whispered, his fingers dropping to her neck. "You deserve the world," he said softly. His eyes fell to where his fingers ran lightly over the ridges of her throat from where the ties had been. "Yet all I bring you is pain and fear."

She shook her head. "That's not true, Cade. You know that isn't true."

"I know that you are the most incredible woman I've ever met. And I'll never be able to repay you for everything you've done for me."

Olivia blushed. She knew how he could repay her. He could fall in love with her the way she had fallen in love with him. She had realized it the other day when they were making tortillas and she couldn't imagine her life without him.

But she was dreaming again. He already had a life with his daughter, and the last thing he needed was a new relationship to complicate things.

She stood on tiptoe and gave him a quick kiss. "Take your bath before your water gets cold," she ordered, and she forced her mind off the temptation he posed. She had to keep focused on everything she needed to do tomorrow. It was going to be a long day.

Chapter Seventeen

S ERENA HAD BEEN expecting her any day. So when Olivia tapped lightly on the back door of the house, Serena was there within moments, holding two heavy saddle bags.

Serena frowned at the pale light beginning to spread into the sky. "This early?" she asked in disbelief.

Olivia nodded without saying anything, and Serena's eyes narrowed on her face. "What's his rush? Okay, forget that, stupid question. I know he wants to get to his daughter. Has he already left?"

Olivia shook her head and gathered the saddle bags from Serena. "I don't know how long I'll be gone," she whispered so softly Serena had to strain to hear what she said. "And you know there is a chance I may not ever come back."

Serena stepped out of the house and circled her arms around Olivia, tears shimmering in her eyes. "Be careful, Vi. I love you. And you are coming home to us."

Olivia hugged her back just as tightly. "I love you, too, Serri. I love you, too."

Before Serena could say anything further, Olivia had turned and vanished off into the early morning darkness to her horse where she loaded the saddle bags, then quickly mounted. She glanced back one final time before turning the horse and nudging it into a quick canter headed out of town.

But she didn't turn fast enough before Serena spied the tears in her eyes, and for the first time in a long time, she returned to her room and buried her face in her pillow so no one could hear her sobs. Olivia was gone.

CADE HAD BEEN riding a solid hour before the hair on the back of his neck stood on end. While he had been traveling carefully, weaving in and out of the wooded area, he had the distinct feeling he was being followed.

He urged his horse into a trot, hoping to gain some slight distance between whomever was following him, and then pulled back into a deep alcove and waited. His horse enjoyed the slight reprieve, and lowered its head and cocked one leg, making the most of the opportunity to rest. But Cade was certain the rest wouldn't be for long.

His instincts were correct when he heard the sound of horse's hooves pounding lightly on the soft earth. The mud had dried mostly, but the earth was still damp enough to muffle some sounds. But whoever it was that was following him, they weren't being extremely cautious or trying to hide their journey.

Cade pulled out his pistol and nudged his horse slightly, bringing it to alert, full attention, jolting it out of the light doze it had slipped into. He kept his body relaxed so the horse wasn't on edge, but every sense was on high alert. He was going to stop the bastard following him and find out why, then decide if he deserved to have his life spared or not.

The sound of the horse's hooves moving from behind him had slowed drastically, to the point that he could no longer hear any sound. Even the nature around them had gone silent. Sweat beaded up on his neck and slid down his back. One of the hardest things he had learned when he moved from the city to Texas was that patience often earned a man what he wanted, especially when it came to hunting.

At the moment, he was tired of being hunted. It was time for the hunted to become the hunter. It didn't take long for his patience to pay off.

The horse moved forward slowly, several paces away from him, and he couldn't get a good look at the rider. But there was a shotgun in a sleeve on one side of the saddle, and a rifle on the other. This rider was ready to go to battle.

The rider stopped suddenly, staring down at the tracks in the ground. *So the bastard had been tracking him.* Cade's anger increased, and along with it, the throbbing in his leg did, as well. Without waiting for the rider to turn on him, he urged his horse out from their secluded space and towards the rider.

He hadn't expected the rider to turn so quickly and aim a pistol at him. But he had been prepared, either way, as he already had his pistol aimed, and his finger already cocking it back. But that was when his motions froze. This was one contingency he certainly hadn't planned on.

"What the hell do you think you are doing?" It took all of his restraint not to yell the question. At the moment he was feeling extreme anger, yet at the same time a sense of joy that he knew he shouldn't feel.

Slowly the rider rode towards him, lowering their weapon and guiding their horse to stand close to his. "I couldn't let you do this alone," Olivia rasped, her voice still damaged from her close brush with death only the day before.

Cade had already lowered his pistol and glared at her. "This isn't your fight."

"Yes it is. It became my fight when... when... there is a little girl out there that needs to be saved. And if I can help with that in even the smallest of ways, it is my fight."

"I forbid it. It is far too dangerous." His heart was racing in his chest as he imagined all the things that could go wrong if they were caught.

She raised an eyebrow at him. "I'll follow you. You have no way of stopping me. So I hardly see how you can forbid it."

Cade nudged his horse until he was right next to her, his knee brushing her knee, facing each other. "Damn it, Olivia, for once will you do the safe thing? For once, will you just do what you are asked to do?"

Olivia's eyes searched his face. "I can't leave you, Cade. And I can't let you leave me. So you see the quandary I'm in. And, after everything you've told me, I already feel like I know Bella. Two of us are better than one. We increase our odds of finding her and getting her to safety. Don't fight me on this, Cade. Please."

Cade pinched the bridge of his nose and closed his eyes closed tightly. When he looked at her, his eyes were stern.

"And what if something happens to you? What will I do?"

"You'll save Bella. That is the mission, and that is all that we need to think about."

Unable to resist the temptation, Cade leaned forward in his saddle and placed a hand at the back of her head, pulling her towards him until their lips met. His lips moved over hers softly, gently, then he slowly released her. Her lips were damp as she settled back in her saddle. "Does that mean that you'll let me join you?"

Cade hung his head as if defeated. "Yes," he said, but then he lifted his head and looked at her with hard eyes. "But you do as I say at all times. I don't want to worry about you and Bella at the same time."

Olivia nodded, a faint smile touching her lips. "We should probably get going then. The day isn't getting any longer."

"WE NEED TO take a break. The horses need water, and we can't afford to drive them into the ground."

Olivia couldn't agree more. She was sore all over from the hours of sitting in the saddle, and the spring weather was toying with them, going from sunny and slightly warm, to cloud covered and a cold breeze. She nodded to Cade, thankful he had found the small area that had a basin of water, green grass, and large oak trees that provided much needed relief from the sun.

She attempted to dismount quickly, knowing Cade

would need help because of his leg. But as soon as her feet touched the solid ground, her knees gave out on her. Much to her surprise, a strong arm that had the sleeve rolled up to reveal the golden hair on his forearm, caught her around the waist and steadied her, and she found herself leaning against his muscular body.

"Take it slow, angel. I'm used to rides like this, you aren't. You should have asked me for a break sooner."

Olivia let her head fall back against his shoulder and stared up into his incredible blue eyes. "But your leg, Cade!" she whispered. "Your leg isn't strong enough for this kind of journey."

He smiled down at her. "I won't lie to you. It hurts terribly. But I'll manage."

She didn't want to move from her spot. Leaning up against Cade, feeling his strong arm around her, she felt safe and more content than she could remember feeling in a very long time. But there was no time for them to waste. Her legs had finally stopped shaking under her, and she could stand on her own.

Cade slowly released her, pressing a kiss to the back of her neck as he did, and Olivia feared her knees would go weak again. Every touch from him, every soft kiss, every slight gesture of affection was tearing her apart. What would she do when he left her?

She gathered the reins of her horse and his and led them to the water while he took the saddlebags and searched for food for them. Having tethered the horses so they could graze, Oliva came back to Cade and sat near him where he leaned against the trunk of a large tree.

"I need to check the dressing on your wound," she whispered to him, shaking her head as he offered her some of the jerky and tortilla that Serena had packed in one of her saddle bags.

"I'm beginning to think you just like to get me naked," he said teasingly, one eyebrow lifted.

Olivia could feel the blood rush to her face as he stood and quickly began to remove his trousers. She kept her eyes averted as he slid them down, and only looked over at him when she knew he was sitting. Like the gentleman she knew he was, he had used his long shirt to conceal his body from her.

She moved forward and began to carefully remove his bandages. The scar was rough and jagged, and she wished she had the skills to make it less than what it was. But she had done her best with her limited resources and the extent of his injury.

She sighed heavily. "Your leg is inflamed and swollen. Traveling this hard could cause you to damage it even further."

"I have no other choice, angel. My daughter is out there, and for all we know she may be caught in the middle of a battle. I have to get to her."

Olivia shook her head at him, then rummaged through one of the saddle bags and pulled out a new jar of the lotion Serena and her Comanche friend had made. She dipped her fingers into the lotion and began to gently massage it into Cade's leg. His low moan of appreciation brought a smile to her lips. Her fingers moved smoothly over his skin, her thumbs pressing into the painful muscle to try and give it relief.

He sighed and leaned his head back against the tree, his eyes closed. Olivia took the opportunity to admire him. His blonde hair, which had grown so much longer while in her care, was tied back away from his face with a piece of leather strap. She had given him a shave only a couple of days earlier, but already his square jaw was dark with the growth of his beard.

His lips were full and firm, and lifted slightly at the pleasure of her touch on his sensitive skin. His nose was almost straight, but there was a slight curve in it that made him even more charming in her eyes. And then there were his eyes. His bright blue eyes that seemed they could see into her very soul.

It was at that moment that she realized his eyes were open, watching her. She blinked hard and felt the blood rushing to her face as she looked back down at his leg. She did her best to concentrate on massaging his leg until his finger hooked under her chin and lifted her face up until her eyes clashed with his.

There was a fire in his eyes, a fire she recognized and it stoked the one within her as well. Without waiting for him to ask, without waiting for him to make the first move, she leaned forward and pressed her lips to his, moving them sensuously as she had learned from him.

He received her kiss with enthusiasm, his hands reaching for her waist and pulling her closer to him. She ran her hand along his face, then down to his neck, then landed on his collarbone. Her fingers felt the strength of his shoulders and her hand slipped lower, dipping inside his shirt to feel the warmth of his chest and the crisp blonde hair.

"Angel," he whispered against her lips, his fingers squeezing her waist.

She knew what she was doing was inappropriate. But she was already destined to live her life as an old maid. She would enjoy her love now, and take pleasure in it while it lasted.

Her heart thundered madly. She loved him. Somehow she had fallen in love with the man that had disrupted her life and made her break all her rules on propriety. A man who had tested her patience, her discipline, and above all, her preconceived notions of the way things should be between a man and a woman.

She pressed into his kiss more deeply, parting her lips for the taste of him. She moved closer, pressing her chest against his. It seemed as if every single fiber of her being was tuned in to his body, the feel of his muscles bunching beneath her fingers, the feel of his heart beating rapidly beneath her palm.

Ignoring propriety all together, she moved even closer to him and placed one leg on each side of him, straddling him with her skirts bunched up around them. He drew in a deep breath at her bold move and his hand shifted to her hips where he pulled her tightly against him. It was in that moment that she realized he desired her, and desired her with a passion that matched her own.

His lips dropped to her neck and she let her head fall backwards, giving him all the access he needed. His hands forcefully gripped her bottom and rocked her against him and she couldn't restrain the soft cry of pleasure. She was desperate to feel more of him, to finally embrace the way lovers embrace, to feel the ecstasy she had only heard were rumors. But she knew they couldn't be rumors. The pleasure she was feeling in his arms at that moment alone let her know that ecstasy was achievable.

Her hands slid into his hair, pulling it free from the leather thong and let it fall loose, enjoying the soft blonde curls. She couldn't contain another soft cry of excitement and pleasure as he rocked her against him. Her breasts felt heavy and ached with a need she knew he could satisfy. With fingers moving quickly, she had her dress down to her waist before giving it a second thought.

Moaning softly, he dropped his head to her breasts, slowly teasingly, pulled a taut nipple into his mouth. When he suckled upon it, she arched against him, her breathing so ragged and her heart racing in her chest so fast she feared she would pass out on him.

"Angel." He breathed against her wet nipple. "Sweet, sweet angel."

His lips found her other nipple and suckled upon it just as hard and before she knew what she was doing, she was hastily moving their clothing, trying to get closer to him. His teeth nibbled on the sweetly throbbing nipple, and she nearly had their clothes parted, ready to ease the ache that had built to a firestorm inside her.

He rocked her against him again, hard this time, and she whimpered as something deep within her clenched in a pleasurable pain. "Do you want this?" he asked breathlessly against her ear, his breathing just as ragged as hers. To make his point he pulled her against him again, and this time she could feel intimately the pressure against her, the pressure that would be relieved soon.

"Yes, oh, Cade, yes," she whispered urgently. "I want this, Cade. I want you, all of you."

He pulled her head down for a deep, passionate kiss as his hand fumbled with her skirts. Finally, his hand had penetrated the sea of fabric and his fingers ran lightly over her swollen, damp need and he kissed her through her shuddering gasp of pleasure.

This time she rocked against him, hard, realizing her ache was about to be soothed. "Oh, yes, Cade. I want you. I want this, Cade. I love you so very much!"

Suddenly his motions stopped and he was gripping her waist again, squeezing it tightly, his eyes closed and his breathing rapid.

"Cade," she whispered, and moved against him and he moaned and she could tell he wanted this as badly as she did. But something was holding him back, and he held tightly to her waist, controlling her movements as his breathing slowly came under control.

When he opened his eyes, the blue was sharp and focused. "What did you say, Olivia?" his voice was still hoarse.

Olivia didn't understand why he had stopped. They were so close. So very close. "I love you, Cade. I want to share everything with you, including my body. And I want to claim your body as mine, for as long as you'll let me have it."

A shudder ran through him, and he let out his breath slowly. "Angel, you can't love me. You can't."

Much to her surprise he was pulling up the sleeves of her dress and gradually refastening the bodice. "I-I don't understand. Cade, isn't this what you wanted, too? Don't lie to me. I could feel it. I could feel *you*."

He was already lacing up the rest of her dress and he shook his head at her. "No. It was wrong for me to take advantage of you like that."

"Take advantage of—well, I never!"

"Exactly," Cade said sharply, looking at her with his intense blue eyes. "You've never been with a man. You don't know what it is like."

"From everything I could tell it was going to be something incredible!" She wished she had her voice. Her statements coming out as hoarse rasps weren't helping her.

"It would have—I mean, it is—with the right person, it is amazing. But I'm not the right person for you, Olivia. You can't love me. I can't let you love me."

Olivia was in stunned shock when he slipped her from his lap and began to very quickly pull up his britches and stuff in his shirt. He had his britches laced and was turned away from her, leaning against the tree.

He had turned her away. She had been so terribly wrong, so terribly, terribly wrong. She had thought he desired her, that he saw her differently than the other men she had encountered in her life. She had thought he would treasure her and enjoy this precious time together. She had been a fool.

"Olivia," he said finally, turning to face her, but she held up her hand as she stood and brushed off her skirt and gathered the jar of balm for his leg.

"You don't need to say anything else. You've said enough." She concentrated on placing the jar back carefully in the saddlebag, fighting hard to keep her tears from falling. She was a complete idiot for thinking any man would find her desirable.

She wasn't prepared when Cade caught her arm and pulled her up to face him. His expression was tight and hard to read. "I don't think you understand me, Olivia."

"I understand you perfectly well, Cade. Please, allow me to save what little dignity I have left and let me gather the horses. We've wasted far too much time here."

A myriad of emotions swept across his face quickly before he released her and let her go to the horses. It was as she untethered the two horses that Olivia allowed only a few tears to fall. But a few tears were all she would allow. She wouldn't be a fool ever again.

Chapter Eighteen

THEY RODE UNTIL dusk and, despite the chill in the air, Cade wasn't willing to risk the danger of a fire. Olivia had come prepared with a thick blanket and used her horse saddle as a pillow. Cade, too, had brought a thick blanket and, for a moment, he considered asking Olivia to lie with him so they could share each other's warmth.

But she already had her back to him and was wrapped tightly in her blanket before he even had the chance to ask. He sighed heavily and wrapped the blanket around him, used the saddle blanket from his horse as an extra layer of warmth, and rested his head against his horse's saddle.

He had hurt her. God, it had felt so incredible to hold her the way he had, to touch her so intimately, and to know that if he wanted, he could feel sweet release with her. And she had been so passionate in his arms. He had never had another woman so free and loving in his arms. He had never had a woman desire him in such a way, so intently, with every fiber of her being.

Even in the early stages of his marriage, his wife had treated lovemaking as a chore, a task required of her as his wife. And after she had passed, he had sought comfort in the arms of a couple other women, but their movements had been awkward, hesitant, and nowhere near as tantalizing as Olivia. He had made the mistake of forgetting his pledge to himself, that he wouldn't be with her because it wasn't right. She deserved a better man, and he couldn't be the man to take away her virginity. That would ruin her forever.

But then she had whispered the deadly words. "I love you." He couldn't deny it—hearing her utter those words as she was writhing her sweet body against his had nearly been his undoing. But instead, after a few seconds, it was as if someone had thrown a bucket of ice water on him.

She couldn't love him. Everything about him was wrong for her. She had been caught up in the moment and uttered the words out of passion, not out of true love. Or, at least, that was what he hoped it was.

The alternative was an even bigger problem. Every person he loved in his life either died, or, in Bella's case, was being used as a pawn in a war. He had loved his wife, though it was more fondness than love, but it had still hurt when she had died when Bella was born. And he had loved his son more than words could express. Bella was all that he had left, and he didn't know if she was even still alive.

It was a curse for him to love someone. And, in his mind, it was just as much a curse for someone to love him in return. He didn't know if he was capable of returning the unconditional love that Olivia seemed to be offering him. The idea of Olivia being hurt because of his actions, or because she simply loved him, was more than he could bear.

He rolled over in his blanket, trying to get comfortable.

The desire in her eyes when she looked at him... it was something he had never thought he would see. And on top of that, his desire for her had nearly clouded his ability to think at all. He had wanted her. He had never wanted a woman more in his life. But he would be damned if his own desires hurt another person in his life. She had already been through far too much for his sake.

He turned again and lay on his back, trying to focus on anything else to get some sleep. It was as he lay there that he heard her. Her teeth were chattering and she was letting out soft gasping sounds as she tried to gain warmth.

To hell with her anger. She could be angry at him in the morning after she had a relaxing warm sleep. Picking up his saddle and the saddle blanket he was using for extra warmth, he moved to wear she lay.

"What do you think—" Her words were cut off as he pulled her out of her tightly wrapped blanket and into his arms. He then wrapped both blankets around them, lay down, and spread out the saddle blankets on top of them as well. He then settled down with his head on his saddle, and her head on her saddle.

She didn't make any further protests, but his own body did. He hadn't thought through his actions and how they would bring her close to him, where he could smell her fresh scent, and feel her soft form near his. Damn, he wasn't going to get sleep no matter what he did.

TRAVEL WAS SLOW. Olivia continued to ask for breaks, but the real purpose was for the sake of Cade's leg. If she told him that, though, he would hardly stop at all. Serena had packed the saddlebags well, and they certainly weren't lacking for food.

But Olivia found it hard to eat. She realized she had been a fool to think she was attractive, to think that a man could ever want her in the way a man wanted a woman. But she had thought, she had felt, as if Cade desired her in that way. But it very well could be the fact that he hadn't been with a woman in a long time, and he had thought he could lower his standards to her.

She was past the point of being sad, and had even gotten past the point of being mad at Cade. She couldn't force something that didn't exist. But she hated herself. She had even gone so far as professing to him that she was in love with him. Which was the truth, but she wished she had kept it to herself.

In spite of her bruised pride, she still insisted on massaging the balm into his leg each day. She would make sure Bella got her father back in as good of condition as possible. Much to her relief, he didn't try to talk to her when she was working on his leg.

During their travel they didn't talk either. They rode in silence, heading east, following behind Santa Anna. As they went through small towns along the way, they would meet various people who would speak of Santa Anna's journey, the destruction he left behind, and the young girl that rode with one of the camps. They also learned of the Goliad Massacre, where Santa Anna had ordered the execution of four hundred Texians.

While the news was disheartening, the information about a young girl in one of the camps gave them continued hope. Many of the people grumbled that Houston was retreating instead of fighting, while still others believed the United States would come to their aid once they were close enough to the Louisiana border.

They had been traveling for nearly a week when Cade felt it was safe enough for them to have a small fire and Olivia cooked them fresh biscuits and bacon. Coyotes howled in the distance as they sat near the fire, eating the first warm food they'd had in a long time.

Olivia ate for the first time in nearly two days, and the biscuit filled her stomach quickly. The bacon had been a nice change to the dried jerky, and she hoped Cade enjoyed it as much as she had. He'd been eating consistently, but he was bound to be ust as tired of the dried venison as she.

After placing the remainder of the biscuits carefully to the side of the fire and covering them with the heavy cast iron lid, she gathered her blanket and saddle blanket together, and was just reaching for her saddle when a tanned hand reached around her and grabbed it.

She turned and found herself nearly nose-to-nose with Cade, his blue eyes watching her intently. "What-what are you doing?" she stammered, caught off guard by his proximity. She had done everything she could to give him distance, since that seemed to be what he wanted from her.

"We need to talk," he said softly, his eyes never leaving

hers.

Olivia swallowed hard. "There isn't anything for us to talk about," she replied reaching for her saddle, but he held it out of her reach.

"The hell there isn't. I'm tired of a week of your silence. The first few days I thought it was because your throat still hurt. But you are talking just fine, now, and you need to understand some things."

Olivia shook her head and began to step around him, but his hand caught her upper arm, holding her still.

She looked over at him with surprise. "I don't understand, Cade. What do you want from me?"

He sighed heavily and released her, turning to place her saddle where she would sleep for the night. He proceeded to grab his own items and placed them next to hers and waited patiently for her to move. Slowly she walked towards him and spread out her blanket and saddle blanket the same as they had every night, where they would be wrapped together for warmth against the unusually cold spring nights.

He gestured with his hand for her to lie down, and she wondered if he had changed his mind and decided not to talk with her after all. She felt relief and disappointment at the same time. She craved the sound of his voice, craved his gentle touch, craved the things they had before she had made a fool of herself. She had ruined everything between them.

She stretched out on the blanket, taking her usual position where she would be facing away from him. "No," he said, and she looked at him quizzically. "Turn around. Tonight you're going to face me and you're going to listen to what I have to say."

Hesitantly, Olivia rolled to her other side, watching him with trepidation. What was so important that he needed to talk to her? She already knew the truth as he had made that quite obvious when he had pushed her away. She was there to help him find Bella, and she wouldn't back out of that decision, no matter what he had to say. Perhaps that was what he wanted to talk to her about. Perhaps he no longer wanted her on this journey with him.

He settled down alongside her and brought the blankets over them, creating the warm cocoon they had become accustomed to. Olivia found herself facing him directly, her eyes meeting his, and she instantly looked away. She wasn't ready to face him.

Cade reached up and cupped her chin, tilting it up until she raised her eyes to his. "I've missed you, angel. I've missed you so very much. And I know it is my fault, and I'm going to try to fix it. But I need you, more than I realized or wanted to admit."

Olivia's eyes searched his, trying to comprehend what he was saying. "I haven't gone anywhere," she replied. "How can you miss me?"

He closed his eyes for several moments then as he opened them, his fingers on her chin relaxed and traced her jawline softly. "I've missed this, angel. I've missed being able to touch you, to feel you, and to hear your voice." He leaned in closer to her, and her heart was racing. "I've missed being able to do this," he whispered, and his lips brushed over hers lightly, then with more intensity.

Olivia should pull away—she was allowing her heart to be vulnerable to pain all over again, but she didn't care. She loved this man, and if he wanted to touch her, to kiss her, then she would enjoy every bit that she could.

She returned the kiss with enthusiasm and he deepened the kiss as his fingers buried in her hair. When they broke apart, they were breathless.

"God, how I've missed you," he said roughly.

Olivia shook her head and pulled back slightly. "I don't understand, Cade. I don't understand how you could want this from me."

"You don't understand—how can you not understand this? For a month we have shared touches, caresses as we passed each other, sweet kisses whenever the opportunity arose. Don't you crave it? Or have I hurt you so badly that you don't want anything from me anymore?"

Olivia's eyes flew to his. "You didn't hurt me. It was my fault, and I see that now. I just—I had just hoped..." She closed her eyes as tears began to build behind her eyes.

"Talk to me, angel. I can't fix anything if I don't know what all I did wrong. And I know I have made a terrible mistake, but I want to rectify it."

"A terrible mistake? It was a mistake to be honest with me?" Olivia shook her head and would have rolled to her back had his arms not moved around her, keeping her close to him.

How could she talk to him when she wanted to cry out all of the pain in her heart?

She drew a deep breath. She would confess to Cade why

she had been aloof. And perhaps then he would be grateful, knowing she had finally come to the right mind. But his actions in the moment spoke of a different story, and she was completely confused. It was best to just confess.

"I've known for a very long time how unattractive I am to men, to the point that sometimes they can't even bear laying their eyes on me. But with you... with you, I feel like a woman. A true woman who can be kissed and caressed the way lovers do. I feel as if you find me appealing, not revolting, and I want to be every bit of a woman with you."

"Olivia—"

"Please, let me finish. I know you have been without a woman for a long time. And I know that men have needs, and are willing to make sacrifices in order to have those needs met. But I had forgotten how undesirable I am when in your arms, and I became far too brazen. I tried to push you into desiring me as much as I desire you, but you could not lower yourself to be with me. Even though your body had a need, you couldn't bring yourself to be with me."

"Of all the—"

"I understand, Cade, truly, I do. I know the names they call me in San Antonio. I know that no man wants to touch me. It is my fault for thinking it would be different with you, and I'm sorry that I put you in that position."

"Olivia, stop." His voice quivered with emotion, and she couldn't tell if it was anger or frustration, or perhaps it was relief that she had taken the burden off of him to explain what had happened between them.

Her eyes lifted to his and his blue eyes shined brightly in

the moonlight. Everything about him, from his soft blonde hair, to his incredible eyes, to his square jaw and even his slightly bent nose, made her love him and desire him. But it wasn't meant to be.

His fingers reached up to trace her eyebrows, the curve of her jaw, the bow of her slightly parted lips. "You are, without a doubt, one of the most attractive woman I have ever seen. Anyone who said or thought otherwise was either blind or a fool. You had horrible things done to you in the past to make you feel unattractive. But I thought you were past all of that! Can't you see how incredibly beautiful you are?"

"Please, Cade, please don't do this. Please don't tell me these things to make me feel better. I've caught glimpses of myself in the mirror and even I couldn't tolerate looking for long. Don't tell me these lies to try to make me feel better about myself."

Both of Cade's hands captured her face and her startled eyes met his. "I'm not lying, Olivia. You are exquisite. I could simply watch you all day and be happy the entire time. You are beautiful. I don't know why they were so determined to make you think you are anything less. But they were wrong. If I didn't find you attractive, how could I do this?"

His lips crushed hers, his hands moving from her head down to her collarbone where his thumb traced the hollow of her throat. His hands finally settled on her waist and squeezed gently, pulling her closer to him.

They were both breathing heavily when he pulled away from her, and Olivia's heart raced.

"Why?" she whispered. "If you desire me, why did you push me away? What did I do wrong?"

"You didn't do anything wrong, angel. It was all my fault."

Oliva watched him, confused, and then her gaze fell to his lips, swollen from their kiss and all she wanted was to kiss him again, to feel his tongue grazing her lips, asking permission to enter and tease her to heightened levels.

"You can't love me, Olivia. You can't."

Olivia pulled back away from him slightly, watching his eyes more closely. "What do you mean? I can't change the way my heart feels for you. And while you are with me for only a short time longer, I wanted to take full advantage of my love for you. I know there will be no other after you."

"Don't love me, angel. Everyone who has ever loved me is either dead or currently a prisoner of the Mexican military. My wife died. My son died. And they have Bella. If they capture you and know you are close to me, you will die also. I can't let that happen."

"I am a strong woman, Cade. And even stronger because I love you. And I will continue to say that, no matter how much you don't want it to be true. I love you. I love you so very, very much."

Cade's lips came down on hers firmly, and she sighed with pleasure as his tongue tasted her. His arm circled around her and pulled her closer, holding her tightly as his mouth continued its assault. Her own hands moved up and ran through his blonde hair, tugging gently as the desire rose within her.

His lips pulled away from hers and began to trail down her jaw, then her neck, and she arched her head back, giving him full access to her skin, becoming vulnerable once again to the power of his touch. He moaned his approval softly, but with reluctance he stopped his caress and his fingers tightened on her waist. "I can't, angel. I can't do this with you."

Dazed, Olivia shifted her head to look at him, her eyes full of desire and love. "What? What can't you do?"

"This," he said squeezing her waist and allowing his hands to travel a little higher and lightly brush her breasts. His hands were shaking as he pulled away from her and ran them down his face. "Olivia, you deserve a far better man than me. I have nothing to offer you—no stability, no home, not even my love. I can give you my desire, my passion, and I crave being with you intimately more than you will ever know. But I can't take this beautiful gift that you offer to me when it belongs to a man far better than me."

Olivia closed her eyes for several seconds, trying to regain control of her emotions. But it didn't seem to be working. When her eyes opened they were still full of love and desire. "There is no other man for me, Cade. Nor will there ever be. You haven't been listening to me."

"I've heard everything you've said, angel. And that doesn't change the fact that you should have a better man. I want you to have the beautiful life you deserve, Olivia, and that won't happen with me."

Olivia smiled softly at him, and her fingers traced his eyebrows, his high cheekbones, his firm lips. "I know what you believe. And I know how I feel. I know that you will leave once you have Bella and that you will no longer have me in your life. Knowing that, I want to soak up as much time with you as I can possibly can. Unless you don't want me to. If you want me to stay away from you, I will."

"God, I know I should tell you yes. I know I should tell you to stay as far away from me as possible. I know I should try to make you hate me so that you will never be at risk for any pain, either from me or my enemies. But the selfish part of me wants to enjoy you and enjoy the brief time we have left together."

"So which side of your odd logic wins?" she asked him in a voice barely above a whisper.

His eyes collided with hers in the moonlight, and the small flames from the fire that was beginning to go out made it seem his eyes were dancing. "I choose you, angel. I choose you."

Chapter Nineteen

NEWS TRAVELED SLOWLY across Texas, and as the devastating blow to the Alamo traveled east, the newly founded government of Texas took flight. Fearing Santa Anna's further aggression, they left what was to be the new capital of the republic, New Washington, and headed east, towards Harrisburg.

Santa Anna scented their fear, and took off in pursuit of the fleeing government, ready to put an end to any and all who still thought the revolution had a leg to stand on. When he reached New Washington, he had been furious that the Texian government had fled.

He ordered his men to destroy the town and, even from a distance, Cade and Olivia could see the smoke of the burning town. April twelfth, he crossed the Brazos River, along with his large force of military strength.

The news came to Cade and Olivia as they traveled, meeting some people on the path carrying a few of their precious belongings with them, trying to get as far away from Santa Anna and his ruthless military as possible.

The rains had been falling again, leaving Cade and Olivia drenched for nearly a week. The stench of the burning town mingled with the rain as they rode through New Washington. The devastation to the town was hard to witness, but they pressed forward, knowing they were getting closer.

They huddled together at night, and they enjoyed sweet, loving embraces, but Cade made sure it never went past that. As much as he desired her, he wouldn't take advantage of the unusual situation they were in. He knew it frustrated her, and it was driving him insane. So, instead, he got her to start talking. They both started sharing stories about their lives as they lay facing each other, laughing softly in the night air. It wasn't what his body craved, but it was what his soul demanded.

Cade was overjoyed that Olivia desired him as much as he desired her. But he knew how little he had to offer her, and he wasn't going to put her in a position where she would look back on their time together and regret it. Her love though… her love was what made it capable for him to get through the day.

He had never thought he would be loved by a woman again, and even doubted if he was ever truly loved by a woman. Certainly not with the passion and unconditional love Olivia offered him. His wife had offered him respect. But it hadn't been love. But he had been in love with her. At least—he thought he had. He enjoyed her presence, enjoyed coming home to her, and couldn't have been more grateful for the children she had given him.

What he felt for Olivia was different. He craved her presence. He craved the sound of her voice, or the brush of her hand. She brought him comfort and solace, and she created a desire within him no woman had ever done. The realization made his chest tighten. Dear God, he was in love with her.

The ferry rocked on the choppy water, drawing his attention back to the moment. Olivia stood by his side, her eyes looking out across the frothing water with unease, her hands clinging to the railing. On the other side they would come upon Santa Anna's troops.

Cade wrapped a protective arm around her, and she leaned into him, seeking his warmth and strength. "All of this rain has caused the river to swell. But the ferry is solid and we can make it across. It will just be rough."

She glanced up at him and gave him a shaky smile. "I'll be very thankful once we are off this blasted thing."

A log floating in the river bumped into the ferry, causing the entire thing to shake, and Olivia grabbed ahold of Cade's hands. She gripped them so tightly he could feel his fingers going numb. He smiled down at her and pressed a kiss to her forehead. "On the bright side of things, the rain has stopped."

A few men suddenly yelled several comments and the ferry was turned loose and instantly began bobbing and heaving across the water. Cade widened his stance, bracing himself against the pitch and sway and kept a tight hold on Olivia.

The ride felt like hours, though it was closer to just a half hour. Olivia was holding on to him as if she never intended to let him go, and she wobbled as she was finally able to step off the ferry and on to solid ground.

Cade observed the area around them and frowned. Hundreds of horses had pounded through the area recently, turning it into a muddy marsh to plod through. They were certainly on the right track.

After gathering their horses and fighting through the mud, they were finally able to mount up, and Olivia looked over at Cade. "We're almost there," she said. "You'll have her back in your arms very soon."

Cade's heart leapt at the thought. To hold his sweet little girl again, to smell her hair, her soft skin, and tickle her with his whiskers until she was laughing hysterically was a dream he had never thought possible.

And it wouldn't have been—not without the woman riding close to him. If she had turned him away that fateful night—if she had told him "no" to his request for help, he would have died from his wounds.

Olivia looked over at him and smiled. "You seem to be in deep thought. Care to share?"

He felt his throat close up briefly. This incredible woman had given him everything, including her heart. He had nothing to offer her. He had no home, he had no future. He barely knew what he was going to do with Bella once they rescued her. All he had to offer Olivia was his love, but that wasn't enough. She needed a man that was going to provide for her, take care of her, and make sure she was happy for the rest of her life.

"I don't know how to thank you enough for what you have done," he finally said, urging his horse to ride up alongside her. He reached out and grasped her hand. "I never would be this close to Bella if it hadn't been for you."

A blush crept up her neck and made her cheeks flame red at his praise. "Oh, Cade," she said softly, "I've done little except irritate you and drive you close to madness with my attempts at healing you. I'm thankful that it has paid off and that you are strong enough to take Bella and rebuild your life."

Cade squeezed her hand then released it and turned his eyes to the beautiful countryside they rode through. The tall pines provided incredible shelter from the sun, and the scent in the air was fresh and energizing. He had witnessed many areas of Texas, and was amazed that each and every place was different, from dessert land, to the ports along the coast, to the great prairie land he had built his home on, to this beautiful forest.

"We're probably a half day's ride away from their rear regiment," Cade said, returning his mind to what lay ahead. Bella wasn't his, yet. They still had to go through the process of sneaking her out of the Mexican camp, and neither he nor Olivia knew what they were in for.

Olivia's eyes drifted upwards and his followed to see the dark clouds that were rolling in, blocking out the sun. They had finally dried off for the first time in days, and the idea of getting drenched again was highly unappealing.

Cade's eyes searched their surroundings and, much to his surprise and pleasure, he spotted a break in the trees where an old, ancient tree had hollowed out and petrified, creating the perfect resting place for them to weather through the storm. "Over here." He turned his horse towards the break in the trees and Olivia followed, hesitantly at first, but then more eagerly as she saw where he was headed.

By the time they had their blankets and saddlebags in the log, a light drizzle had started, and within minutes the sky burst open and the rain pounded the outside of the log. They adjusted their blankets and the saddlebags and enjoyed a light lunch of dried meat and cheese to the sound of the rain.

Sighing with contentment, Olivia turned and nestled up against Cade, laying her head on his shoulder. "We are so close. Bella is so very close to being in your arms again."

Cade wrapped his arm around her and rested his chin on the top of her head. "She's close but so far away, angel. It's as though I can see her, but I can't reach her. I feel as though I'm stuck in this swamp mud around here."

OLIVIA GRABBED CADE'S hand and interlaced her fingers with his. "You will hold her in your arms again soon. What will be the first thing you want to tell her?" she asked, trying to draw his mind on some more positive thoughts.

"That I love her. And that I've missed her so very, very much."

Olivia squeezed his hand. "She will feel the same way. What else do you want to tell her?"

His chest rumbled with a slight chuckle. "I want to tell her about you, of course. The bravest woman I've ever known in my life. How you rescued me from the Mexican Army and brought me to her."

It was Olivia's turn to chuckle. "Don't you think that is a

bit exaggerated?"

"It's how I feel." He leaned down and she lifted her face to his, anticipating the sweet taste of his lips on hers. The kiss was gentle and light, not asking for anything from her, yet Olivia could feel the passion he held back.

She pulled back slightly, looking up into his eyes, then her gaze roved over his cheeks, his slightly crooked nose, and his lips. This could be the last time she would ever see him again, depending on what happened on the morrow. She wanted his face branded into her brain, so that even when she was eighty or older she would remember him, and remember him exactly as he looked in that moment. The sun was beginning to set, casting unusual shadows across his face, and he had a thick beard growing, covering parts of his face.

"What thoughts run through that mind of yours?"

His voice rumbled against her body and she realized she'd been staring at him. "You look better without a beard," she said, smiling.

He feigned a shocked look on his face and began to try to tickle her neck with his beard, and he soon had her laughing so hard she could barely catch her breath. God, how long had it been since she had laughed like that? How long had it been since she had allowed any type of joy in her life? She had always thought it was disrespectful in the face of her parent's death. But now… now it seemed right.

Having finally regained some of her composure, she settled back into Cade's arms. "So, what are your plans to rescue Bella? I don't think they'll just let us walk into the camp, do you?"

Cade shook his head. "No, they won't." He sighed heavily and pulled her sideways so that she could face him. "I think… the absolute best plan is for you to stay here."

"What? Stay here? Why on earth would I do that? I can't help you from here!"

"And you won't be in any danger here, either."

"Oh, no. You are not going to walk out on me, Cade. You know that I am just as invested in finding your daughter as you are." She pulled away from him and turned, facing him, trying not to grind her teeth in frustration.

Cade ran a hand down his face wearily. "I don't want to fight with you about this, angel. We have no idea what we're going into to try to get Bella. And you'll certainly be noticed."

"You haven't been paying attention to all of the information we've been getting. Santa Anna has women traveling with them to keep the men—satisfied. A woman in their camp won't be an unusual thing." She crossed her arms and raised an eyebrow, daring him to say something.

"And what if they are only allowed in one part of the camp and you go waltzing into an area where you don't belong? And what if you are spotted by one of the soldiers that has eaten at the *cocina*? There are too many things we don't know enough about." He shook his head at her.

"That's why we have to scout the camp before we enter. We'll know what we need to do. You *did* say you were a spy for the Texians, didn't you?" Olivia could feel her face getting flushed as her indignation grew.

Cade reached out and caught her shoulders. "Angel, I

can't let anything happen to you. Between you and Bella, you are the two most important women in my life. I can't lose you."

Olivia was momentarily stunned. He had just said she was one of the two most important women in his life. And that he couldn't lose her. Did that mean he wanted a future with her? Did that mean—

"Besides, if I don't return you in one piece to your sisters, they will do far worse to me than the Mexican Army ever could," he said with a lighthearted grin, unaware that he was crushing her heart with his attempt at lightening the feelings around them.

"Cade, I want—I *need* to be able to help with Bella. I can't stop here."

His fingers squeezed her upper arms almost painfully. "You aren't listening to what I'm trying to tell you. It is too dangerous. I can't let you go."

Olivia's anger threatened to boil over. "You have no right to tell me what I can or can't do. I've come this far, and I intend to see this through to the end."

"And it may very well be the end of you. Listen to me, Olivia!" He shook her slightly. "Listen to me! I've seen what these men are capable of. I've seen how they treat women, especially Texian sympathizers, and it is a terrible thing. I won't be able to live with myself if something happens to you. All it takes is for them to find out you're a Texian. And they'll figure that out rather quick."

Olivia saw the genuine fear for her in his eyes and felt tears burning the backs of her eyes and her throat. He had already been through so much... had seen so much, things that no man should ever have to see. And she took hope from the concern in his eyes. Perhaps he truly did have feelings for her, but just didn't know how to express it the right way.

"Angel... please. You have to listen to me and stay here. I can't protect both you and Bella at the same time."

Olivia bit back her retort that she didn't need him to protect her and that she had been protecting herself for years. But, for the time being, she needed to pacify him, at least for a little while. He would see differently in the morning. She would make certain of it.

She reached up and placed her hands on his face, lightly stroking his beard. "Alright. If that is what you need from me... then that is what we should do." She did her best to seem defeated, to make him think she was disappointed, instead of inwardly plotting what she would really do.

Chapter Twenty

THAT NIGHT, UNLIKE most of the other nights, had been warmer, and they had enjoyed lying together in the log, teasing each other with sweet kisses wherever they could find a bare piece of skin. But they were too exhausted to go very far, and fell asleep wrapped in each other's embrace.

Olivia knew something was wrong the moment she woke up. She was tense, and it felt as if there was a rock in the bottom of her stomach. She turned within the log and realized Cade was gone.

She gasped, noticing the sun was already peeking through the trees and scrambled out of the log, praying with all her might that she would find him out there, warming up some of her leftover biscuits. But he was nowhere to be seen.

Neither was his horse, his guns, his saddle, and his saddlebags. He had left her. The realization hurt... it stung so sharply she sat down hard on the ground. He had left her without even saying goodbye, knowing this could very well be the last time she would ever see him.

Once he found Bella, she was certain he would return with her to East Texas to rebuild his ranch. She would never see him again. She clenched her hands into fists.

No. She wouldn't let him do that to her. She was going to get to tell him goodbye, she was going to get to see Bella and hold her and kiss her as she had imagined, and then—only then—would she be ready to say goodbye. He would not steal that from her.

Quickly, she began to gather up her belongings and saddle her horse. She had planned all along that she would head to Harrisburg, ideally using a different path than Cade so he wouldn't catch her again, and then help with the search for Bella.

She wouldn't be able to tolerate not knowing what had happened to that innocent girl, nor could she watch Cade put his life in unnecessary danger in order to save Bella when Olivia could help him.

As soon as she had gathered up all of her belongings and loaded them in the saddlebags on the horse, she mounted and took off at a fast trot, heading just north of the direction Cade had taken. She would veer back onto the path once she was close enough to the camp and wouldn't be at risk of Cade sending her back.

Suddenly, she heard a noise coming from up ahead, and she hesitated, pulling her horse to a stop. It was voices. Male voices, speaking in Spanish.

With her heart racing, she leaned low over the horse and urged it forward slowly, until she could just make out the two men. Their backs were to her, but she recognized the white uniform of the Mexican soldiers instantly.

Slowly, quietly, she slid off her horse and grabbed her rifle. She couldn't shoot them outright—the sound would carry way too far. But she had to do something. Gripping the rifle tightly with sweaty palms, she advanced on them.

The talk amongst each other was loud enough that neither one of them noticed her approach until she was almost upon them. One of the soldiers turned in surprise and she swung her rifle as hard as she could and heard the loud crack as it hit his head. He tumbled to the ground and began to roll down the slight incline she had just climbed, nearly taking her with him.

But she dodged him at the last second as she swung her rifle again. But this soldier was already prepared for that attack and grabbed the butt of the gun before it struck him and gave her a terrifying smile. Using the rifle, he yanked her closer to him, speaking in a cooing voice to her in Spanish, saying things that were making the very tips of her ears turn red.

He pulled her in closely and, as he tried to lean in to place his disgusting lips on her skin, she brought her pistol up that she had kept hidden in her skirts and struck him as hard as she could in the back of the head. The crack was an awful sound and he fell hard, tumbling down to join his partner on the ground.

Olivia stood still for several minutes, trying to catch her breath and coming to terms with what she had just done. She had probably killed both of the men, considering the force she had hit them with, and the large bulges on their heads. Oh, dear God, she hadn't wanted to kill anymore, but, it was as Cade had said—it was war.

To be on the safe side, Olivia took vines that she found

lying around and tied the men's hands and feet, making sure there was no way for them to get free without having some help. And, given the condition they were going to be found in, Olivia doubted they would want to tell anyone what had happened even if they did survive.

She hadn't planned on the delay, and knew moved Cade closer to the encampment than she would like. She wanted to be with him when he first went into the camp. With determination, she mounted her horse again and took off at a fast trot, her eyes probing everything around her and trying to stay as close to the trail that he would have taken as possible without being detected.

Everywhere she looked there were discarded items. Entire pieces of furniture, expensive pottery, even heirlooms, wasted by the roadside, abandoned by the Texians as they heard of Santa Anna's approach. They feared for their livelihood and for their families but, in the end, they had made the choice that would allow them to flee certain death that much faster.

The last report Cade and Olivia had gathered was that Houston's men were headed towards Harrisburg, where it seemed they might actually finally engage with Santa Anna's men, who had just arrived there the day before, furious at having lost the fleeing newly-founded Texian government that had traveled on even further.

But with Houston approaching Harrisburg as well, there was a good chance battle was inevitable, and that meant sweet Bella could be caught in the crossfire. Olivia wasn't the only one consumed by these thoughts. She could only imagine the pain Cade was going through, wondering if he had taken too long to heal, or if he had paused too many times along the journey, and could lose her before he even got close.

Lost in her thoughts, Olivia wasn't prepared when her horse stumbled and nearly fell to his forelegs, and she was pitched forward. She had no chance to grab the pommel of the saddle to catch herself and was tossed about, landing so hard on the muddy ground that she felt sharp leaves and twigs cut through her clothes and into her skin.

But she had been prepared enough to keep her gun with her. Before her assailant was upon her she had her pistol out and cocked and aimed at his head. She couldn't see his face as he was blocking the sunlight, but she didn't care. She hadn't come this far to lose everything now.

Her finger tightened on the trigger before the gun was ripped from her hands and she was yanked to her feet, all in the same motion. "Give me that damned thing," a familiar voice growled. "If you were going to kill me you would have already done it. I swear, woman, you test even the sanest man…" His voice trailed off as he turned to head back to his horse, tucked away behind thick shrubs where she wouldn't have been able to see him.

Or maybe she would have if she'd only been paying attention. "That's a bit of a stretch, don't you think? Referring to yourself as a 'sane man?'"

Cade turned to face her, leading his horse behind him. "Yes, yes, you're right. I'm completely insane. And do you know who has made me insane? You! You! It's as if you just want to go looking for trouble. You ride towards hostile territory with your head in the clouds, and you think *I'm* the one that's insane?"

Olivia could feel a fine trembling in her hands and clasped them together tightly so he wouldn't see. "I told you all along that I intend to help you get Bella back."

"But not like this! Not like this. You have a home and people who love you dearly who expect you to return to them safely. You keep careening through these woods like this, and you'll get caught and maimed and murdered in no time."

He is really angry. She grimaced inwardly. There was a small vein at the base of his neck that throbbed with each of his rapid heartbeats, and it was all because of her actions.

"Let me help rescue Bella. Please, Cade. I must help."

"She is my daughter. This is my responsibility. And twice now you've demonstrated you have no idea how to sneak up on someone, let alone follow at a distance where you won't be noticed. You're a risk, Olivia. A risk I cannot and will not take." He looked back to his horse and tightened the cinch and was about to mount when he turned back to her.

"If you try to follow me, or if you even go on your own wayward trail, you will leave me with very few choices. And the one I like best is tying you to that horse and smacking its rear until it runs all the way back to the ferry."

Olivia placed her hands on her hips. "You may have me at a disadvantage when it comes to sneaking up on you, but I am not as inept as you think." She turned from him and stomped over to her saddle bags and pulled out a bundle of white clothing. White Mexican Army uniforms.

Cade froze, his eyes fixated on what she held.

Then his eyes lifted to hers and she couldn't tell if his anger had calmed slightly or escalated significantly. "Where. Did. You. Get. Those." Each word was clipped and seemed forced from his lips.

His anger had escalated. She almost wished she could put the garments back and that he could forget he ever saw them. But, she was an honest woman, so she would tell him the truth.

She stood straight and tall, her usual stance when she wasn't being disarmed by Cade. "I came across two sentries on my way. They weren't facing me, and I was able to incapacitate them with my guns. Then I took their clothes and tied them up."

"You did what?" Cade exploded.

Olivia lifted her chin. "You heard me. I took care of the threat and I gained us something to help us sneak through the camp."

Cade's hands clenched and unclenched, and he was breathing harshly through his nose. Within two strides he was gripping her by the arms, hauling her up on her tiptoes so that she was nearly eye level with her. "I heard no gun shots. What did you do?"

"I—well, I hit them. In the back of the head. With quite some force. I'm afraid I killed at least one of them."

He released her and took a step back, running a hand down his face, staring at her as if she were unlike any creature he had ever seen before. "You're impossible," he whispered, "absolutely impossible."

Olivia wasn't sure what he meant by that, but she was in his arms again, yet this time he was kissing her, pressing his lips against hers in a way as though he wanted to claim her, to mark her as his forever. And she loved every second of it.

When they broke apart, their lips were dewy and they stared at each other breathlessly.

Finally, Olivia broke the silence. "So this means you're taking me with you?"

CADE KNEW HE should be angry. Olivia wasn't supposed to be with him, and he would be much more comfortable easing up on Santa Anna's camp thinking she was safe in the log he had left her in that morning.

He should have known she would come after him. Hell, maybe he had even hoped she would come after him. Nothing felt normal anymore without her. Riding in silence he had felt as if he was missing something, something very important. And he had finally realized it was Olivia.

For even when they rode in silence together, there was a connection, a warmth, a feeling. He'd been missing that all morning long. Until the hairs on the back of his neck had stood up and he knew that someone was trying to track him.

He had rigged the trap to stumble the horse and pitch the rider, and his heart had nearly lurched into his throat when he had seen the black-haired beauty who was starting to become his world go flying in the air and hit the ground.

But his fear over her being hurt was quickly outweighed

by his indignation, and he had wanted to put her on her horse, smack it with his leather reins, and watch the horse race away to a safer place for Olivia. Why did she have to be so stubborn?

Without turning his head, he observed her from the side. They had already changed into the white uniforms, and while his was a tad too tight on him, hers was loose, almost to the point of being baggy. But she still looked good. Even with her hair bunched up underneath the hat. He was surprised at how grateful she had been that the hat could pull down past her damaged ear. He knew it bothered her, but he hadn't realized how much.

Her smooth olive skin was exposed all along her neck and at the open collar, and his thoughts began to drift to some of their more intimate moments they had experienced together. He shifted in his saddle and forced himself to focus back on the camp ahead of them. The woman had such an incredible impact on him. He desired her with a ferocity he had never felt before.

He suddenly pulled his horse in and looked over at her. "Do you hear that?"

Olivia nodded. "A camp. A large one."

"Let's dismount and walk the horses in. Try not to make eye contact with anyone. I can assure you some of these men will remember you if they see those incredible eyes of yours."

He hadn't intended to pay her a compliment, but it had slipped out, and the incredible smile he received in return made it worth it. How was he going to make it without her when he left? Bella would be his again, and that was all he needed, right? No, there would be a vacancy in his heart, and he wouldn't be haunted by her memory for the rest of his life.

Perhaps if he got his life back in order, perhaps if he could get established once again, he would be able to ask her to be his wife, to be able to provide her the kind of life she deserved. But that could be years away, and by then someone would have charmed her into being their wife. He would be too late.

Her smile faded. "Don't you think some of your captors might be in this camp? Your eyes aren't so easy to forget, either."

Cade turned to dismount, not wanting her to see his smile. He was hoping to find some of his captors and was eagerly anticipating doling out some justice. There were many wrongs that needed to be corrected. But he wasn't about to let his desire for vengeance overcloud what he needed to do to rescue Bella. And, now, he had to focus on Olivia's safety at the same time.

He looked over and saw she had dismounted as well. She gave him a smile, though he doubted she realized it was a weak one and she was trembling slightly. "Are you ready?" she asked, gripping the horses reigns tightly.

"Do everything as I tell you. Keep your head down and look exhausted. Fortunately, these uniforms already have enough dust and mud on them to prove the long trek Santa Anna forced upon his men. If anyone tries to talk to you—"

"I know what to do. You continue to forget that I'm a spy, too, just like you."

His lips twitched in a grin. "A spy that I've caught twice."

Her eyes narrowed. "You've been lucky."

His eyebrows lifted and he nearly broke out into a laugh, but they were too close to the camp for him to make such noise. "We'll have to continue this conversation later. Let's go find Bella."

Together they moved forward, their boots occasionally slipping in the mud, but it wasn't as bad as it had been. When they came through a set of brush, Cade had to restrain his reaction.

The camp was huge. There were tents everywhere, stretching nearly as far as the eye could see, and soldiers gathered around campfires, or practicing in drills. They were able to move to the area for the horses unnoticed, and then turned to face the camp.

"Where do we start?" Olivia whispered, her eyes wide as she absorbed the same magnitude that Cade did.

"There are at least six hundred men here, if not more. I doubt the Texians have anywhere near this number. It will be a slaughter, just like the Alamo." Cade's stomach knotted up at the thought.

"No," Olivia said firmly. "No. Houston is strong, and I'm certain he's gathered a strong army. We must have faith. If we don't, then who will?"

Cade looked over at her and wished he could kiss her. He wanted to do nothing more than to pull her into his arms, hold her, and take in some of the courage and will-power that such a tiny woman could carry.

His face must have conveyed his thoughts, as she

blushed. "We must remain strong and loyal to the cause. We cannot doubt them. Not now, when victory is so near."

He nodded and they placed the horses with the others. Cade's eyes were searching the surrounding area cautiously when he suddenly felt Olivia tugging on his shirt frantically. He turned to her quickly, afraid she had seen someone she knew. But instead, she was looking off into the distance and Cade's eyes slowly followed hers.

Camped several hundred yards away was the Texian Army. Cade blinked several times, thinking it was an illusion, or a fabrication of his mind because he wished so strongly to see the Texians. But there they were, the ragtag group of men that were giving everything they had to win independence. But there appeared to be so few of them, and his heart sank.

He glanced back at Olivia and she had tears in her eyes. "They're here," she whispered. "Finally, Houston is here to face Santa Anna!"

Cade nodded. He was happy, but he was terrified at the same time. "Our time is being cut very short, angel. We must find Bella before the battle begins." He lifted his eyes to the sun. It was no later than 8:30 or 9:00 in the morning.

Olivia closed her eyes briefly and swallowed hard, and he knew she had just realized the magnitude of the situation they were in. All around them the soldiers were making preparations for battle, and it was only a matter of time before they or the Texians attacked.

Cade put a hand on her shoulder and squeezed it gently, but with enough force to draw her attention. "It's time. Let's go."

Chapter Twenty-One

THEY WERE WRONG. Santa Anna wasn't setting up camp. He was preparing for battle. His scouts were riding the terrain, judging the distance between them and the Texian army, and continuously came back with additional information. The morning was running late, and while Olivia and Cade had quietly moved through the ranks, acting as if they were helping prime the weapons, while they were actually removing gun powder, there had been no sign of Bella.

And then the order had come for them to move forward. At least, the cavalry was to move forward. Cade pulled Olivia to an area of soldiers at the rear of the regiments, both of them trying to remain inconspicuous in their movements. Even as far back as they were, they were able to anxiously watch the advancement of the cavalry.

Olivia was trembling and doing her best to hold herself together. She nearly jumped when Cade spoke low near her ear, but was able to contain the reaction.

"They must be keeping her close to Santa Anna. We haven't been able to get very close to him and his top aides. It would make sense that he would keep her near him."

Olivia nodded, afraid to speak, afraid her feminine voice

would reveal herself to the men around her. Cade squeezed her shoulder gently, trying to reassure her, then straightened to watch the attack and praying that the Texians were prepared.

The cavalry drew closer to the Texian camp and they played the same horrific trumpet call they had used at the Alamo. For a moment, Olivia felt as if she was going to be sick. The sound of those trumpets made it feel like the men were screaming and dying all over again, and she struggled to pull in a deep breath and calm herself.

The sudden sound of a cannons exploding made her jump and her eyes searched the area desperately, wanting to know who had fired first. Smoke was hovering around a small copse of oak trees on the other side of the field, and the cavalry began to turn away.

They had only gone a short distance before they turned to attack again, but the cannons had been pulled out further, and they went off again, enormous booms that seemed to shake the very earth they stood on.

The Mexican cavalry pulled a full retreat, returning to Santa Anna's camp, having lost a couple of horses in the small skirmish. Olivia wanted to let up a light cheer, thrilled that the Texians had made a stand and were proving they were a force to be reckoned with. She had to focus on containing her smile and presenting a stern face.

Santa Anna began to bark orders and the officers passed the orders down the line. They were to start unloading the pack mules and begin fortifying the area with all sorts of equipment, saddles, brush, bags of flour, and many other items. Much to Olivia's disappointment, the men were following their orders explicitly, and were doing a damn good job.

Cade grabbed her by the arm and directed her towards the work, and she realized they had to stay busy and look like they belonged, or they could be in a world of trouble. Olivia did her best to appear like a man, making her stride wider and powerful-appearing, and began to grab saddles and haul them to the site to create the breastworks.

Not far from her, Cade was grabbing large bags of flour and beans, and it flashed through Olivia's mind how much the Texians could use such simple food. They had been living off the land, and barely at that. The Texians were thin and hungry.

Suddenly, an extremely loud *boom* reverberated and Olivia fell to her knees, covering her head. Her ears were ringing and her heart was lodged in her throat. But when she dared to lift her head and look around, several of the Mexican soldiers were laughing and pointing at her.

Cade quickly stepped in and shouted at her in Spanish. "Get up, boy! Haven't you heard a cannon before?"

"*Si, si,*" Olivia stuttered, scrambling to her feet and picking up a couple more saddles, doing her best not to show that her arms were beginning to shake from the exertion.

The men around her were still laughing and even shoved her lightly as she passed them. Briefly she made eye contact with Cade, but she couldn't tell how he felt, as his face was guarded.

She suddenly felt very alone and, for the first time, genuine fear began to creep into her heart. She didn't belong here. But she had to help Cade find Bella. She tried to focus on Bella to take her mind off of the pain in her arms as she attempted to move quickly among the soldiers.

The resounding double boom of the cannons on the Texian side of the field filled the air. It was quickly greeted by the boom of Santa Anna's cannon, the Golden Standard, as he had dubbed it. The volley back and forth seemed to last forever. But then the sound of the cannons was interrupted by the Mexican Army that had stationed themselves on a small island near the two camps.

Olivia paused for a little while, her eyes fixated on the island as the Mexicans drove the Texians away. Their two cannons were turned onto the island and fired, forcing the Mexican infantry to make a hasty retreat. At the same time, the Mexican Army withdrew the Golden Standard. All of the Mexican Army was now in an area surrounded by hard woods with a piece of high prairie in front.

Work renewed to fortifying the camp, and Olivia worked tirelessly, keeping her head down and trying to keep her eyes on Cade. There was still a chill in the air, even though it was already late April, but it was a welcome chill as the work was hard and she was building up a sweat.

As she worked, she tried to move further and further towards the Mexican officers, trying to get close to the tents that had already quickly gone up. Her gut told her Bella was in there somewhere and she just needed to find the right tent. But every time she started to get close, someone would slam something into her arms and tell her to haul it to the breastworks.

"Mount up! Mount up!"

The call startled Olivia and she watched the cavalry race to their horses just as the Golden Standard fired off again, the sound of the blast causing her weak hearing to get even weaker, and made her bad ear ache painfully.

She rushed to the breastworks, as did several other soldiers, to see what was happening. Much to her shock, the Texians were riding out onto the plains in a blatant attempt to capture the Golden Standard. But the Golden Standard opened up on them and the Mexican cavalry charged forward.

Olivia wasn't aware she was holding her breath until she felt a pain in her chest as her lungs were beginning to complain. She drew in a shaky breath as she watched the Texians retreat and the Mexican cavalry charged after them.

But more Texians fired off from within the woods, holding back their enemy until the Texians had reloaded and made a second charge at the Mexican cavalry, and again they were driving the Mexicans back again.

Olivia's hope increased until she heard the voice of Santa Anna barking out orders in Spanish, sending two companies of riflemen. They opened fire for what felt like hours to Olivia, but probably only lasted fifteen minutes at the most. One of the Texian cannons was rolled out, but, much to Olivia's fear and disappointment, the Texians were forced to retreat.

Random gunfire cracked across both sides of the field for a long time, and it became so common, Olivia no longer jumped at the sound. But evening descended quickly, and both sides fell silent as they all prepared campfires. Both sides of the field were brightly lit with the glow of the flickering flames, reminding Olivia of the smoldering remains she had seen when they had passed through New Washington, witnessing the destruction by Santa Anna.

In the darkness, Olivia tried to seek out Cade, but it was near impossible. And she didn't want to appear lost or as if she didn't know anyone and then get hit with a bunch of questions she couldn't answer.

Suddenly, a hand grabbed her upper arm and yanked her to the darker side of the camp, and she began to fight before she looked up to see Cade's bright blue eyes staring down at her. She had to use restraint to prevent from throwing herself into his arms and holding on to him with all of her strength.

"Shh, shh," he whispered into her good ear. "I know it has been terrifying, but it's what we had to do."

"But we still didn't find Bella. She's in this mess some-where… why haven't we found her?"

"We will. We just haven't had the time. And in this darkness, we don't stand a chance." Cade frowned as he looked around them, constantly on the alert to anything unusual, or someone listening who didn't need to hear the conversation.

"So what do you propose we do? Lie down with the en-emy?" Olivia's palms were sweating. She was already having a hard enough time being around them without wanting to draw a gun or knife on each and every one.

"No. Tonight we sleep with friends."

CADE DRESSED QUICKLY against the chill, thankful to feel his own clothing touch his skin once again. When they had deposited the horses and taken the saddles off, he had grabbed their saddlebags and hidden them in a cluster of bushes. No one would find them unless they were looking for them, and, fortunately, his gamble had paid off.

Olivia sighed as the dress slid over her head and he smiled to himself. He turned to look at her and saw that her hands were trembling so badly she was having a hard time with the bodice of her dress.

"Let me," he whispered softy, stepping towards her and reaching out to gently cover her hands with his own. Her skin felt like ice. "We need to get you in front of a campfire as soon as possible." He frowned, wondering if her chills were entirely because of the weather, or if there were other things causing her to tremble.

"You've been so brave today," she said, allowing her hands to fall away and letting him fasten her bodice. "You move around with them as if you belong."

His eyes shot to hers. "That is the only way to not draw attention to yourself. You have to become one with the enemy."

Olivia shook her head. "I tried, but I wasn't very successful. They looked at me as a source of humor, not as a comrade."

Cade smiled down at her. "It was rather humorous when you fell to the ground and covered your head when the cannon fired."

Olivia's eyes narrowed as she looked at him. "I suppose it would be to anyone who hasn't been hit with shards of a cannon ball and lost half of their hearing."

Cade's smile quickly vanished and he felt guilty. "That isn't funny, you're right. But none of these men know that story. It did afford me the chance to speak with you, so that if anyone saw us talking again, we'd have an excuse."

She nodded and she looked up into his eyes, searching them for answers, as he finished with her bodice. The firelight glittered in her eyes. "We're going to find her, Cade," she said with strong conviction in her voice.

"I know." His smile returned. "As long as you are by my side, I have confidence we can do anything."

She looked at him with shock. "But you didn't want me to come. You wanted me to stay back there."

"I know this will come as some surprise to you, but occasionally I'm wrong. I'm glad you are with me. Two sets of eyes are definitely better to look for Bella. I just wish you weren't exposed to danger."

She flashed him a smile, something she rarely did when he first met her. But now, more and more often, he would see her with a whimsical smile, or a smile of pure joy. He liked to think he had some part in cracking open the walls around her heart. But if that was the truth, what would happen to her when he left her? *It's for her best interest that I should leave.* But a part of him nagged, telling him he was lying to himself, and would be lying to Olivia if he did leaxxve her.

His fingers lingered at the top of her bodice, and he wanted her. Right then, right there. To hell with whoever would find them. He needed her. He leaned in to kiss her and she rose on her tiptoes to meet him halfway. He moaned with pleasure and wrapped his arms around her, and suddenly realized she was still shivering.

Cursing his randy body, he pulled away from her and looked across the field. "Now comes the difficult part."

OLIVIA LOOKED OUT over the field as well, seeing the fires shining brightly on the other side. Cade grabbed her hand, forcing her attention back to him. "It's time to go. Just follow me and do exactly as I say."

Olivia nodded, and they took off, headed towards the field, moving at a slow pace, crouched down low so they stayed behind the shrubs and brush. The tall grass played to their advantage. Moving low on their stomachs, the crawled forward using their arms to drag their bodies behind them.

Every few minutes, Cade would hold up his fist, his warning for her to stop and be quiet. They would stay that way for well over a minute before, through the deductions Cade made, they moved forward once again.

The ground was cold and in some of the damp spots there were crystals of ice. While they had experienced a pleasant evening the night before, another cold wind had blown in, bringing with it freezing temperatures, and the wrath of Santa Anna.

CADE KEPT A constant eye on the Mexican camp, feeling more and more relaxed the further they moved away from them, yet, anxious at the same time, knowing he was moving away from his baby girl. He would be back for her, though, and this time he wasn't going to stop searching until he found her—or was killed first.

The last thought chilled him more than the icy ground. If something happened to him, who would take care of Bella? Where would she go? Probably back east to be with her snobbish grandparents who thought he was out of his mind to go and build a new home in wild territory. Which, if he died out here, they were probably right.

They were about one hundred yards away from the camp when they came face-to-face with two muskets pointed at them, the tips nearly touching their noses. "Looks like we found some certified Mexican scum looking for secrets about us," one man spoke, then turned and spit the juices from his tobacco on the ground.

Cade was grateful Olivia wasn't talking, and was staying put. It was best for her to go along with what he did. He raised his hands and held them over his head and, to his relief, she did the same.

"We come to you in peace. We are Texians who have been hunting Santa Anna's men for the past couple of months. We have valuable information to pass on the General Houston."

The other man attempted a laugh that was much more

like a snort. "They just want you to take them straight to the general. Well, they get points for having big—"

"Shut up, Gomez." At least now they had one name and knew who was in charge, at least, for the moment.

"Where you from?" he demanded from Caleb.

"Originally Columbus. Most recently from San Antonio."

"No one survived the attack on the Alamo, *hombre*, so you just lost your life." He cocked his gun and settled his finger on the trigger.

"Wait!" Olivia cried out desperately. "I can vouch for this man. He was badly injured by the Mexican Army and came to my home naught but a day before the battle at the Alamo. He wanted to fight so much. When he learned the Alamo had fallen, he was devastated."

"I'm sure he was, sweetheart. Now say goodbye." He spat another stream of tobacco.

Olivia stood slowly and the men became nervous, not sure whether she was the immediate threat or if Cade was. She stood tall and regal, much like he remembered seeing her the first time he had met her. And then she did something that made his heart nearly stop.

She stepped in front of the gun.

Chapter Twenty-Two

"OLIVIA!" HE GROWLED. "Get behind me."

"You're-you're one of the Torres sisters, aren't you?" The second man said stuttered.

"Yes, I'm one of the Torres sisters. And I can vouch that this man is a Texian, same as you and I, and we have been within Santa Anna's camp. We have valuable information to share with your officers."

The man holding the gun on Cade seemed mesmerized by Olivia, and Cade took full advantage of the opportunity. He grabbed the gun and shoved it backwards, hard, and the butt of the gun slammed into the young soldier's nose. He yelped in pain and Cade ripped the gun free of the man's hands and turned it on the two privates, obviously just farm boys who had wanted to see a little action but had no idea what war was really about.

Cade stood slowly and, with his free arm, he grabbed Olivia and wrapped his arm around her waist. Then, amazingly, he handed the gun back to the other soldier. "I'm sorry about your nose, but it was my only chance. Now, would you mind taking us to see Sam? General Houston, I mean."

The two men looked at both of them with wary eyes.

Finally, the second man stepped forward and lowered his rifle. "I will, sir."

Cade smiled at him and clapped one of his big hands on his shoulder. "Thank you, private. But I must ask...where did either of you get tobacco when you are so low on supplies in general?"

***

HE GRINNED AND Olivia guessed he was probably only sixteen or seventeen years old, far too young to witness the horror of war. "Not anymore, sir. We, uh, well, we commandeered one of their supply boats."

The other man next to him rolled his eyes. "What he is tryin' to say is that we stole it."

Olivia and Cade both fought hard to contain their laughter, and their eyes met, full of mirth. "I'm very glad you were able to get some vittles for the men," Cade spoke calmly, even though all he wanted to do was set his head back and laugh heartily.

"Now," he continued, "will you take us to General Houston?

"Yes. But you gotta look to be prisoners we've caught. If we just show up in camp with two strangers, we could all be shot."

"I take no issue with that," he said, and again he spoke calmly, even though his nerves were starting to fray. They could very well have killed both of them for being Mexican spies and never said anything else on the matter.

"Put your hands back up, now, and walk in front of us. If you even attempt something suspicious-like, we'll shoot you. Ya'll understand what I'm sayin'?"

"Yes," Cade and Olivia said in unison.

THEIR EYES MET and he wanted to be mad at her for placing herself in the line of fire to protect him, but her beautiful eyes glittered with hope, and he lost all desire to be mad at her. He would talk to her about it later. He had to make her understand how valuable her life was to him. He had to let her know how much he loved her.

That thought made his palms sweat more than having the gun pointed at his back. How could he tell her he loved her when he didn't have anything to offer her other than his heart? And, on top of that, she'd gain a daughter instantly. Could she love Bella the way he did? Could she be the mother that Bella needed? Or did Olivia want to only have her own children and would decline his love because of what came with it?

All along he had been thinking he had nothing to offer her if he fell in love with her. Now he realized he had many things to offer that would drive away most women. He felt as though his heart was suddenly being clamped tightly. He loved her—he needed her. And she had already professed her love to him. But he couldn't give her what she needed.

The eyes of many Texian soldiers turned on them as they walked into the camp. Olivia followed his instructions and didn't make eye contact with anyone. He did the same, though his eyes did scan over the faces quickly as he kept his head down, making sure no one could see him. And his heart began to race.

They were paraded through the camp towards one of the larger tents, and Cade did everything he could to keep his face averted from all within the camp. He couldn't afford for anyone to identify him.

One of the Texian soldiers nodded at the two men that were escorting them and held open the flap to the tent. They were pushed inside where a few men sat around a wooden table, discussing the Mexican Army's position.

"What is the meaning of this?" A voice boomed with indignation, and the two soldiers that had escorted them inside stepped forward, their chests puffed out proudly.

"We caught these here Mexican spies trying to sneak into our camp," one of them, the one chewing the tobacco, announced proudly.

Cade finally lifted his head and smile broke out across his face. "Sam," he said with warmth and respect.

A towering man with large sideburns that went all the way down his face to his cheeks turned from the table and looked at Cade, his expression at first suspicious. But it swiftly changed and a smile touched his lips.

"Cade Barret, as I live and breathe. You are a sight for sore eyes." The giant man stepped forward and held out his hand and grabbed Cade's extended one, and pulled him in to slap him on the back affectionately. "I'd heard you were either dead or stuck with the Mexicans, being tortured to death. I'm happy to see that neither are true."

The other soldier, the one who wasn't chewing tobacco, stuttered, "B-but, general he's—he's a spy for the Mexican Army!"

Sam Houston closed his eyes and pinched the bridge of his nose. Finally, he opened his eyes and looked at the soldier. "How old are you, son?" he asked, his tone not revealing whether he was mad, amused, or irritated.

"Eighteen, sir!" The young soldier stood straight and rigid, his chin lifted with pride.

"Eighteen," Sam Houston sighed. "Son, go back out with your fellow soldier here and take back your post. This time, watch for some genuine Mexican spies or soldiers."

The boy looked in disbelief at Cade, then at General Houston, then at his buddy, who was already turning and beginning to head out. He looked back at General Houston one more time, then raced after his friend out of the tent.

General Houston turned back to Cade and placed a hand on his shoulder. "It's good to see you, Cade. I'm sorry to hear about what happened to your family."

"That's one of the reasons I'm here, general."

General Houston's eyebrows lifted and his eyes finally drifted over to Olivia, who stood slightly behind Cade. He looked her up and down quickly, then let his eyes slowly drift back to Cade. "I certainly hope that you have a reason for bringing this woman into my camp."

Cade pulled off the wide-brimmed hat he wore and ran a hand through his hair, then placed the hat back on. "She's helped me to get here and if it weren't for her, I probably wouldn't even be alive."

Sam Houston stepped around him and approached Olivia with a serious expression on his face. "I owe a debt to Mr. Barret, and therefore, I owe a debt to you, Ms…"

"Torres. I am Olivia Torres."

General Houston hesitated, then a small chuckle escaped him. "You are the *fria* sister, aren't you? From San Antonio? Your reputation precedes you."

Cade saw Olivia stand a bit straighter, her pose nearly becoming rigid, and her expression hardened. "You are correct, general. I am indeed the *fria* sister."

Cade wondered what would happen if he punched the top general of the Texas Revolution. He suspected he would be hung for treason but, at that moment, seeing how Olivia's past haunted her all the way to this side of Texas made him want to force the general to apologize. But, it was foolish. Olivia had deliberately taken on that persona for more than one reason, and it was because of her choices she would be met with people who pictured her this way.

"It is an honor to meet you, General Houston," Olivia said politely, giving him a small curtsey.

Again, General Houston chuckled. "I can't remember the last time a woman treated me with such respect. Young lady, how did you end up all the way out here in the middle of this mess?"

"I brought her with me to tend to my wounds," Cade said, sliding his arm around her waist subconsciously. It was a movement that was caught by General Houston's keen eyes, but he said nothing about it. Instead, he focused on what Cade had just said.

"Wounds? I heard the Mexican Army took you prisoner, but I know nothing of your injuries."

"Colonel Ramirez is determined to see my death. He already killed my son, and he tried to kill me when I escaped them. He sliced my leg to the point that I couldn't walk. I made it away from him, but I don't know how. I made it to Olivia's house, having heard they are Texian sympathizers. If Olivia had turned me away…"

"Cade is a strong man. I only aided in his recovery."

"Sounds like you did more than that," General Houston replied. He glanced around at the men that were in his tent. "Give me some time to catch up with my friend here."

"But General Houston!" one man exclaimed.

"The Mexican Army could be on the move at any—"

"I can have five damn minutes of privacy with an old friend!" He barked at them, and without saying another word, they took off out the tent, some of them still grumbling.

General Houston sighed heavily and ran his hands over his sideburns, smoothing down some of the wild hairs that showed signs of turning grey. He turned back to the table and leaned upon it heavily, staring down at the map that had been sketched together. It showed the positions they held, as well as what they knew about the positions of the Mexican Army.

"Tell me everything," General Houston said to Cade as he poured a small cup with two fingers of whiskey, handed it to Cade, then did the same for Olivia and himself.

Olivia stared at the whiskey she held as if she had never seen it before. Then she drew a deep breath, tilted her head back, and downed the whiskey in one large gulp. The expression on her face as the whiskey burned down her throat would have been comical had they not been in the middle of a war.

"You're at a major disadvantage, here, Sam. The two men who betrayed me to the Mexican Army are camped just about one hundred feet from you. It wouldn't surprise me if they aren't sharing all of your knowledge with the Mexican forces any time they get even remotely close."

"Damn it to hell!" General Houston slammed his hands down on the table, causing the lamp to vibrate dangerously close to the edge of the table. Then he straightened his tall frame and turned to the tent flap and marched to it in just a few long strides. He jerked open the flap and barked at one of his guards who came to him and listened intently to the general's instructions.

General Houston stomped back into the tent and a few minutes later there was a commotion outside, and it sounded as if two men were starting to voice adamant protests, and then there was sudden silence. "If that was only the worst of the problems I'm dealing with," the general grumbled under his breath.

He poured himself two more fingers of whiskey and downed it quickly. Then he wearily sat down in his chair, his knees bumping the bottom of the table. "Talk to me, Cade. Give me good news."

"I wish I could, Sam. God, you don't know how much I

wish I could." Cade located another chair and urged Olivia to sit down, even though she tried to insist she was fine and could stand. The general watched them with a knowing eye.

"So, tell me what the problem is with Colonel Ramirez? What does he have against you? Killing your family wasn't enough for him?"

"That's just it, Sam. He didn't kill Bella."

The general's eyes narrowed. "What are you talking about?"

"He took her hostage, sir," Olivia spoke up. "He took her hostage to use for their cause."

"She isn't—she can't be the one... oh, God, Cade, is she the little girl they've been parading around on the trail?"

Cade squeezed his eyes closed, then finally looked at the general, his heart full of fear, anger, and the mad craze for revenge. "Yes. Yes, she is. And we've heard on the trail that he has a boy, now, too. So he's using two different children to manipulate the people to do what he wants."

"Good God, Cade... I can't even imagine what you're going through." The general leaned back in his chair, crossing his arms over his chest. "But knowing you as I do, you are doing something about it."

"Colonel Ramirez took me out of the game for a long time. A lot of time I could have spent looking for Bella. But, instead, I've been laid up, learning how to walk again."

"That would explain your limp." The general's eyes drifted over to Olivia, who had remained silent as the two men exchanged words. "So, young lady... how did you end up in this position of caretaker?"

Olivia shook her head. "I'm not a caretaker at all, sir. I'm just as eager to find Bella as Cade. I'm here because I want to be, and, yes, Cade needed some help in the beginning, but he's in fine health, now."

"That's good to hear, because I need some reliable men. These men out here are just itching to cry mutiny and take over. I know they are thirsty for revenge but, hell, there has to be a strategy. There has to be a plan."

"I wish I could ride alongside you, Sam, but I've got to find Bella. I can't let her be in the middle of a battle. Not my little girl."

The general shook his head. "I understand. Truly, I do. I wish there was a way I could force you to stay, but I know you already—you'd defy me anyway. What can I do to help you?"

"We just need a safe place to sleep for the night. I'm not comfortable sleeping with the wolves. Can we bed down over here?"

"There's not much for comfort, but, yes, you can certainly stay here. Anything for my favorite lawman."

"I'm sorry, what was that?" Olivia had been listening to the conversation, but the last sentence really grabbed her attention.

The general chuckled. "He hasn't shared with you some of his crazy stories? He's one of the best lawmen I've ever had the pleasure to work with. He always made sure there was justice for all, and fought for it harder than anyone I've ever known." General Houston looked at Cade with what appeared to be a sense of admiration.

Cade could feel Olivia's eyes boring into the back of his head and wanted to tell his good friend, even if he was the general for the revolution, to keep his trap shut. But he shouldn't be keeping secrets from Olivia, and she should hear his past. But there were other things going on that had a higher priority.

"My life as a lawman is in the past," Cade said with determination. "I'm ready to help with the revolution as our top objective."

"Having you over there when we finally engage with them could be extremely helpful for us." He hesitated, his eyes looking over Olivia and Cade. "You could start as soon as you get back, if you're able to sneak around the camp enough. You could destroy some of their ammunition, keep their saddles far away from the horses, things like that."

"We won't have to worry about that. They've used the saddles as part of their breastworks."

One of Houston's bushy eyebrows lifted at Olivia's words and he tilted his head slightly. "Ms. Olivia, are you able to help us with our map?"

Olivia stood and looked over the map in a quick review and nodded. "Absolutely. They are located in some of these little island areas that are more of a swamp between the trees than land. So it may prove an opportune area for attack."

For over an hour, Olivia and Cade shared information with General Houston, making several marks on the paper that was their "map." Finally, the general knew he needed to speak to those who were in his immediate command to lay out their plans for the following day. He gave Cade a firm handshake and embraced him briefly. "I look forward to seeing you on the other side, once we've defeated this tyrant."

Cade nodded. "Same here, Sam. It will be a glorious day when Texas gains her freedom."

General Houston then turned to Olivia and a soft smile lit up his face. "Had I known I would've had someone as beautiful as you in my camp today, I would have tried to make myself more presentable. But since you've been around this ugly fellow for the last several weeks, I'm sure I've still been a welcome change."

Olivia laughed lightly. "Of course, general. I, too, look forward to seeing you on the other side and witness the beginning of something incredibly great for the people of Texas."

He bowed over her hand and kissed the back of it lightly. "It has been an honor, Ms. Torres. And you certainly do not match the description I've heard rumored. Take care of yourself and"—he jerked his head in Cade's direction—"take care of him, please."

Olivia's smile seemed to light the tent brighter than the lamp placed on the tale, and Cade wanted to pull her out of Sam's grip and make sure everyone and anyone would know she belonged to him, and only to him. But he restrained himself, and they finally exited the tent, after Sam had already notified the two guards at his entrance to be sure they received the best campfire and at least a couple of saddles to lay their heads. It was going to be a long night.

Chapter Twenty-Three

DESPITE THE FACT that the temperatures had started to warm up some during the days, the nights were still brutally cold. Olivia could see her breath plume in the air as she exhaled and, subconsciously, she wrapped her arms around herself.

Cade came across a couple of soldiers that camped near a large fire, and used some of the few coins of American currency he still had to convince them to part with their bed rolls and a spare blanket.

They moved to an area of the camp that wasn't as congested, but still close enough to the soldiers for protection, and Cade went to work putting together a fire for them. By the time he had a good one roaring, Olivia had been able to pull together some leftover beans and bread from a nearby group of soldiers, and had also gathered them a canteen of cool water. It was by no means a feast, but it would be a welcome break to the dried beef they'd been eating the last several weeks.

Olivia gave the canteen to Cade first, and he drank from it gratefully after having to blow on the dampened tinder to get it to finally ignite. The rain was causing havoc on a lot of things, not just the traveling. Frowning down at the damp soil, he finally placed one of the blankets that had a sleeker side down and quickly placed the rolls where their heads would rest.

It was with a sigh of relief that they both sat down on a nearby stump and began to dig into the meager portions. Olivia watched Cade closely, waiting for him to provide her with an explanation for what he had revealed during their earlier conversation with General Houston, but he remained silent as he used his bread to mop up the last bits of the sauce the beans had been cooked in.

She began to feel frustrated, the same frustration she had been struggling with ever since she found out that he was much closer to General Houston than he had ever implied to her. It wasn't as if he owed her an explanation of all of his relationships, but she had thought their relationship was close enough at this point that he would have wanted to tell her about such a thing.

And then the revelation that he had been a man of the law? Maybe she hadn't asked him enough questions as they got to know each other. But he had stated to her that he had been raising cattle, and that he was about to go on his first trail drive with his own cattle this spring when he had been taken by the Mexican Army.

She glanced down at the food in her small tin bowl and realized she had eaten every last bit without even tasting it. She gathered her bowl, then took Cade's from his, and used a bit of water from the canteen to clean it out, as little as it actually needed to be cleaned concerning that they had practically licked them dry.

Exhausted beyond means, she made move towards the blankets. Cade's hand shot out and grabbed hers, pulling her back towards him. She gasped as she was spun around and landed in his lap.

His face was level with hers, and his eyes were serious. "How are you, angel? I know a lot has been thrown at you today."

Olivia closed her eyes and sighed heavily, resting her forehead against his. "That's the lightest way to say it, Cade," she whispered, bringing her hands up to thread through his hair.

She waited for several long moments, expecting him to begin explaining himself, but he was silent as they leaned against each other. Finally, Olivia couldn't take it any longer, and she pushed herself to her feet and went to the blankets. The chill from leaving Cade's arms literally and figuratively struck her. It seemed the temperature had dropped another ten degrees since she had been pulled back into his arms. And he had certainly left her cold with his lack of information.

She settled down on the soft ground and was about to wrap the blanket around her when Cade slid in tightly behind her and wrapped them up intimately. "You know, angel, it's okay to tell me when you're mad at me."

Olivia turned her head, but her hair blocked her view of his face. She spun around in his arms and lifted herself up on one elbow. "What makes you think I'm mad at you?"

He leaned in towards her. "When was the last time you

passed up the chance to kiss me goodnight?"

Olivia stared him down. "You usually fall asleep by the time I kiss you goodnight."

"You just think I'm asleep. Besides, I'm awake for all of the kissing before that," he said, arching an eyebrow at her.

"It's been a long day for both of us. I'm exhausted. Aren't you?"

"With you, angel, I will *never* be too exhausted for that."

Olivia fought the smile that was threatening to pull at the corners of her mouth. "We've also never been camped so close to others."

"Are you afraid these brave men around us are going to hear your charming laughter? Good point. I won't tickle you tonight. I don't want anyone coming around to check on us."

"Cade, how could you hold back on telling me that you are good friends with Sam Houston? And, better yet, why didn't you tell me about your experience as a lawman? Don't you think these would be things you should share with me?"

"Ah, and now the truth finally comes through."

Olivia withheld the punch curling up in her fist. "Is that your answer?"

He flashed her a smile and she began to turn back around, but he wouldn't let her, and his smile quickly turned to a look of remorse. "I'm sorry, angel. I'm sorry. I know there are some things that took you by surprise tonight."

"Why, Cade? What did I do that made you think you couldn't trust me?" Olivia couldn't stop the ache in her heart, as well as its rapid pounding as she waited for his response.

"It had nothing to do with trust. I just... well, I just couldn't have you thinking about me a certain way."

"I certainly think of you a certain way now," she said through gritted teeth, trying to hold back her anger.

Cade's expression was exacerbated, and she didn't understand why. Didn't he understand that *she* was the one that had been kept in the dark? *She* was the one that had been caught off-guard and put in a vulnerable position?

Cade shook his head. "I don't think I'm doing a very good job of explaining myself."

"Shall I get you a bitter shovel to fling around your piles of crap? What did you think was going to happen when it came to light that you are one of the best friends to the man who is leading our charge against Santa Anna? And exactly how did you expect me to react to hearing that you were a former lawman? Seriously, Cade... why keep so much from me?"

"If I told you I was a former lawman when I first met you, how would you have treated me? And then, if I followed up that statement with the fact that I am extremely close to General Sam Houston, you would have laughed at me till you cried. You still might. There are very few people who know my background, but I will share it with you if you want me to."

Olivia glared at him. "All of this time—all of this time that we've been together, that you've told me about your life, that you've told me about your children, and your time out east... All of this time, and you neglected to include this information because you were worried that I would laugh at you? That's the most ridiculous thing I've ever heard."

Cade propped himself on his elbow so he was closer to eye level with her. "It's not that you would just laugh at me. It's that you would laugh at me because you wouldn't believe me. You would think I'm a complete fake, fabricating stories to garner your help and, even better, your attention. And, I didn't know how much I could trust you, either."

"You didn't—you didn't know how—" Olivia sputtered and her nails dug into the skin of her palms as she fought the incredible urge to punch him. "I saved your life. I have spent countless hours trying to make sure you lived. And you didn't know if you could trust me?"

Cade closed his eyes briefly, as if trying to maintain his composure. "You forget that you were a stranger to me from the beginning. I knew you were an ally to the Texians, but that was all I knew. And considering the fact that I had just been betrayed by a man I considered a true friend and loyal Texian, you can surely understand why I was so hesitant to trust anyone."

Olivia wanted to stay angry with him, but what he was saying made complete and perfect sense. He was right to be wary and cautious given what he had gone through. "But still, Cade, why couldn't you at least have shared with me that you are a lawman?"

"Was. It's in my past." He rubbed his eyes with his thumb and forefinger. "I don't like to talk about it much," he said, lowering his hand and looking her in the eyes. "I was the sheriff for the small town we lived near—Columbus,

Texas. I enjoyed it thoroughly."

Olivia was confused. "So why do you not like to talk about it?"

"What do you think when you learn that someone was a sheriff, or a Texas Ranger, or any representation of the law?"

"I think that person is strong, brave... and can protect me and my loved ones."

"But I failed at that, don't you see? I couldn't even protect my whole family. How can I protect an entire town? I know they've replaced me by now, and I pray for the person who did. The weight you carry on your shoulders—the responsibility..." His voice trailed off.

"Cade, what happened to your family was because you were betrayed. It has nothing to do with you being a man of the law."

"Yet you will look at me differently. You will think of me as greater than I really am. Because there is a sense of responsibility that comes along with carrying a badge. But I no longer have that badge, Olivia. I lost it the day I lost my son because I couldn't protect him. I lost it the day my daughter was kidnapped. I am no longer a man of the law. I'm a man seeking revenge, and there is nothing lawful about that,"

Olivia finally understood. And her heart ached for him. She reached up and placed her hand along his cheek, and he held it there firmly, the turned his head and kissed her palm.

His eyes looked at hers beseechingly. "You understand now, don't you? You understand why I didn't tell you everything?"

"I understand. I just wish you had told me sooner and

that I didn't have to learn this way. I wish you would have trusted me sooner."

"I trusted you. But how could I even bring up the topic without it seeming pompous or arrogant? No, this has worked for the best. And now you carry all of my dark secrets. I'm terrified to learn all of yours." He teased, a slight smile touching his lips.

She shook her head. "I've always thought you are pompous and arrogant, so if you had told me all of these things, it wouldn't have made me think any differently about you."

Cade chuckled and wrapped his arm around her waist, hauling her closer to him. "We're going to find her tomorrow, angel. I can feel it."

Olivia pulled his head to hers and kissed him passionately, her lips moving eagerly over his, and he moaned in pleasure. Slowly he rolled her, his hand cupping the back of her head, until she was flat on her back and he lay halfway on top of her.

He broke away from their heated kiss to her disappointment, but moved on to press kisses to her jawline, and slowly moved down to her neck. She arched her neck, giving him greater access, and affording him a better view of the mounds of her breasts already peaked hard and ready for his touch.

His lips moved down to her collar bone, and she sighed with pleasure. She was going to let him take the lead on this one and just lie back and enjoy. She would just enjoy the sweet caresses of his fingers on her body and relax in the warm, comfortable bedding...

TEASINGLY, CADE KISSED her collarbone, then nipped it lightly with his teeth. But when it didn't illicit any response from her, his eyes darted to her face and he let out a low chuckle. His angel had fallen asleep.

REVELRY SOUNDED CLOSE to four in the morning of April twenty-first on the Texian camp's side. Cade and Olivia were already in the grass, carefully making their way back to the Mexican camp. They cringed slightly as the drummer marched through the Texians camp, rousing the slumbering soldiers. But he made sure to steer clear of General Houston's tent, as their leader had specifically requested to be awoken later in the morning so he could finally catch up on some much needed slumber.

They reached the Mexican Army's camp before the soldiers had even stirred. They quickly made it to the spot where they had the white uniforms stored, but Olivia stopped before she donned the garments.

"Why should I wear this?" she whispered. "There are several women moving in and about the camp, tending to the soldier's needs and bringing the food to them. I can do that."

Cade continued pulling on his uniform, but his brow was furrowed with thought. Finally, he nodded his head. "That is probably for the best. It was obvious yesterday that you were unable to do some of the heavy labor, and it could cause too many questions. This will be less suspicious."

Together they let the small, cluster of shrubs that had served as their dressing room and crept back to camp. They nearly jumped out of their skin with the revelry suddenly started to play for the Mexican side, nearly a full hour later than the Texians.

But the tensions in the camp were high as the Mexican Army seemed certain the Texians were going to attack by daylight. Olivia busied herself refilling canteens for the soldiers, while Cade moved through the camp slowly, his eyes constantly seeking tiny legs and feet and shiny brown hair.

Olivia listened to the various conversations among the men in the camp, and they didn't understand why they weren't attacking, instead of having to wait for the other side. They also bragged amongst themselves that they would take down this insurgence the same way they had destroyed General Fannin's men and the men of the Alamo. She made sure their canteens held a bit more dirt and grit.

The morning hours waned on, and the camp became even more restless. But Santa Anna continued to order them to be on the lookout... not just for the Texians, but also for General Cos and his men who were due to arrive soon.

Word that General Cos was coming disheartened Cade and Olivia, especially when they learned the large number of men he was bringing with him. By midmorning rumors circulated that Cos was going to appear, leading hundreds of men to join Santa Anna. If the rumors were true, Santa Anna would have nearly fifteen-hundred men compared to General Houston's eight hundred. They would be outnumbered nearly two to one.

Cade and Olivia continued moving through the camp, performing as the other soldiers and women did, keeping their heads down, though. They couldn't afford to make eye contact with anyone who might recognize them. Fortunately, Cade wore a hat that covered his startling blue eyes, one of his defining features, and Olivia wore her hair down instead of in a bun, and it would be virtually impossible for anyone to recognize her without that.

Around midmorning, Cade and Olivia snuck off into a secluded oak copse where they embraced briefly, offering each other comfort. "I haven't seen her, Cade. We're going to have to find a way to check the tents."

"That's going to be near impossible with all of the officers going in and out. Unless we come up with plan to explain why we are sneaking in to those tents—"

Suddenly the atmosphere around them seemed to change. There was a lightness, an almost cheerfulness. Cos's men had arrived.

Chapter Twenty-Four

SANTA ANNA WAS addressing his troops, dressed in his fine uniform, his decorated hat upon his head. He was magnificent to look at, Olivia had to admit. He was a striking figure. But his eyes were cold and heartless, and his words were hard.

In Spanish, he told the troops that the Texians were too afraid to attack them, and that they hid just across the field of grass, hunkered down like little children. He told them that the new "government" the Texians had established had fled in terror when they heard that General Santa Anna was headed their way.

He bragged that his magnificent cavalry had already driven back the Texians, and that they were trapped, with no way to escape. Victory was theirs to rejoice in! And since the Texians were such cowards, the Mexican Army deserved some much needed rest and relaxation as soon as they had finished their lunch. And if the Texians didn't make a move on them by dusk, they would take matters into their own hands.

He praised them for all the success they had already had, and he talked about their incredible overtaking of the Alamo, and how he had made certain that none of the traitors had survived. Olivia's stomach clenched, and the image of Lorenzo's laughing face flashed through her mind. How was Angie ever going to raise her child in this harsh world without a father?

Then, unbelievably, his dismissed them, telling them to get their food and take a *siesta*. Cade and Olivia looked at each other in disbelief. How could they possibly be taking a nap at a time like this? Their enemy was just on the other side of a field, potentially preparing to attack at any moment.

Olivia looked back at Cade with excitement in her eyes. "This is our chance, Cade!"

"What are you talking about? They're all going to be in their tents now."

"And they will be asleep. Or, well, or distracted by the women that are here to entertain them. We can at least take the chance of peeking into tents to see if we can find Bella. It is worth the risk—now more than ever."

Cade shook his head and looked at Olivia with disbelief. "I can't let you put yourself in such a risky position. I just can't let you—"

Olivia placed her fingers over his mouth. "I'm not asking your permission. It's what I'm doing. You have the choice to join me or not."

She turned and began to walk off, but Cade grabbed her and pulled her back close to him. "Olivia…" His fingers ran through her hair and trailed down her face. "I can't lose you. I need you."

Olivia's heart pounded. Did he mean what he said? Did

he really need her? "Cade, I love you. I will always love you. No matter what happens."

He shook his head. "You shouldn't. You have no reason to love me. But, God, I'm so grateful that you do." He dropped his head to hers and kissed her deeply, his hands cupping her face.

When they pulled apart, they were both breathing heavily. Olivia caught Cade's hands and slowly pulled them away from her face and had the distinct feeling that he was telling her goodbye. And she realized suddenly that he actually might be telling her goodbye in reality. Once they found Bella, he would return to his ranch in Columbus and would begin his life all over again.

She fought the tears that burned the back of her eyes. "We must split up. It will give us a better chance to find her."

"No, I cannot let you wander around these men without protection. You know very well how dangerous they can be." His face had hardened, and his eyes were intent upon hers.

"Cade, we have very little time, and you know it. Let's go find Bella."

Cade squeezed his eyes shut and he pulled her to him once more and pressed a kiss to her forehead. "Be careful, angel."

Olivia pulled back and did her best to give him a strong smile. "Of course. You too."

She turned away from him quickly so that he wouldn't see her tears. She craved to hear him say the words "I love you," but she was wishing for too much. His world revolved around his daughter, as it should, and she didn't play a role in his future.

She moved out of their secluded area slowly and blended in with the crowd and Cade did the same a short time after her. She moved towards the tents that were at the far end of the encampment to begin her search and rapidly wiped at her face to remove her tears. She wasn't known to cry, and the fact that she was doing so because of a man made her angry with herself. She had constantly told her sisters to never let a man get to their heart because he would have the power to crush it. And she had done exactly that.

Several of the soldiers had found a place where they could lie down and immediately fell asleep. It was obvious they were exhausted. Olivia actually had to step around several of them as she made her way to the farthest tents.

She was silent as she pulled back tent flaps and peeked inside. Fortunately, most of the tents were small, and she was able to quickly scan them. Some held sleeping men, others held men that were engaged in activities she had never seen before with some of the women who had joined them.

But there was no sign of Bella.

Olivia prayed Cade was having more success. She prayed he already found Bella and was moving her as far away from this danger as possible. Would he try to find Olivia and get her away from the battle that loomed, also?

In her heart she hoped he would, but her mind told her the logical thing to do was to flee as quickly as possible. He needed to get his daughter to safety, and he knew Olivia well enough to know she could hold her own.

The day wore on and the sun moved across the sky and, yet, Olivia could not find Bella. But there were so many tents and so many places where a child could be hidden, she could be at it for days and still not find her. After searching through a small storage area, Olivia stepped out into the sunlight and stretched. From the position of the sun, she figured it must be close to three o'clock in the afternoon, if not later. She looked at the next tent, drew a deep breath and moved onwards.

Before she had made it to the tent, the sound of rifles firing pierced the silence, and there came several shouts and the screams of men—screams of anger, screams of battle, screams of pain. The camp came alive in a rush, but it wasn't fast enough.

Shouts of "Remember the Alamo!" and "Remember Goliad!" rang through the air, along with the rifle volley, and it was rapidly moving in her direction. Cade! She thought desperately. Cade was near there, far closer than she, and he could be hurt. She hiked her skirts up and began to run towards the last place she had seen him when suddenly horses flew over the breastworks, and the Texians fired their weapons on the Mexican Army.

She skidded to a halt and dashed inside one of the tents, seeking some form of protection. God only knew what was going to happen now with the battle in full swing. She turned and peeked out the flap of the tent and saw the Mexican Army in all states of attire grabbing rifles and frantically trying to shoot and then prime and fill with gun powder again. But they were getting mowed down by the

Texians, until even the Texians were having a hard time reloading their weapons and began to use them entirely for the purpose of beating at the heads of their enemy.

A sound came to her over the bedlam, a soft sound and she concentrated hard to hear it better. It sounded like... like someone was crying. Olivia whirled around and her eyes searched the tent, and she saw that it was more than likely an officer's tent, since the cot was slightly nicer, and there was room for a desk.

And there was someone underneath that desk, huddled into a small bundle, crying into her knees. Olivia's heart was pounding, and she slowly kneeled down to get a better look. Could it possibly be...

The small girl huddled under the desk had gorgeous sandy brown hair and was rocking back and forth, her soft sobs bringing tears to Olivia's eyes. "Isabella?" she asked softly.

The girl hesitated in her motions, but refused to lift her head yet. "Bella, I'm here with your father. We're here to take you away from this terrible place."

She lifted her head just barely and Olivia had to hold back her gasp. Cade's incredible blue eyes stared back at her, frightened, yet hopeful. She hadn't realized how young the child really was, and she wondered at the girl's fortitude to make it as far as she had.

Olivia climbed underneath the desk to huddle with Bella. "Everything's going to be okay now, Bella. Your father and I are here. You are safe."

With a sob that was louder than her earlier ones, she

jumped forward and into Olivia's arms and held onto her so tightly, Olivia wondered if she was going to choke her. Then she pulled back, looked at Olivia, and with tiny hands she smoothed Olivia's hair away from her face.

"Are you my Mama?" She was still at the age where forming her words was difficult, but it was clear enough to Olivia what the girl was asking. And she had no idea how to answer.

However, her lack of answer seemed to be all that Bella needed. She threw herself against Olivia, wrapping her small arms tightly around her neck, and settled her head under Olivia's chin. She had light hiccups in lieu of the sobs that had been racking her tiny frame earlier.

"Scared," she whispered, curling tightly into Olivia's lap.

Olivia searched for the words to say. She lightly ran her hand through the girl's incredibly smooth and shiny hair, surprised that she had been cared for so well given the conditions they were under. Then again, they wanted her to be presentable to get the people to give up information about the Texians movement.

"Shh." She soothed Bella. "Everything is going to be okay now. You're safe with me and your papa."

Bella pulled back and looked at her with wide eyes. "Papa? Papa is here?"

Olivia smiled at her through the tears that she couldn't seem to control. "Yes. Yes, Papa is here."

"Mama, why you cry?" She used her tiny fingers to wipe at Olivia's face, and Olivia's heart clenched.

Dear God, if she could be this child's mother, she would

be immeasurably happy. But it wasn't to be. But Cade was going to take care of her, and would soon enough find a woman near Columbus that would be a good fit for him and for Bella.

"I'm just so happy to see you, sweetheart," she said, her voice rough with her tears. She couldn't resist pressing a kiss to her soft cheek. "We've missed you so much."

"Where Papa?"

"He's close, baby, he's real close. We just have to wait until it is safer to go find him."

"Boom, boom," Bella said, covering her ears as the cannons exploded, and she hunkered down in Olivia's lap again. Olivia hovered over her, wrapping her arms around Bella, trying to make sure that, should any stray bullets come through, Olivia would be struck before Bella.

She rocked her back and forth for several minutes, whispering prayers to God and calling upon every saint she could remember to watch over them as the cannons burst and the bullets whizzed around.

Slowly, very slowly, the sounds traveled further away from them. Olivia held her breath for a long moment, and realized the fighting has moved away from the camp. She looked down at Bella and smiled. "We're going to go find Papa, now. Won't that be wonderful?"

Bella's tears had been fading, and her smile struck Olivia at how much it was like Cade's. It was as if she was the feminine version of Cade—and a much prettier one, too. But the similarities were striking, and every time she looked at Bella she was reminded that she was about to say goodbye to them both.

She gathered the young child tightly in her arms and slid out from underneath the desk. Bella wrapped her arms around Olivia's neck and her legs around her waist, making it very obvious that she was going to stay stuck on Olivia for as long as she possibly could.

Olivia didn't mind the loving embrace and held Bella tightly as she pushed herself completely out from under the desk and managed a less than graceful attempt at standing with the weight of Bella pulling her in ways she had never experienced before.

A sense of disappointment hit Olivia suddenly. This would be something she would be a pro at if she was a mother. She would have the knowledge of how to shift her own body weight to pick up a child, to carry the baby on her hip, to provide for a baby in every way a mother was supposed to provide.

But there wouldn't be another moment like this for Olivia. She would hold more babies, she was certain, as Angie and Serena moved into that phase of their lives, but she would always come second. Because, without Cade, there was no future of being a mother ahead for her.

Bella lay her head down on Olivia's shoulder, and Olivia could feel her Bella's breath blowing sweetly across her skin. She closed her eyes for several long moments, just enjoying the situation.

Angie and Serena would try to convince her there was another man out there for her, but she knew without a shadow of doubt Cade was her soulmate, and anyone else wouldn't be able to receive her full love, and that wouldn't be fair for them. She really was going to die an old spinster.

The thought brought a smile to her face. At least the gossips in town would have enough to talk about for years once she got back since they would be able to speculate on why she had disappeared so long from the *cocina*.

But her mission, at the moment, was to get Bella back into the safety of Cade's arms. She didn't want to go through the camp, because she was quite certain the carnage was not something Bella should see.

Thinking quickly, she grabbed a letter opener from the desk and stabbed the canvas at the back of the tent and made a long cut down. Dropping the letter opener, she cautiously peeled back the canvas, and was relieved to see that there were no soldiers nearby.

Carefully she slid through the slit that she made, holding Bella to her chest. She looked both ways, but there was no sign of any soldier. She had to get to the Texians. That was the only thought running through her head. The Texians meant safety and also more than likely meant Cade would be there as well. Unless he was still looking for Bella, or he was hurt…

Olivia pushed the negative thoughts from her mind, and concentrated on the task at hand. From where she was currently positioned, the Texian camp would be ahead and to her right. A light drizzle had started, and she wished she had grabbed a blanket from the officer's tent before leaving, but she was too far gone now.

She could hear random gunshots in the distance, and

Bella tightened her arms around her. "It's alright, Bella. They're far away now. They can't hurt you."

Olivia forced her feet to move through the thick mud, rounding around to the other side of the tents where she could finally see the field that lay between the Mexican and Texian Army. To her right were the breastworks that had been built—but they stood no more. The amount of destruction and death in the Mexican camp was unbelievable. And it wasn't all men from the Mexican Army that lay on the ground. She recognized several Texian faces.

"Bella, you need to close your eyes, now," Olivia said, though her voice was quivering. "I need you to keep your eyes closed until I tell you to open them. Can you play that game with me?"

"Yes, Mama."

Olivia felt as if her heart was being ripped from her chest every time Bella called her "Mama." How was she going to explain this to Cade?

Cade. Just the very thought of him made her want to run across the camp in search of him. But she had to be careful. She had to make sure that all was safe for Bella before she did anything.

Moving slowly, she made her way through camp and watched closely for any movement. But the encampment was empty, and there was death and destruction all around them. She began to move quicker, ready to get away from the sights and smells, and didn't want to risk the chance that Bella could open her eyes and see some of the carnage.

Finally, she cleared the camp and was out in the open

field that divided the two camps. She just had to make it to the other side. With determined strides, she began to cross, forcing her legs to move when all she wanted to do was fall to her knees and scream. Would she find the same carnage in the Texian camp? Had the Texians fallen to the Mexican Army with the overwhelming size of their camp? Or had the Texians succeeded with their surprise attack?

From the corner of her eye, she saw movement and she instantly crouched down in the thick grass. "Stay quiet, Bella, sweetheart, stay quiet."

"I will, Mama," Bella whispered, and Olivia couldn't help but plant several soft kisses to Bella's cheek as she watched the movement. In the afternoon light, Olivia began to make out the images of the men walking along, and her heart jumped into her throat.

She stood and began to run, as best she could with Bella in her arms, towards the men. "Cade!" she cried at the top of her voice.

A few hundred yards away from her, one of the taller figures stopped and looked in her direction, then he turned back briefly to the other men and they all began to race towards her.

"Cade!" she cried again, her elation and excitement nearly unbearable.

"Shh. Mama, you said quiet."

Olivia laughed at the innocent remark, but was suddenly drawn up short by a man who stepped out of the tall grass from behind one of the knolls and approached her at a deadly pace. He was too fast—there would be no way to escape him.

Cade was still advancing, though he was still too far away to help. "Bella, I need you to stand," Olivia ordered quickly, and Bella did exactly as she was told and Olivia rushed towards the nearest tent, but was yanked to a halt by the man grabbing a handful of her hair and yanking her backwards. She withheld her cry of pain and placed shoved Bella behind her as she felt the him moving around her.

Colonel Ramirez stepped directly in front of her and she realized he was the officer that had been hunting for Cade at their *cocina*, and was also the one that had bragged about slicing his leg. Which meant... dear God, this man had killed Cade's son.

Olivia kept Bella securely behind her and faced their enemy with determination. She was not going to let him have Bella. Never.

"Olivia!" Cade yelled, coming over one of the small hills and getting incredibly close to them.

Colonel Ramirez turned quickly, pulling his pistol from the back of his pants. "Stay where you are, traitor!"

Olivia kneeled down quickly, hoping she would find some sort of weapon to use to defend them. Her hand wrapped around the muzzle of a bayonet and she lifted it, rapidly checking it for ammo. Both rounds were spent.

The colonel turned back to her, saw what she held in her hands, and shook his head in disapproval. "*Senorita* Torres, it is so unfortunate that we should meet under these conditions."

Olivia bared her teeth at him in a false attempt at a

smile. "The battle is over, colonel. Go back to your troops and leave us alone."

"Back to my…" He gave a loud bark of laughter then returned his gaze to her. "You don't even know what has happened, do you?"

Olivia continued staring him down, keeping Bella nearly hidden behind her skirts. She wouldn't give him the satisfaction of an answer or even guess at what he was referring to.

He laughed again, but there was no mirth in the sound. "You won, you little fool. You and those heathens that call themselves 'Texians' have captured most of the army, at least the few left that they didn't kill."

Olivia's heart was pounding rapidly out of fear from what this man might do, as well as elation. They had beaten Santa Anna. That meant they were finally free and the war was finally over. "Then you should be a prisoner as well, shouldn't you? Leave us be. Run and try to escape if you wish, but leave us be."

"Only a coward would try to escape. But I can at least kill a couple more of you traitors before I am taken prisoner."

"Colonel Ramirez!" Cade shouted, having come down the slope of the hill while the colonel had been distracted by Olivia. "Your issue is with me. Face me like a real man and we can settle this once and for all."

The colonel held the gun on Olivia as he turned sideways to face Cade. "I'll get to you soon, traitor. But you're going to watch your woman and daughter die first."

Cade began to step forward, his face full of rage, but the

colonel pulled back the hammer on his pistol, making Cade stop instantly. "Don't rush this for me," he said lightly. "I want to enjoy killing all of you. Even your friends who stand behind you will die by either my gun or my blade today. It should have happened far sooner."

Olivia couldn't let him kill Cade and certainly not Bella. Holding the bayonet in her hand she lunged at him, a growling scream in her throat. Startled, he stumbled backwards and she lunged for his gun.

The struggle between the two of them was difficult, and Olivia bit down hard on his hand, hard enough to taste blood and he roared in pain. From the corner of her eye she saw Cade rushing towards them, and realized she could not let him gain control of his gun again, for he would surely kill Cade.

She struggled with him, keeping a firm hold on the bayonet. And then a gunshot tore through the silence.

Chapter Twenty-Five

CADE RAN THROUGH the muddy field as fast as he could to get to Olivia and Bella. He had nearly fallen to his knees earlier when he had seen Bella alive and strong, and the relief and joy had nearly been overwhelming.

But now Olivia was fighting for her life, and for Bella's, from a madman intent on destroying his family. Time seemed to stand still when the sound of the pistol shot pierced the air. Olivia and the colonel continued wrestling for the gun, before Olivia finally gained control of it. With hands that shook she backed away from him, holding the gun pointed at her.

But she had already wounded him dearly. As they had struggled, she slammed the sharp, jagged edge of the bayonet into his neck, and he was carefully trying to pull it out as he stared at Olivia with pure hatred.

But it was more of a mistake for him to pull it out, for when he did so, his blood began squirting from the wound, and he tried desperately to staunch the flow of blood with his fingers, but it was too little, too late. His face grew incredibly pale, and Olivia turned quickly to Bella, blocking her view and smiling down at her.

"Now, you see? That bad man can't get to you anymore. It's all over." But Bella didn't seemed calmed by the news. Instead, she was staring at Olivia's dress. Olivia looked down and saw blood all over her. "Bella, I'm fine. That man just bled a lot."

"Bella!" Cade was running to them again, but it didn't seem as if his legs could move fast enough.

"Papa? Papa, papa!" Bella took off for Cade, and when they reached each other, Cade swept Bella up in his arms, lifting her high, then bringing her in for a tight hug. "My dear, sweet Bella. Are you okay? You weren't hurt were you?"

Bella smiled at him, then wiped at his cheeks. "Why crying, Papa? I'm okay."

He hadn't realized he had started crying, but it didn't surprise him. The joy pouring through his heart couldn't be contained. "I'm just so very, very happy to have you back, sweetheart. You don't know how much I've missed you."

Bella stopped wiping at his cheeks and frowned at him. "Scratches. Papa, your face has thorns."

Cade laughed through his tears. "Papa needs to shave, and will do so very, very soon." He kissed the top of her head, her cheek, her neck, and inhaled her sweet, youthful scent. She had grown so much since he had last seen her. It had been nearly three months. Never again, he vowed to himself.

Suddenly, she was wiggling in his arms, trying to get down. "Papa, down!" She grunted in frustration and reluctantly he set her on the ground, but was startled when she took off and started running away from him. "Bella!"

"Mama! Mama!"

She nearly made Olivia fall when she threw her arms around her from behind, and Olivia turned, a beautiful smile on her face as she gazed down at the child that was his only life.

"Mama, up." Bella had her arms extended out to her and Olivia instantly reached down and picked her up, moving her to her hip in a way that seemed almost natural to her. "Don't leave us, Mama."

Olivia's eyes jerked to Cade's, and he was doing his best to hide his surprise and disbelief. Bella had never been warm with other women that they met in town or a neighbor from a nearby ranch visiting. Instead she had been shy and reserved, and had stayed very close to Cade or her brother.

And for her to call Olivia "Mama," he was completely stunned. He moved towards them, a half smile on his face. "Were you trying to leave us?" Cade asked softly. "Now that I have Bella, have you decided all is finished?"

Olivia's eyes searched his. "I wanted to give you a private moment together. I will never leave without saying good bye." She closed her eyes and swallowed hard. "Bella, you are heavier than I thought." She went to her knees and set Bella on her feet and smiled at her.

Cade kneeled down next to them and watched Olivia with something close to amazement. "Bella has never called anyone 'Mama.' What happened between the two of you?"

"Mama made the bad man go away," Bella answered.

Cade smiled at Bella, then looked back at Olivia. "I can't thank you enough for everything you've done. You've saved me and now Bella. You truly are an angel."

He leaned forward and wrapped a hand at the back of her head and pressed his lips to hers, grateful beyond words to have his daughter back in his arms, along with the love of his life. He pulled back and tasted something coppery in his mouth. Blood?

He looked at Olivia and she had a small drop of blood running down the corner of her mouth, but she seemed unaware of it. "I'm so happy you have Bella back. You can move forward with your life now."

"Olivia, are you hurt somewhere?" he demanded urgently, but her eyes had a glazed look as she hugged Bella.

"I love you, Bella," she said softly.

When she turned to him, there were tears in her eyes. "I love you, too. I will forever."

"Angel, where are you hurt. Talk to me, please!" His eyes drifted down to her bloodied dress and he saw that the blood had spread even further. He felt along her dress until she gasped, and he could tell she was trying to restrain her cry of pain. "God, Olivia, you've been shot. That bastard shot you."

Cade stripped out of his shirt rapidly and pressed it up against Olivia's wound, and he was scared at how fast it was getting red with her blood. His eyes searched the horizon where his friends had been, and they were slowly moving towards them. "Get help!" he yelled towards them. "She's been shot! Get help!"

Two of the men turned and took off towards the Texian camp. "Papa, what's wrong with Mama?" Bella asked, her eyes brimming with tears.

Cade didn't know how to answer her. Olivia was starting to lean against him, and his eyes jerked from Bella back to Olivia, and her eyelids were drooping. "I love you," she whispered again.

"Angel, stay with me, please. I can't lose you. Please, stay awake."

But she had no control after the massive loss of blood, and she fell limply in his arms. He lifted her quickly and looked down at Bella who now had tears falling down her face. "Everything is going to be okay," he said, though he didn't know which one of them he was trying to reassure. "Just stay close by me. We have to get her some help." And, with that, he took off as fast as he could across the muddy ground towards the Texian camp. Dear God, let everything be okay.

Pain. Blinding, white hot pain. It consumed her and wouldn't allow her to breathe. Dear God, why was she in such horrible pain?

She tried to open her eyes, but her lids felt weighted down. She needed to see what was going on. She tried to breathe deeply, but every attempt only seemed to make the pain worse.

"Easy, Olivia, easy. Help is on the way."

The voice was very familiar, but she was struggling to put a name to the voice. She fought against the darkness pulling at her and was able to gradually open her eyes slightly, and she would have gasped had her body allowed it.

"Lorenzo?" Her voice sounded odd—strained and breathless.

He smiled at her warmly and kneeled down so he was closer to her. "You're going to be alright, Olivia. Fatima and Gabriella are helping you, but it is going to hurt."

Olivia's mind raced. Fatima was her aunt, and Gabriella was her cousin. But they both lived in Corpus Christi. Why were they here? Or had she lost a giant chunk of time and been moved to Corpus?

"Why are they here? How are *you* here?" The image of his face in front of her was spinning, but she wasn't going to let her eyes close until she had answers.

He picked up one of her hands and held it gently between his two large ones. "Your sisters got word to Fatima about where you were headed, and they knew there would be the need for medical help should a battle occur. They've been tending to our wounded soldiers until you... well, until you were brought to us. They're gathering what they need to tend to you now.

"As for me... Bowie sent me on a special mission just days before the Alamo fell. I was able to sneak out and past Santa Anna's troops and began on a hunt for General Houston to come to our aide. By the time I made it, the Alamo had fallen. I stayed on with General Houston, and I know Angie has been worried, but I haven't been able to get word to her. I can't wait to see her."

His image swirled a little faster and she felt the darkness

pulling at her but she still had so many questions. "Fatima…"

"She's on her way, Olivia. She's going to be with you very soon. Just stay strong and hold in there. We know how strong you are."

"Cade…" She managed to say before the darkness swallowed her.

WHAT SHE HAD thought was pain before was nothing like this. She heard someone sobbing and realized it was her own sobs. She forced her eyes open, and Gabby was staring down at her, wiping at her face with a towel.

The sight of her cousin's sweet, innocent face helped lessen the pain, but not enough. "Gabby," she cried, "Gabby, make it stop, please."

Gabby's usually cheerful face was pinched with concern. "Mama, she's getting worse."

Olivia's eyes turned slowly and she saw Aunt Fatima leaning over her from the other side of the bed and she tried to reach for her. "*Tia*," she whispered. Her aunt, or *tia*, looked up at her with eyes full of compassion.

"It will all be alright, *hija*, just try to stay still."

There was a stabbing pain in her side and she couldn't stop herself from crying out.

Gabby looked over at her mother. "She's getting worse, Mama."

Fatima frowned deeply. "You know what must be done."

The pain was burning, stabbing, consuming. "Please, *tia*, please… make it stop." But Fatima was focused on something else, concentrating hard on whatever she was trying to achieve.

"Do as I said, Gabby," Fatima ordered curtly when Olivia began to twist to avoid the pain.

Olivia's eyes drifted back to Gabby, and she saw Gabby pouring a liquid onto a cloth, and she suddenly knew what she was about to do. "No, Gabby, please don't. I don't want—"

Gabby placed the cloth over Olivia's face and Olivia felt desperate to breathe as she was assaulted by the smell of the chloroform and tried desperately to avoid it, turning her head from one side to the next. But then the tent went out of focus and she sobbed one last time before giving in to the darkness once more.

✂

THERE WAS SUCH a deep silence around her, Olivia wondered if she was dead. Was this what it felt like to die? To be surrounded by silence and no feeling, no knowledge of anything around her—to just float?

The gentle sound of trickling water greeted her ears, and she jumped slightly when a cool cloth pressed against her forehead. Her quiet, still existence had been disrupted. She opened her eyes slowly and her eyes felt gritty and dry.

Gabby smiled down at Olivia, pressing a rag against her forehead and face, and Olivia realized the feel of the cool cloth actually felt good. "Gabby." She tried to speak, but her voice was just a hoarse rasp.

"Hi," Gabby said, "I've missed you so much. I just wish I wasn't seeing you like this."

Olivia tried to look around, but found herself too weak to even turn her head. "What happened?"

"You don't remember? Well, we've seen this with many patients who have gone through something as terrible as you have." Gabby smoothed the cool cloth down Olivia's temples. "You were shot, Olivia. It's a true miracle that you are alive."

Olivia stared at the tent ceiling. "Where are we?"

"We're still at San Jacinto. You haven't been asleep for long. You were only shot yesterday."

"The Texians?"

Gabby smiled broadly. "Enjoying victory as much as they can. They still haven't found Santa Anna… that coward is hiding somewhere around here. He couldn't have gone far. But the Mexican Army lost soundly. We are finally a free republic."

Olivia tried to smile, and hoped it came through that way, as her energy was still so low. "Where's your mother?"

"She's tending to a few of the Texian soldiers that were injured. We were expecting to come out here to help them. We never expected that we would be treating you, as well. Just wait until your sisters find out what you did."

"Lorenzo…"

Gabby's smile grew brighter. "He's already on the road back to San Antonio. He can't wait to see Angie."

This time Olivia was certain that her smile came through. "He is going to be very surprised."

Gabby cocked her head in curiosity, her eyes searching Olivia's face. "Why is that? Angie didn't give up on him, did she? Oh, he will be devastated if she is with another man."

Olivia felt sleep pulling at her again, but she had so many more questions to ask, so she fought it off with all of her ability. "You will find out soon enough. You and your mother will be coming to our house in a few months to welcome a new addition to the family."

Gabby nearly squealed in glee. "There's going to be a new baby in the Torres home!"

Olivia's thoughts turned to something less pleasant. "Have many of the soldiers left?"

"Some, yes. They were eager to get back to their old lives. Several have stayed to watch what happens once Santa Anna is found. Can you believe he is such a coward? Well, I shouldn't be surprised. It is the type of behavior we should expect of such a horrible man."

Olivia had stopped listening when Gabby had said that some of the Texians had let to return to their old lives. Cade was gone. And Bella, too. She was certain of it. She never would have thought it possible to fall in love with someone as deeply as she had with Cade. The loss of him tore at her heart and made her ache.

Just like her father, Bella had stolen her heart as well. To know that both of them were gone was devastating. They had already essentially said their goodbyes. And he wanted to get back to a normal life. And he very well might know that her injury was fatal.

Her eyes refocused on Gabby. Sweet Gabby, only fourteen, nearly the same age as her sister Serena, already did so much to help her mother care for the sick and serve as a midwife. She was wise beyond her years. She was wringing out the cloth again to place on Olivia's forehead, but she was biting her lower lip, something she usually only did when she was anxious about something.

"Am I going to die?" Olivia asked bluntly, needing to know the truth.

Gabby's head whipped around to look at her, her eyes wide. "Olivia! Don't think such things. You have me and mother here to help you."

"You didn't answer my question," Olivia replied, feeling the ache in her heart easing.

It was best that Cade had left with Bella. He shouldn't have to live through her death, and shouldn't have to explain it to Bella, either.

"You need to save your energy, Olivia. You need to concentrate on healing."

Olivia sighed and closed her eyes. Without Cade and Bella, she was better off dead anyway.

Chapter Twenty-Six

C ADE SAT BESIDE Olivia's bed, holding her hand in both of his, staring at her pale, lifeless face. If only he had noticed the wound sooner, if only he had gotten her to help sooner... But he couldn't turn back time. And now she was dying, and he hadn't even been able to tell her he loved her.

He took the rag Gabby had given him and bathed her feverish forehead with the cool water. The bullet had gone through her side, striking her in a very vulnerable area. Fortunately, it appeared no major damage had been done, but it was a vicious wound, and Fatima had to make the hole even larger so she could get the bullet out.

That afternoon, after she had been shot, he had been re-lieved to find that Fatima and Gabby were Olivia's family, and he knew they would take special care of her. But it had taken three men to hold him back from charging the tent when he had heard Olivia's screams of pain as Fatima tried to pull out the bullet and the surrounding fragments.

The bullet and particles were gone, but the wound had been so large she had a cross stitch forming and "X" on her side. And now she battled infection. If her fever didn't break by the next day, Fatima was going to reopen the wound to try and find the source of the infection. He could only imagine what kind of pain that would put Olivia through.

He lowered his head and couldn't stop the tears. *Dear God, don't take her from me. Please, don't take her. I need her in my life more than I need the air in my lungs. She is the love of my life. I cannot lose her. Please, God. Please.*

Suddenly, a warm hand touched his cheek lightly, and a hoarse voice whispered, "You shaved."

Cade's head jerked up and Olivia was staring back at him, though her eyes were bright with fever. He smiled at her and tried to discretely wipe away his tears. "Yes, I did. For Bella, and for you, angel. I want to look my best for you."

She gave him a weak smile and her eyes drooped, but she kept talking. "I thought you left with Bella. Why are you still here?"

"I wouldn't leave you, angel. I couldn't leave you. I love you too damned much to leave you."

Her eyes opened more and searched his face. "What did you just say?" she whispered.

"I love you, angel. I've loved you for a very long time. I've just been a fool and haven't told you."

Silent tears spilled from her eyes, running down the sides of her face. "I love you, too. I love you more than I could ever put words to. I never thought I would find love, and never in my wildest dreams did I think that love would be returned."

He smiled at her and leaned down, pressing his lips to hers in a gentle kiss, then trailed kisses down her jaw to her neck. Slowly, he pulled back, looking at her with loving tenderness. "God, I love you so much," he whispered.

Olivia gave him a weak smile and her hand trailed down his face as if trying to remember everything about him. "And there's Bella," she murmured. "I love that sweet little girl. Will I get to see her before... before..." She paused, unable to put the words out there that she wanted to see Bella one more time before she died.

"You aren't going to leave me, now, are you?" he asked, trying to keep the tone of his voice light, but his throat was tight with more tears. "I stayed for you—from the very beginning. From the moment I met you, you became one of the reasons I wanted to live. You and Bella. You can't leave me when I fought so hard to stay with you."

She closed her eyes for several long moments, and Cade was certain she had slipped back into the darkness. But the tears continued flowing from underneath her eyelids, and they gradually opened, and he was struck again by her beauty. He had no idea how no one had secured her as their wife, but he was mighty glad they hadn't.

"May I see Bella?" she asked, her lips trembling in her attempt to smile.

Bella must have been eavesdropping at the tent flap, something he had noticed she was very good at doing, and she rushed inside. "Mama, mama, mama!" she cried, and before Cade could stop her, she had pulled herself up onto the cot and was snuggling up against Olivia.

"My sweet Bella," Olivia whispered, pressing kisses to her forehead, "I love you so much."

"I love you, too, Mama. When can we play?" Bella was smoothing Olivia's hair away from her face with the palm of her hand, making her hair look like a tangled mess.

Olivia pulled her down to her and once again kissed her forehead and her cheeks. "I'm very tired, *hija*. Some other time?"

"Tomorrow?"

Olivia was staring into blue eyes identical to Cade's. "Yes, tomorrow. We'll play a game."

"Promise?" Bella pushed her, determined to make sure she got what she wanted.

"Yes," Olivia said softly. "I promise."

Bella, satisfied with the answer, pulled out Olivia's arm, snuggled down into her side, and secured Olivia's arm around her. She was asleep within a matter of seconds.

Olivia looked at Cade and again gave him a weak smile. "She calls me Mama. Why? Do I look like her mother did in a photograph or something?"

Cade shook his head. "My wife was very, very light colored. She would burn in the sun if she was in it for more than ten minutes. And her hair was a mix between blonde and red. We do have one picture of her, but, trust me, you look nothing like her."

"I wonder why, then. Why does Bella call me Mama?"

"Because she sees in you the same things I see. A strong, loving woman, who will do anything and give everything to protect her and make sure she is happy and safe. You saved her life, angel. Do you realize that? That bullet was meant for Bella, not you."

Olivia blinked her eyes hard. "It was worth it," she whispered, looking down at the small child wrapped around her in the small cot. Then her eyes went back to Cade. "Does it bother you that she calls me Mama?"

He shook his head. "Not at all. It actually pleases me that she is so comfortable with you. It is obvious that she loves you."

Olivia's eyes were beginning to feel heavy. "Will you stay with me just a little longer? I know how sick I am, Cade. And I don't want you or Bella to have to deal with my death. If you decide to leave soon, I understand. Will you please just stay a few minutes with me? Just let me hold her for a moment…"

Before Cade could reply, she had fallen back asleep. He leaned down and kissed her forehead, and then Bella's forehead. "We aren't going anywhere, angel," he whispered, then resumed pressing the cold rag to her forehead, silently praying for a miracle.

*

CADE CAREFULLY PACKED his saddlebags with the necessary provisions to take care of him and Bella until they made it home. Fortunately, the Mexican Army had more than enough items to be divided out so that he would easily have a meal three times a day for both of them.

There had been extra blankets, as well, and he had grabbed several, knowing that he would face the soggy ground and cold nights again. He had tin plates and a small cooking pot and pan, and even utensils, which he doubted he would even use, given how much more convenient it was to just use his fingers when out on the trail.

Bella wasn't far away, picking a bouquet of fresh spring flowers while talking and humming to herself. He shook his head. Women. He would never understand them.

All around him, men were packing up and tearing down tents. Santa Anna had been caught a couple of days ago, trying to pretend to be a private. He was wearing the simple white uniform and it was obvious he had been attempting, poorly, to live off the land for the last few days.

But as he was brought in with a few other prisoners, his soldiers recognized him and began saluting him and address-ing him as the general. He was forced to reveal the truth of his identity, and he was immediately taken to a separate area to be held under guard.

Sam had been injured in the battle, though not gravely. He had been hit in the ankle with grapeshot and was unable to walk on that one leg. They took him out under one of the larger oak trees so that he would have shade, and brought Santa Anna to him.

Within a short time, Santa Anna signed papers agreeing to grant freedom to Texas and to retreat with his army back to Mexico. It had been an incredible thing to witness, and every Texian there roared with triumph that they were officially free of his tyranny and could finally go home and know they wouldn't be forced to live by laws that were designed to punish them for merely pursuing their dreams.

Cade glanced over at the tent where Olivia had been kept

and wished he could burn it to the ground. But instead, he went to it and found Gabby inside, gathering up some of the items they had left before they departed.

"Back to Corpus for you?"

Gabby turned at his voice and smiled. "Yes, though I wish I was going to San Antonio. It's my hometown, you know. I look forward to every chance I get to go there. And now since Angie is pregnant, I'll get to go there with Mama a couple of times and then assist with the birth when that day comes."

Cade wanted to laugh at her barely contained excitement. She looked as though she wanted to jump up and down and cheer. "I know she'll be in good hands with you and your mother. I can't thank the two of you enough for all that you did for Olivia."

Gabby's eyebrows lifted. "She's family. Shouldn't we be thanking you for all that you did to help her?"

"I only sat with her and talked to her through her fever. I truly didn't do anything."

"She loves you. Just the sound of your voice brought her comfort."

It was Cade's turn to lift his eyebrows. "Did she tell you she's in love with me?"

Gabby laughed. "She didn't have to. It was obvious."

Cade looked back at the small cot Olivia had been on, and there were stains from her blood. He swallowed hard to contain his emotions and turned away from it. "We are on our way now," he said. "It has been a joy getting to know you, and I look forward to seeing you again soon."

Gabby walked over to him and gave him a big hug. "I know this has been hard on you and your daughter. But it's over now. Rest, and enjoy your journey. I, too, look forward to seeing you again soon."

Cade nodded and stepped outside the tent, his eyes adjusting to the sunlight. Bella had obviously finished picking her bouquet because she was no longer in the field where he had last seen her. But he knew where to find her.

Underneath the shade of one of the oak trees, Bella was sitting in Olivia's lap, handing her the bouquet and chattering up a storm. Olivia was nodding to everything she said and smiling as she ran her fingers through the little girl's long hair. He paused for a moment, soaking in the sight, wanting to remember it forever.

Finally, he approached them and stood next to Olivia who sat in a comfortable chair. Bella looked up at him and grinned. "I got flowers for Mama."

"And some absolutely beautiful ones, too," Cade said, making sure Bella saw him inspecting the bouquet. "But none of these flowers are as beautiful as the two of you."

Bella giggled and Olivia looked up at him with a smile, and he leaned down to kiss her, softly, sweetly. When he pulled back he knew he really was looking at the two most beautiful women in the world.

"So you are about to leave, then?" Olivia asked, and he could hear the sadness in her voice.

"Yes. We have the horses packed and saddled, and everything we should need to get home."

Olivia swallowed hard and nodded. "There are a few soldiers from San Antonio that are going to escort me home. They are honorable men, and I feel safe with them."

Cade nodded slowly, then shook his head. "I don't feel comfortable with you traveling home with strangers."

"They're hardly strangers. I know their entire families. I'll be safe, Cade. You must stop worrying about me." She looked down at the bouquet in her hands, then back up at him. "So are you going to rebuild your home? Do you think your cattle will still be there?"

Cade shook his head. "Rustlers will have gotten to them by now. No, there's really nothing left for us back there except terrible memories."

"What will you do then?"

"Well, word is they are looking for a new sheriff in this growing town, and the job is mine if I want it."

"Oh, Cade, that's wonderful. Where is it?"

"San Antonio."

He waited and watched it register on her face what he had just said. When it fully dawned on her he nearly laughed at the expression on her face. "So, you're—you and Bella— you're coming to live in San Antonio?" The hope in her voice made his heart thunder.

He kneeled down in front of her. "Only on one condition."

"What?" she asked breathlessly.

Cade looked at Bella. "Just like we rehearsed, okay?"

"Okay!" she said with enthusiasm.

Then, in unison, "Will you marry me?"

Epilogue

T HE SOUND OF their boots on the porch alerted everyone in the house that they had company. Serena was the first to the dining area with her apron on, holding a pitcher of water, a smile plastered to her face that anyone who knew her knew the smile was not meant to convey joy.

Olivia was the first through the door and the pitcher of water crashed to the floor. Serena cried out in joy and ran to her sister, but Cade stepped between them quickly. Serena shot him a "go to hell" look and drew back her fist.

"No, Serena, no. It's okay. It's just… It's just…"

"She was shot, Serena. I'm trying to stop you from hurting her. She's okay, but still very, very sore."

Serena's eyes shot to Olivia's face and Olivia gave her a half-hearted smile. "Maybe you aren't the only wild and crazy one in this family," she said, her smile growing bigger as Serena stepped forward and delicately hugged her sister.

"I never thought I'd see you again. I prayed, Olivia. I even went to church and the holy water didn't burn me. Lorenzo told us… when he came home he told us you had just been held up. But I knew he was trying to protect us. That *pendejo* is terrible at lying."

"Serena!" Angie's voice floated in the room. "I've told you not to say things like that—Olivia? Oh, praise the Lord! Olivia!" Following Cade's directions as he had done to Serena, Angie hugged Olivia, then hugged Cade. "Thank you for bringing her back to us."

Olivia smiled brightly. "We brought something else back with us." Olivia reached behind her and very slowly a sandy brown-haired little girl peeked out from behind her skirts, then moved forward to stand in front of Olivia. Olivia carefully kneeled down and whispered into the girl's ear then stood again with Cade's aid.

The little girl twisted her fingers in her dress, then took a deep breath and spoke loudly, "My name is Bella. And... and..." She looked up at Olivia. "What else, Mama?"

Serena and Angie both drew in a deep breath at the word and Lorenzo walked into the room, smiling brightly at all of them. He went over and embraced Cade, then gently embraced Olivia, then bent down and placed a quick kiss on Bella's cheek. "Glad to see you all finally made it home." He moved back over to Angie and she swatted at his arm. "Why didn't you tell us Olivia had been shot?"

He moved around her and wrapped his arms around her, his hands resting lovingly on her growing belly. "There was no need to have you worry. Not in your condition."

"I'm pregnant! Worry is an everyday thing for me right now!"

"So I've noticed," he muttered, and then chuckled and pressed kisses along her neck.

"I see she's forgiven you for not sending her a note that you were alive." Cade observed, watching the loving couple.

"She realized how dangerous it was. Any letters could be tracked back to our locations. I couldn't take the risk... to her or to the cause."

"How long did it take you to get her to agree with you?" Cade asked, a chuckle in his voice.

"About a week," Lorenzo responded dryly, giving Cade an unappreciative glance.

"Has everyone forgotten about the surprise that has just been dropped on us?" Serena asked in shock.

All eyes returned to Bella and she squirmed slightly under the stares. She turned to Olivia and tugged on her skirts. "Mama, up?" she asked, stretching her arms up. Cade lifted his daughter and carefully placed her on Olivia's hip, and Olivia wrapped her arms around her, giving her a quick kiss on the cheek.

Cade looked around at all of them and felt joy expand in his heart, a joy he had never felt, and had never allowed himself to feel. "I am very honored to announce that Olivia has agreed to marry me."

"Us, Daddy!" Bella piped in. "She marries us!"

Cade laughed. "Yes," he said. "Olivia has agreed to marry me and my daughter Bella. I need to speak to her grandparents, first, though, so please—"

"Young man, if you didn't ask her, I was going to hunt you down." *Abuelo's* voice came into the room as he and their grandmother walked in, smiling fondly at all of them.

Cade dropped his head to hide his smile and glanced over at Olivia, who was smiling brightly at all of them. When he looked up, he was surrounded by all of the smiling, joy-filled family that would soon be his.

But the smile on his bride-to-be's face was worth more than anything. "I love you, angel," he whispered, pressing a kiss to her forehead.

Olivia looked up at him, turning her radiant beauty on him. "I will always love you, Cade."

The wedding was an incredible *fandango*. Not only were they celebrating Olivia and Cade's marriage, they were also celebrating the exit of the Mexican forces that had agreed to leave Texas forever.

The festivities were only halfway over when Cade got a hold of Olivia and took off to the hotel, where they would celebrate their night as a married couple. "Cade! What are you doing?"

But the loud cheer from the partygoers only encouraged him and he swept her up in his arms, taking long strides to the hotel. Before Olivia could catch her breath, they were in their room and he was laying her down on the bed.

"Now," he said softly, "I can finally enjoy what I have wanted since I first laid eyes on you."

Olivia smiled, even though tears of joy and overwhelming love shimmered in her eyes. And then she welcomed him into her heart, her soul, her mind, and her body. Theirs was a love that would last beyond time.

The End

If you enjoyed Texas Desire, you'll love the next book in…

The Texas Legacy Series

Book 1: *Texas Conquest*

Book 2: *Texas Desire*

Book 3: *Texas Heat*

Available now at your favorite online retailer!

About the Author

Holly grew up spending many lazy summer days racing her horses bareback in the Texas sun. But whenever Holly wasn't riding her horses or competing in horse shows, she was found with pen and paper in hand, writing out romantic love stories of the wild west.

Later, in her professional life, Holly worked just blocks from the Alamo in a unique setting where the buildings were connected with basements and tunnels. The exciting history of Texas, the Alamo, and working in a historic building dating back to the 1800's inspired Holly to write about the Texas Revolution, and has evolved into a series all about Texas becoming the great State it is.

Today, Holly lives in a small community just south of San Antonio, with her husband and two children. On the family's 80 acre ranch, surrounded by cattle during the day and hearing the howl of coyotes by night, Holly has endless inspiration for her writing.

Thank you for reading

Texas Desire

If you enjoyed this book, you can find more from all our great authors at TulePublishing.com, or from your favorite online retailer.

CPSIA information can be obtained
at www.ICGtesting.com
Printed in the USA
FSHW022032221119
64433FS